S0-BFB-161

Proof Perilous

"Your attentions go too far, sir," Phoebe declared. "I do not return your interest."

"Perhaps I would believe you if you could look into my eyes and say that," the Earl of Devenham quietly replied.

I am strong, she thought. I can do it, this one time. He will believe me then, and be gone.

She looked into his intense blue eyes. "I am looking into your eyes," she said in carefully measured syllables. "I am not interested in you. I want you to leave me alone."

"Your words say no, but your heart says yes," Devenham said. "If you have truly fooled yourself, let me prove it to you."

His lips were gentle yet demanding, seeking. She struggled for only a moment. The searing desire she had thought dead, or at least banished forever, was pouring through her again—as lips that had tried so hard to lie surrendered to the delicious torment of passion's proof. . . .

SIGNET REGENCY ROMANCE
Coming in April 1995

Emma Lange
A Certain Reputation

Anne Douglas
Miss Caroline's Deception

Margaret Summerville
Double Masquerade

AT YOUR LOCAL BOOKSTORE
OR ORDER DIRECTLY
FROM THE PUBLISHER
WITH VISA OR MASTERCARD
1-800-253-6476

The
Persistent Earl

by

Gail Eastwood

A SIGNET BOOK

SIGNET
Published by the Penguin Group
Penguin Books USA Inc., 375 Hudson Street,
New York, New York 10014, U.S.A.
Penguin Books Ltd, 27 Wrights Lane,
London W8 5TZ, England
Penguin Books Australia Ltd, Ringwood,
Victoria, Australia
Penguin Books Canada Ltd, 10 Alcorn Avenue,
Toronto, Ontario, Canada M4V 3B2
Penguin Books (N.Z.) Ltd, 182–190 Wairau Road,
Auckland 10, New Zealand

Penguin Books Ltd, Registered Offices:
Harmondsworth, Middlesex, England

First published by Signet, an imprint of Dutton Signet,
a division of Penguin Books USA Inc.

First Printing, March, 1995
10 9 8 7 6 5 4 3 2 1

Copyright © Gail Eastwood-Stokes, 1995
All rights reserved

 REGISTERED TRADEMARK—MARCA REGISTRADA

Printed in the United States of America

Without limiting the rights under copyright reserved above, no part of this
publication may be reproduced, stored in or introduced into a retrieval system, or
transmitted, in any form, or by any means (electronic, mechanical, photocopying,
recording, or otherwise), without the prior written permission of both the copyright
owner and the above publisher of this book.

BOOKS ARE AVAILABLE AT QUANTITY DISCOUNTS WHEN USED TO PROMOTE PRODUCTS OR
SERVICES. FOR INFORMATION PLEASE WRITE TO PREMIUM MARKETING DIVISION, PENGUIN BOOKS
USA INC., 375 HUDSON STREET, NEW YORK, NEW YORK 10014.

If you purchased this book without a cover you should be aware that this book is
stolen property. It was reported as "unsold and destroyed" to the publisher and
neither the author nor the publisher has received any payment for this "stripped
book."

To Mare,
because "old friendships
are more precious
than diamonds."

Chapter One

"I won't have that man under our roof, Edward. I'm sorry. It is simply too much to ask."

Judith, Lady Allington, stared fixedly out one of the rear-facing windows of the Allingtons' Wigmore Street drawing room, her back turned resolutely toward her husband.

Sir Edward sighed, noting the stubborn set of his wife's slight shoulders. Clearly, he had yet some distance to go before he would win her over to his side of their present discussion. He loved his wife dearly, and in over a dozen years of marriage they had managed to rub along with each other quite nicely, with five children of respectable ages to show for it. But if she felt she was right, she could tend to be headstrong. She had spirit, his Judith.

The baronet stopped pacing in front of the marble fireplace and crossed the carpet to join his wife by the window, as if closing the physical gap between them would somehow improve their point of view. Already the heat of the day could be felt in the sun pouring through the glass.

The Allingtons were still in London, despite the fact that July was turning into August and the summer temperatures had turned the city into an oven. The stone pavements soaked up the sun's relentless heat, baking the remaining inhabitants with callous disregard for either wealth or position. However, the temperature in the Allingtons' drawing room seemed to be rising quite of its own accord.

Edward and Judith's disagreement was an unusual occurrence, but then, in many ways it was an unusual summer. Parliament had stayed in session well into July, delaying the customary exodus of *le beau monde* from the city accordingly. Wellington had finally defeated the little Corsican at Waterloo,

Gail Eastwood

but now no one knew whether France and England were still officially at war, or whether they actually had been, in the past months. While the political questions were debated, and the fate of the man who had caused all the trouble was decided, the flow of wounded coming home continued, and the echoes of skirmishing still sounded in the French countryside.

The Allingtons had not expected these circumstances to affect them. They were still in Town now simply because the repairs to the roof of their country estate had run into delays. Yet, as so often happens, that one unforeseen change in plans had now set new events spinning, causing a small skirmish on the northern fringe of fashionable Mayfair.

"It is not like you to be so judgmental, my love," said Sir Edward. "Devenham is an old friend. He needs our help." Gently taking one of his wife's hands between his, Edward endeavored to position himself where Judith would be forced to look at him instead of the flowers wilting in the garden. "You know I wouldn't ask this of you if I had any doubts about his character."

Judith did look at him then, searchingly. "Do you not think reputation is a reflection of character? You have been out of his circle for a long time, Edward. People change. Waterloo hero or not, he is accounted one of the worst care-for-nothing rakes in England—just like all the Earls of Devenham before him!"

"I do not credit all the tales the gossipmongers spread about him, and neither should you. He hasn't set foot in London in three years. We should feel honored that he has asked to stay with us."

He paused, unsure what to say next. His wife had returned her gaze to the window, and now he looked out as well. He saw at once what had caught her attention.

"That is one of Phoebe's strays, is it not?"

The walled garden, with its formal beds and neat gravel walks, had flourished this summer under the supervision of Judith's sister, Phoebe, who had been living with them for some eighteen months now, since the death of her husband. A tortoiseshell cat was crouched low on one of the walkways, its head clearly following the activities of a sparrow hopping about farther down the path. The cat appeared content to study the bird, making no move to attack.

"They have become quite tame, really, since she started feeding them. I see them in the garden all the time," Judith said distractedly.

Edward narrowed his eyes. "Do you think Phoebe would turn Devenham away if it were up to her?" he asked quietly. He took his wife gently by the shoulders and turned her to face him.

"Oh, Edward, I don't know. She has been through so much. I truly don't know what to do."

The death of Phoebe's husband, Stephen, had shocked the *ton* and devastated the young woman. She had been subjected to cruel gossip to top off her terrible loss, and ultimately the strength and courage Edward knew she possessed in common with his wife had failed. Phoebe had sought refuge in the Allington household, finding a safe niche as a doting aunt and unpaid governess for the children. When they were in London she never so much as set a single foot outside their residence except for the hours she would spend in the garden. Until today.

"Do you not think it a sign that today she has found the strength to attend Lord Tyneley's memorial service? I think it is Phoebe that worries you, not Devenham's reputation."

Judith moved into her husband's arms then and rested her head against his broad, solid chest. "Oh, Edward. What Phoebe has been through has made her so fragile, and she is just beginning to recover. Our home has been her sanctuary. How might it affect her to suddenly have a stranger, a man, thrust in our midst? I fear she's not ready. And bad enough any stranger, but one like Lord Devenham? There is bound to be talk. Why must he come to us? Surely he has his choice of grander houses and higher-positioned friends."

Sir Edward sighed, holding her close. "You love your sister very much, as do I. But she is a grown woman, not a child. She knows she must face the world again. She has taken a courageous step today."

He cupped Judith's small face in one of his large hands and traced the lines of concern on her forehead with the fingers of his other one. "Devenham needs our sanctuary now, love. His wounds have made him very ill. Most of his friends are unattached gentlemen in no position to offer him care. Of those that are not, I dare say most have already left or are leaving Town now that the Season has ended."

"If his friends are so unhelpful, I suspect it is only because he deserves it," Judith said with an unsympathetic sniff.

"In contrast, we will be stranded here for some time," Edward continued smoothly. "We have no daughters of marriageable age to worry over; doubtless Dorrie will fall head over heels for him, but she is only twelve. That we have Phoebe may prove our greatest blessing. Who could be more perfectly suited to nurse him? Phoebe has been a married woman, and she has a talent for nurturing. The maids needn't set foot anywhere near him."

Judith tried to twist away from Edward's touch. "I like that! He can't be trusted around the servants, but you have no qualms about closeting him with my sister!"

In a quick motion, Edward deposited a playful kiss on the tip of his wife's ear, pushing a curl of dark hair and a lace-trimmed lappet from her cap out of his way. "You know they won't be 'closeted.' Besides, the poor man is too ill to misbehave, even if he were such a rakehell as people say." He ran a teasing finger down her nose and reached for her hand, bringing it to his lips. "Trust me, Judith. Have I been wrong so often in all our years of marriage?"

Quite unaware that she was a subject of discussion, Phoebe, Lady Brodfield, sat in St. George's, Hanover Square. She looked down at the tightly clenched hands in her lap and discovered to her distress that no matter how she tried, she could not make them stop shaking. The black silk handkerchief entwined in her fingers was crumpled and wadded beyond recognition, but she did not dare to loosen her grip. She was afraid the trembling would spread from her hands to the rest of her.

"He is gone at last to his heavenly reward, but today we remember Lord Tyneley as he was in life. . . ."

The droning voice of the eulogist floated up from the main floor to where Phoebe sat in the gallery. It seemed unbearably warm there, although the elegant interior of the church normally offered a cool respite from the summer heat outside. She had inched forward to let some air reach the damp back of her black twilled silk dress, but now she pressed against the hard wooden bench, seeking its solid support.

". . . loyal servant to the Crown, distinguished statesman, skilled diplomat, able parliamentarian, devoted husband and father," the voice rolled on.

The church was crowded with mourners attending the memorial service for her father-in-law, the Earl of Tyneley. Stephen's father had been prominent and well-liked. Phoebe felt deep regret that she had had so little contact with the man since Stephen's death. Whatever the failings of his two sons had been, the old earl had been an admirable and kind man. She had learned to love him during her two years of marriage to Stephen. Coming here seemed the smallest gesture on her part—a chance to pay her last respects.

If her family had not still been in London, it would have been too difficult to try to come. But it had not seemed right to stay away when she was so nearby. It was almost as if Lord Tyneley had bestowed upon her one last gift: a chance to test herself and see if she was recovered enough to live a normal life again. She had wanted to prove to herself that she could handle this. She hadn't counted on this sort of betrayal by her own body.

I should never have come, Phoebe berated herself silently. *I was a fool to think I could do this.*

She had purposely slipped into St. George's at the last possible moment and had chosen to sit in the gallery where she thought she would attract no attention. *It should have been all right*, she argued to herself. A spark of anger ignited in the depths of her distress. *I have not had to face anyone, nor engage in conversation. No one here knows who I am.* Besides her unobtrusive seat and late arrival, she had donned a heavy veil that she thought concealed her identity quite effectively. She was not yet ready to be recognized by others.

As it was, she had set herself up for failure. The turmoil of emotion was too great, and the place itself held too many memories. So many times she had been here, among these people, in mourning or in joy. She and Stephen had been married here. The mere sight of the carved pulpit on its six columns had been enough to bring back momentarily all the exhilaration and expectation of that day, in bitter contrast to her present pain. The inspired faces in the painting of the Last Supper had no power to comfort her this day.

From the safety of her perch in the gallery, she had surveyed the throng of black-clad mourners on the level below her. She had recognized Stephen's stepmother, surprisingly discomposed for one normally so unflappable, and various cousins and friends of the family. The family servants were gathered in the back of the church, and the rest of the pews were filled with the members of London's upper circles, including Lord Tyneley's fellow peers and members of Parliament. One person was noticeably absent, and that was Stephen's half brother, Richard, who had not yet come home from fighting Napoleon.

Phoebe shivered, glad to be spared at least the sight of him. Even so, she should have known, she thought, that this test was too difficult. The sorrow of this occasion opened the gates to ever deeper feelings she had been battling.

I must get out while I can still manage it discreetly, Phoebe thought. She was beginning to shake all over. Her fear that someone might recognize her was coming back as overwhelmingly as ever, and she fought a rising sense of panic as she glanced around her to see what obstacles stood between her and the door.

A small collection of other people had already been seated in the gallery when she had arrived, but she was certain that none had taken any notice of her. She was dismayed to discover, however, that she had not been the only latecomer. She realized that she must have been so preoccupied with her own thoughts and emotions that she had not noticed two gentlemen who had taken seats behind her. She would have to walk directly past them to make her escape.

The two were young and fashionably dressed, she noted, regarding them indirectly through her veil. Friends of Stephen? No, she doubted such would be here. But they were far too young to have been involved in affairs of her father-in-law, which left only one other possibility—that they were friends of Richard. In that case, she thought it unlikely that they would know her, even without the veil.

With an effort, Phoebe placed a shaky hand on the rail in front of her and got up. She kept her head down and walked straight past the two men, holding her breath. She saw the astonishment in their faces as she passed them and carefully started down the stairs. She prayed her legs would support her.

As she gained the bottom she began to feel steadier. She had made a dreadful mistake in coming, but she would be all right once she got outside, she was certain. When she saw a knot of people gathered under the church's portico, however, she hesitated, sick with dismay. They would be scandalized that anyone would leave in the middle of a memorial service. The town would be buzzing with speculation later as the gossips tried to identify her.

As she stood there, she heard the clatter of feet descending the stairs behind her. One of the young men she had passed in the gallery stopped beside her.

"Are you ill?" he asked softly. "Can I assist you?"

"No, thank you," she managed to respond. It sounded like a croak to her own ears, and the fellow continued to stand there regarding her as if he had not heard. She shook her head. His presence left her no choice but to proceed on her way, out through the people in the portico and to the hired cab she prayed would still be waiting at the curb.

There was no other way to do it but boldly and quickly. As she pushed her way through the small crowd, her head bowed, she noticed Sir Charles Mortimer, who had always been so kind to her, among those she startled. Would he guess who she was? When she at last reached the safety of the hackney, she discovered clutched in her hand a spring of rosemary that someone must have thrust at her as she went by. She inhaled its scent, blinking back tears. Rosemary, for remembrance. How dearly she wished she could forget!

Up in the gallery, the young man who had approached her returned to his seat.

"Think that was her?" his companion asked.

"Who could say for certain? But the very fact that she was so concealed makes me guess that it was. Who else could it be? She seemed very shaken."

"Who else would have chosen to sit in the gallery? Or to leave in mid-service? Her small size was right. And her figure." A snicker followed. "Nice little number, eh? I doubt the old man could have managed a ladybird on the side like her."

"No, this was definitely a lady. I think it had to be her. She was styled an Incomparable during the season when Brodfield's brother snatched her up. No one else ever stood much of a chance with her. Well, at least we can report that she's in London. That's more than we knew before."

Major John Allen Jameson, Earl of Devenham, lay in a bed at the Clarendon Hotel listening to the low murmur of voices somewhere near him. He had not needed a doctor to tell him he was too ill to travel. He had known it from the way the room refused to stay still, and from his own tendency to drift into sleep at the most unpredictable moments. The sweat that poured off his body, soaking the bed linens, was not merely due to London's excruciating summer heat. The damned saber cut in his upper thigh had opened again during the journey to London, proving that through all the wretched weeks he had stayed in Brussels fighting fever and infection, the wound had never healed properly.

Devenham let out a ragged breath that almost qualified as a sigh. He supposed he should be grateful that he was fighting infection again instead of Boney's army, but he was not. He hated being sick. He would have preferred to face another charge by Napoleon's Imperial Guards than lie helplessly in bed, dependent upon other people. He tried to shift his position and was rewarded with a fresh onslaught of pain radiating from just below his right hip. "Blast and confound it!" he exclaimed softly.

The earl's manservant, Mullins, and the doctor who had been speaking with him both turned toward Devenham, but their conversation did not halt. The doctor shook his head.

"He is in no condition to leave his bed at all, but even a

hotel as fine as the Clarendon is no place for a sick man. Has there been any reply yet to the notes he sent out?"

Mullins's reply was cut off by another oath from the bed. "As far as I know, I am neither dead nor deaf," the earl said. "There is no need to discuss me in the third person as if I had already been called to the hereafter."

"You need to rest, my lord. Mullins can inform me—"

"*I* can inform you of anything you need to know. Mullins has his own duties to attend to." Devenham missed the knowing look that passed between his servant and the doctor.

Precisely at that moment, a knock sounded on the door.

"Note for his lordship," announced the liveried footman Mullins admitted.

The doctor tipped the young man, who was looking about with interest, and hustled him quickly out of the room again. "No need to encourage the curious," he said to the earl. "The gossip mills are full enough of you as it is."

"Hm. A lot of nonsense about Waterloo, I expect. All rubbish." Devenham was so weak, he struggled to break the seal on the letter. "I would rather be dead than be this helpless," he groaned. "I am quite serious."

"Your condition is serious," cautioned the doctor. "After your time in Brussels, I had not thought I would need to remind you not to exert yourself in any way. Would you allow me to read you the letter?"

Devenham let the paper flutter from his fingers onto the blanket and closed his eyes in resignation. A moment later he was asleep.

The doctor retrieved the note and quickly scanned the contents. "It is from Sir Edward and Lady Allington," he told Mullins. "They have agreed to take him in."

Chapter Two

Phoebe had received the news of the earl's impending visit with deep misgivings. She had been shaken by her failure to get through Lord Tyneley's memorial service, and she doubted her ability to cope with the emotional demands she knew nursing the earl would place on her. Engaged in her own struggle to restore balance in her life, the last thing she needed just now was to have dealings with a man—any man, let alone this one.

Why had Edward asked this of her? She had felt too much in his debt to resist, yet she dreaded what lay ahead. She truly felt sympathy for Lord Devenham's physical sufferings, but how would she handle being so close to a man again? Would not her feelings about Stephen rush back to torment her? Would the walls she had built around her heart protect her?

"You would think it was the great Wellington himself who was coming," she remarked with some asperity to Lizzie, the nursery maid, as they readied the children for an escape to Hyde Park on the morning after Lord Tyneley's service. The entire house had been in an uproar since the early hours, the servants flitting about like a flock of jittery sparrows and Judith asking the same questions about their preparations over and over. Edward was anxious and grumpy, and the children were so excited and curious about the "true war hero" who was coming to stay with them, Phoebe thought it best to get them out of the house altogether.

The earl's notoriety was great enough that even she had heard of him. She did not think they had ever crossed paths in the days when she had circulated socially, but the doings of such a man were always grist for the gossip mills and reached even the Allingtons' dinner table. His recent return from overseas had been heralded in the newspapers, and stories of his battlefield heroics were circulating freely amid speculation over what level of promotion he would receive and which ladies of the ton would next catch his eye. Phoebe's heart sank every time she thought of the unwelcome attention that his removal to the Allington home was bound to attract.

Just as she fastened the last button on little William's jacket, she heard the gentle patter of rain against the windowpanes and went to investigate. She had viewed the overcast skies simply as relief from the previous day's heat.

"Oh, dear, perhaps it won't last," she said, but she noticed the sky had darkened. The words had no sooner left her mouth than the water began to come down in torrents. At the same precise moment, she saw a closed landau, a barouche and a baggage wagon come to a stop in the street far below at the front of the house. Major Lord Devenham had arrived.

It would be just now, Phoebe thought, lumping the earl and the rain together in her annoyance and frustration. The earl's visit seemed ill-omened, definitely. Ill-omened and ill-timed.

The pounding of the knocker echoed through the house and the sound of an answering hubbub downstairs at the front door quickly tipped the children as to what was going on. Phoebe cast a despairing eye over them, shaking her head. Dorrie's dark curls and the heads of her three brothers in varying shades of brown and russet were quite literally bobbing up and down with excitement.

"I suppose it would be too cruel to make you stay in the schoolroom," Phoebe said with a sigh. It was obvious that Lizzie, too, had been infected by the children's enthusiasm, although she was making a visible, valiant effort to suppress the fact. Most of the time it was hard to remember that the young servant girl was only a few years older than Dorrie.

"All right, if you promise to be very, very quiet and as invisible as ghosts, you may sit on the stairs up above the second floor landing, where you can see but you won't be in the way," Phoebe said soberly. "Promise?"

"Promise," came the reply from Dorrie, David and Thomas.

Six-year-old William did not join in the reply. "Aunt Phoebe, are there really any ghosts?"

"I've certainly never seen or heard one, William." She bent to give him a reassuring hug. "But that's how quiet I want you to be—so nobody knows you are there. Can you do that?"

The little boy nodded, clutching the ball he had planned to take to the park. "After this, are we still going to the park?"

"No, love, not in the rain. We'll find a game to play instead."

Phoebe straightened and, patting the child affectionately on the head, led the little group from the schoolroom to the top of the stairs. There they settled themselves to watch when the proceedings below should come into view.

Above all things, Phoebe wished to keep out of the way. She knew she would be called when she was needed. Few people were aware that she was a resident in this house, and she hoped to keep things that way for as long as possible. Certainly, Lord Devenham's presence here would not be secret for long. The neighbors were probably already buzzing about the string of carriages in the street outside. The last thing she wanted was to become a new subject of gossip, with her name linked to the earl's.

The commotion in the entry hall was quite evident to the small party gathered on the stairs even though they had no view of it. The stamping of wet feet, the harried voices, the thumpings, bumpings, and oft-repeated opening and closing of the door suggested a household upheaval of major proportions.

"It sounds like an entire regiment has arrived," whispered eight-year-old Thomas. The mixture of awe and wistfulness in his tone showed clearly how much he wished it were so.

"What could be taking them so long?"

Phoebe turned to Dorrie to reply, but the words died on her lips. Out of the corner of her eye she saw the ball William had been so carefully guarding slip out of his grasp. In the suspended moment before she could react, she watched it bounce gently from the second step to the fourth and on down, in increasing arcs with increasing speed, off the wall and around the bend in the stairs. With a little cry, Phoebe leaped up and flew after it.

She was not in time to stop its progress on the second floor landing. On the first floor landing the ball careened off the column supporting Edward's prized statue of Aristotle, leaving the great statesman tottering as the bouncing projectile continued down the next flight of stairs. Close behind it, Phoebe entertained a horrible vision of the earl's entourage meeting the flying missile head-on as they started up the steps at the bottom.

Fortunately, she arrived there before they did. She chased the ball as it bounced off the base of the long-case clock in the passage and managed to capture it just in time to see the large form of a litterman bearing down on her. It was too late to retreat up the stairs. She hastily stepped back into the shallow recess beside the clock.

The litter carrier was at the head of a sizable procession that stretched back toward the front of the house, leaving a mass of wet boot marks on the polished marble floor. Behind him was a second litterman of remarkably similar appearance and build. Both were shedding water from the shoulder capes attached to their coats, and they carried slung between them a litter with the blanket-draped form of another man, who could be none other than the earl.

Beyond them, Phoebe could see what appeared to be a servant, a doctor, Edward, several of the Allington servants, and a number of porters bearing trunks and boxes. At the far end she saw Judith and Mrs. Hunnicutt, the housekeeper, wearing identical expressions of concern. Sir Edward's butler, Maddocks, was making his way along this prodigious line, apparently attempting to reach the head to lead the way upstairs. The littermen stopped right in front of Phoebe, at the foot of the stairs.

Phoebe tried to resist showing any interest in the earl. Viewing him in such a helpless state seemed somehow improper, equivalent to an act of voyeurism. It was a foolish notion, she knew, since she would be tending him in just such a helpless state for some time to come. But lying on the litter he seemed more exposed, more vulnerable, than he would be safely settled in a bed. She battled briefly with her curiosity, but the outcome was predictable.

Devenham lay motionless on the litter, his eyes closed, his brown hair limp upon his pillow, dark where rain or sweat had

made it wet. Phoebe bit her lip as she noted the earl's pallor
and stillness. Despite his obvious illness, he was more handsome than she had imagined, and she had already allowed that
anyone with such a reputation as his would have to be uncom-
monly favored. There was a softness to his features, at least in
repose, that she had not expected in a man of war. She had expected hard angles where she saw graceful, gentle lines. The
flare of his nose and the prominence of his cheekbones were in
perfect proportion to the smooth expanse of his brow and the
curve of his jaw. She was horrified to find she was especially
drawn to his mouth and the noticeable cleft in his chin.

This is going to be even more difficult than I supposed,
Phoebe thought distractedly, feeling the attraction uncurling
deep inside her like a cat awakened from a nap. Hardening
herself against it, she pulled her attention away from Devenham long enough to notice Maddocks taking his place ahead
of the littermen.

The two burly fellows shifted their grip on the litter and
mounted the stairs after the servant. The jostling and change of
angle must have disturbed the earl, for as the procession
started up, his eyes flew open, and Phoebe saw they were an
unforgettable shade of blue—the azure of a clear October sky.
She wondered if he had any idea where he was.

She thought for a moment he seemed to look at her. Then
she could see no more as the next figures in the procession
mounted the stairs in turn, blocking her view. Every person in
the line would have to pass right by her. Some part of her
hoped, ostrich-like, that by ignoring them she could herself be
ignored. It was exactly this sort of exposure she had wanted to
avoid.

"We will probably be needing you in another ten minutes,"
Edward said as he passed, giving Phoebe a most curious look.
No doubt he was surprised to see her there. She realized that
she must indeed look peculiar, standing there staring with
William's ball still clutched to her chest.

"Did you ever see anyone so handsome?" gushed Dorrie as
soon as Phoebe rejoined her charges at the top of the stairs.
"Did you manage a good look at him?"

"He doesn't look very old," said Thomas with obvious disappointment.

"He doesn't look very well," David observed with a ten-year-old's superior attitude.

"Will we get to see him again?" William asked.

Phoebe handed William the errant ball and motioned the children back toward the schoolroom. "The earl is very ill indeed," she told them. "I doubt you will be seeing much of him for a while." When they voiced their disappointment, she reminded them that he had not come on a social call. "He is here because he is too ill to go to his own home, and you must not expect him to pay much mind to you, even when he is better." She doubted such a rake would have patience for young children.

"Remember, too, that I shall be spending part of my time helping with his care. You must promise to mind Lizzie and not get into mischief when I cannot be with you."

"He isn't married, is he?"

"Is he truly a major in the hussars?"

"Do you think he might die?"

"What are we going to play now?"

Phoebe put her hands over her ears and shook her head. "Children! I shall be able to answer all of your questions much better if you'll wait. I have to go down in just a few minutes. The doctor will have instructions for me, and I will probably learn a little more about Lord Devenham. And yes, William, you are all going to play a game now, with Lizzie. What shall it be? Hunt-the-button?"

Minutes later, Phoebe knocked softly on the door of the guest room that had been prepared for the earl. Edward himself admitted her. She had wondered if Devenham would be awake, but she saw at a glance that he was not. She was pleased to find only two others in the room with them. Edward introduced her to the doctor and to Mullins, who did not leave his post by the bed, but bowed respectfully.

Phoebe's eyes strayed back to the earl, taking in again his handsome features. He did not look like any of the things he was said to be—rakehell, card shark, womanizing officer, daring hero. He looked like an overgrown boy. She forced her gaze away when the doctor addressed her.

"I understand from Sir Edward that you are a widow, Lady Brodfield. Forgive me, but may I ask if you nursed your husband before he died?"

"No, my husband died quite suddenly and unexpectedly," she answered with only a small tremor in her voice. Apparently the doctor knew nothing about it. She was surprised by the calmness with which she was able to reply.

"I *do* apologize." The doctor was obviously nonplussed. "The only reason I asked was—"

"It is all right, doctor," Phoebe interrupted him. If he fussed and spluttered, it would only make the conversation more painful. "I understand completely. You are just trying to ascertain whether or not I have any nursing experience. I can tell you that I spent much of my childhood in the country. We did a good deal of our own physicking, of both animals and humans. I am familiar with most of the usual remedies and procedures, if there is nothing out of the ordinary required?"

"Lady Brodfield seems to have a natural gift, Doctor Fortens, although she is too modest to say so," Edward added approvingly. "I think you will find her an able assistant."

The doctor looked at Phoebe dubiously. How well she recognized that look! She had become accustomed to it almost as soon as she was old enough to catch a man's eye. She had learned that men found her attractive, and that look said, "Can a woman this attractive also be capable?" She forced an encouraging smile.

"I see," said the doctor, turning his eyes toward his patient and the loyal servant beside the bed. "Well, I suppose we must be grateful for your help. Mullins here cannot care for his master around the clock, although he is inclined to try.

"As you know, Lord Devenham was wounded at Waterloo. I have no wish to offend you. Will you permit me to speak frankly? He has a deep saber cut in his upper right thigh, really just a few inches below his hip. He was very lucky that such a vicious cut did not break the bone. In fact, he was doubly lucky. He was wounded in the left shoulder covering the retreat from Quatre Bras the day before. He patched himself up and went on as if nothing had happened. I don't know why the damned fool didn't bleed to death after the second wound," he added softly, shaking his head as if talking only to himself. Recovering suddenly, he said, "I beg your pardon, Lady Brodfield!"

"Pray go on."

"He was fortunate enough to find a bed in Brussels, where he and Mullins have been these many weeks since the battle. He survived the fever from the infection and his wounds seemed to be healing well, as I understand it. He believed himself strong enough to make the trip home. Unfortunately, the rigors of the journey have set him back. His shoulder is doing well, but the leg wound opened again, and he is back to the state he was in at Brussels, having only come this far on his journey.

"I have dosed him rather heavily with laudanum so he would not suffer too greatly the discomforts of this move. His dressings need frequent changing, and he needs constant attention to combat the fever. I will leave you some basilicum for his wound, and some laudanum for the pain. You know that it is essential not to exceed the number of drops that I prescribe?"

Phoebe nodded.

"I regret to say that he is not a very cooperative patient."

Phoebe smiled a genuine smile at that. "Do you not find that to be the case with most of your male patients, Doctor Fortens?"

The good doctor had the grace to return her smile. "Perhaps I should not say so, but I find the earl to be particularly stubborn. It seems only fair to warn you. The laudanum will be a helpful ally, as long as you are careful with it. It is essential that Lord Devenham be kept quiet and inactive. The blood loss and the ravages of the fevers have left him weaker than a newborn."

The doctor paused, and began to arrange on the table beside him a small collection of bottles. "I have no wish to frighten you, but you must know the seriousness of what you are undertaking. He is not altogether out of danger yet. I have told him this myself, but he does not seem to care."

The doctor suddenly sounded tired and discouraged, and Phoebe felt sorry for him. At the same time, she heard in his words the sound of a challenge. If Devenham didn't care to get well, why had he bothered to put Edward and Judith to such trouble as to have him here?

She glanced at Mullins and for a moment their eyes locked. In his she thought she could read both hope and determination. Obviously, he cared, even if the earl did not. That in itself was interesting, something to be tucked away for later consideration. Meanwhile, she could be determined, too. No patient in her care would be allowed to languish if she could help it. She tried to convey that message to the manservant in her steady gaze, and was pleased to see him smile. She did not have to like the earl to want to make him well.

The forces at work in the earl's body were every bit as much at war as the grim armies conjured up by his brain. The restless, tortured dreams from his fever mixed with other-worldly opium visions both fantastical and soothing in an ebb and flow that mimicked perfectly the varying tides of battle. He somehow knew that the dreamworld was of his own making; nevertheless, he could not escape from it.

He had been surrounded by flames—no matter which way he turned, he had faced walls of fire. Choking on smoke and nearly drowning in the sweat that poured off his body, he knew there was someone beyond the walls of flame—someone who needed him. Somehow he had to get through. Then, as he moved through the fire, the leaping flames had become horses pounding toward him and past him with wild, rolling eyes. French cuirassiers' blades flashed in the strange light.

He saw his friend Brownell riding through the smoke ahead of him, going the wrong way, he thought, but he couldn't go after him, for his own horse had been shot out from under him. So he shouted, lost in the dark chaos—shouted for Brownell, shouted for a horse, shouted for an end to the nightmare. And then before him he saw his friend Fitzmorris, pinned to the ground by a French bayonet, reaching his arms out for help.

Blood and sweat mingled as he cradled his dying friend. The dream seemed too real, for he could even smell the putrid odor of the smoke and sweat. Yet suddenly the grotesque dancing shadows around them were chased away by a flood of light, and a sense of soothing comfort came over him. He smelled rosemary, only it wasn't rosemary, for it was mixed with something else, a light, airy, delicate scent he couldn't identify.

He surrendered to it gratefully, exhausted, and for a moment he floated. He floated through clouds and looked down upon vast cities that appeared to be made of gold. Through their streets marched processions of great personages he thought he might know. His sense of relief was so great, he wondered if he had died. He saw eyes watching him—cool, gray eyes filled with sadness and anxiety. But then the clouds seemed to darken and roll in upon him.

When he adjusted his eyes to the thick, heavy darkness, he was in his father's stables, and now it was not Fitzmorris cradled in his arms, but a dog—the too-still form of a young spaniel who had failed to take his brother Jeremy's instruction. Jeremy was there, standing over them, the smoking pistol still in his hand. The weird, green smoke curled upward with a peculiar, twisting motion and seemed to illuminate the scornful expression on Jeremy's face.

"Do you want me to tell Father that you cried over a dog?"

Each word cut like a French saber.

"Do you want me to tell Father that you cried?"

The same words came out each time the apparition of his dead brother opened its mouth. "Do you want me to tell Father?"

Yet Devenham could not stop his tears—they flowed down and seemed to cover him all over. They were as cold as ice—as cold as the chill in his heart.

"Cried over a dog . . ." echoed his brother's voice, but the stable had faded and now he saw eyes again instead—not just eyes, but a sea of faces. He saw his parents, looking at him with intense disapproval, and a dozen laughing young women with eyes as empty as the poor dead pup's. He saw Fitzmorris's face, and a dozen French soldiers, all dead, all empty-eyed. He began to shake and to feel the anger inside that warned him he was still alive, in hell. He knew for certain it was hell when the darkness closed in on him again and he heard the sound of hundreds and thousands of wings, flapping all around him. Cold terror gripped his heart so hard it seemed to stop altogether, and for a moment he could not even breathe.

Phoebe had been awakened by her abigail gently shaking her shoulder.

"I'm sorry, my lady. Mrs. Hunnicutt says I'm to wake you. Goldie says it's the earl—seems he's worsening again and his man is asking for you to help him."

Phoebe pulled on the dressing gown the young woman handed her and pulled the sash tight in a decisive gesture. She lit her bedside lamp from the abigail's candle and carried it out into the hall, her mind already racing ahead.

"Ask Mrs. H to heat some of the milfoil tea I made for Lord Devenham, and have Goldie bring a large basin of cold water. I will need more linens and cloths, too, Mary Anne."

She felt sorry that the servants would lose sleep, but she silently blessed the rigid hierarchy that required the footman to wake the housekeeper to wake the abigail to wake her mistress. She would need all of their help. She tapped softly at the door of Devenham's room and let herself in.

Mullins had been seated as close as possible to the earl's bed, obviously intent upon his master, until Phoebe entered. As she did, he jumped to his feet and came toward her with alacrity, showing a face haggard from exhaustion and worry.

"Please f'give me for disturbin' your rest, milady." Mullins was small and dark and looked to Phoebe about as un-English as a man could appear. It surprised her each time she heard him that he did not speak in the accents of an Italian or a Spaniard. He spoke instead with a broad, flat country accent.

She waved his apologies aside. "You did the right thing," she assured him, feeling her breath catch in her throat as she approached the bed.

The major lay sprawled in the tent bed, to all appearances quite lifeless. The bedsheet was pushed down to his waist, and not a scrap of clothing covered the lean, muscular display of his upper body. Her gaze took in the curling hair that covered his chest and arms, and the angry red scar that marked the injury to his left shoulder. Every inch of his exposed skin was glazed with sweat.

Phoebe swallowed hard, trying to hide her shock. It was not so much the sight of his body that caused her to tremble. She had been married, after all. It was a sudden, tingling memory of touch—the excruciating memory of intimacies shared with Stephen, the only other man she had ever seen so exposed.

She tried to cover her reaction by adopting a detached, efficient attitude. "The next few hours will be critical," she said, although she guessed Mullins already knew that. She hesitated as she bent to put a hand on the earl's forehead. She scarcely needed to touch Devenham to register how hot he was—the heat radiated from him in waves. In the face of such a fever, concern for propriety was quite rightly brushed aside.

"Have you been applying damp cloths to his skin?" she asked needlessly. On the floor beside Mullins's chair sat a basin full of damp wads of cloth. "I have sent for some fresh ones, and a new basin of water." She reached for a wad and, smoothing it out, spread it gently across Devenham's chest. "Let us apply another one to his poor head," she told Mullins. "Although they are warm now, they are still cooler than he is."

But even as Mullins handed her the second cloth, the earl began to stir and moan softly.

"'E's still havin' these spells o' restlessness," Mullins said. "It's the delirium. 'E had it bad before, in Brussels."

Phoebe nodded, attempting to place the cloth as Devenham rolled his head on the pillow. "We *must* keep him cool. We may even need ice. When is he due for his next dose of laudanum? We could increase the dose by a few drops, to help calm him."

"Not for another 'alf an hour," Mullins answered, his doubts written clearly on his face.

Devenham was becoming increasingly restless. Even as his servant and Phoebe watched, he suddenly began to shout, flailing his arms as if warding off unseen assailants.

"This won't do," said Phoebe, helplessly retrieving the damp cloths. "Sh-h. It's all right." She hoped somehow her soothing tones might penetrate to her patient's fever-wracked brain. She glanced anxiously at the bottles of medicine on the bedside table. "If he moves too much, he'll disturb the dressings, or even reopen his wound."

"Aye." Mullins was wrestling with the earl, trying to get him to lie still again. His task was not easy, for Devenham was considerably larger.

"We will give it to him now," Phoebe said decisively, moving to the table and picking up the bottle of laudanum. As she did, there was a tap at the door and the footman they called Goldie entered with a basin of water, followed by Mary Anne with an armful of towels, her eyes as big as saucers.

"Thank you, Mary Anne. Would you see if Mrs. H would bring up the tea?" Phoebe wanted to get the young maid out of the room as quickly as possible. She had no doubt that a full description of the earl's appearance would soon be circulating among the younger women servants, between embarrassed giggles. "Goldie, would you stay? We may need another pair of hands."

She measured out the dose of laudanum and mixed it with water from the decanter on the table. "Now, gentlemen. If one of you would hold down his arms, and the other hold up his head, let us see if I can coax Lord Devenham into drinking this. I'm afraid we have another long night ahead of us."

Chapter Three

Devenham had dreamed he was lying in a wind-ruffled field, watching clouds borrow worldly shapes as they paraded across the sky. The air teased him with the delicate, unidentified scent tinged with rosemary that was by now familiar to him, and nearby he had heard the sound of children's laughter, full of joy and innocence. He awoke to the featherlight touch of a hand upon his forehead.

With consciousness came the headache and lingering fatigue that plagued his waking moments. Despite the discomfort, he knew at once that the scent and the touch were real. He knew they were a woman's. He opened his eyes.

The hand withdrew instantly. All he saw above him were the generous muslin draperies of the tent bed in which he lay, surrounded by softly filtered morning light. He shifted his head on the pillow so he could see who was there.

The young woman had retreated several paces from the bed with an audible intake of breath. Was she afraid of him? As his vision slowly focused, he saw she was dressed in a sleeveless, dark gray morning dress with a deep square neckline; her arms and throat were covered by the gathered white fabric of her chemisette. A simple lace cap concealed only part of her dark hair. Her face was oval and small-featured except for a large, fine pair of eyes. He could not make out their color, but he thought he knew what they would be.

"I won't bite," he managed to mumble, "despite what you may have been told."

She did not move any closer, but merely shifted the cloth she had been holding in one hand to the other. He felt gratified to see that at least she smiled. "You have been in no condition to, my lord, up until now," she said in a soft, pleasant voice. "Welcome back to the world of the living."

He grimaced. "'Thank you' would be the proper response, I am sure, but I suspect the dream world I have just been in was more pleasant, present company excepted."

She did not seem to notice the compliment. A look of concern immediately crossed her face. "Are you in pain?" She glanced quickly at the watch pinned to the bodice of her dress. "'Tis nearly time for your medicine. Perhaps I could—"

"*No.*" The response came out more sharply than he intended. "If it is laudanum, I do not want it," he added. He was in pain, but he would not admit it. Just being awake was precious to him, and being able to think was even more so. For now, he was willing to pay the price. In a gentler tone he commanded, "Come closer, where I can see you."

She took one cautious step toward the bed. She was really quite lovely.

"It is only reasonable that we should study each other," he said, pausing to gauge the effect of his words. "But you have had the advantage over me."

She took another step closer, which brought her within an arm's length from the bed. Her eyes were gray—the lovely, luminous gray that he had expected from his haunted dreams. Finely shaped eyebrows as dark as her hair arched gracefully above them.

"I gather that we have been *companions* for some time," he added with a mischievous inflection.

A tint of pink washed across her cheeks and her eyebrows drew down into a stern frown.

"I have been helping your man, Mullins, nurse you for the past three days, my lord, while you have been senseless with fever. That is all."

"Of course." He treated her to his infamous, lopsided grin. Ladies usually found that devastating. "That is precisely what I was referring to. Coming from a man in my condition, what else could I possibly have meant?"

She blushed, and that response sent a little thrill of victory through his feeble body. Dealing with this woman was going to be quite pleasurable—a welcome distraction since, apparently, he was going to live.

"Madam, you are a delight. I must confess that although I am certain we have been properly introduced, I must not have been sentient at the time. Could you find the kindness in your obviously warm heart to tell me who you are? Perhaps you would also enlighten me as to where the devil I am, if you'll pardon my expression?"

The expression on Devenham's face conveyed an innocence that did not match his tone, Phoebe noted. His voice was deep, rich, and expressive, easily conveying first his suggestive playfulness and then, by subtly shifting tones, a certain cynicism followed by the slightest hint of impatience.

Oh, he was skilled at this game. In such a brief exchange of words, he had already managed to compliment her, embarrass her, and plant suggestive thoughts in her mind that she was not altogether sure she had needed his help to produce. How could he look so innocent?

She decided that his impatience was the most honest of the feelings she had detected, however, and she felt some sympathy for him. Guilt followed quickly. Here she was bristling at a man who could have easily slipped through death's door in the last few days. How could she be so unfeeling?

She smiled and dipped a curtsy. "I am Lady Brodfield, Lord Devenham. You are in the home of Sir Edward Allington and his wife."

The earl's lopsided grin appeared again for a moment, this time even broader than before. "Ah, Edward. I knew I could rely on him. Old friendships are more precious than diamonds, Lady Brodfield. Too many in the world fail to learn that."

He paused, as if searching his reserves for more energy. "New friendships, of course, are golden. Shall we be friends? I am honored to make your acquaintance, albeit under these rather regrettable circumstances. I must thank you for the time you have already given to my care. Will you forgive a sick man's curiosity if I ask if you are related to Sir Edward?"

She nodded, clasping in both hands the damp cloth she had used earlier to wipe the perspiration from his face. "Sir Edward's wife is my sister," she said simply. She preferred not to volunteer any further information.

Lord Devenham rolled his head back on the pillow to his original position and closed his eyes.

"Our conversation is tiring you," Phoebe said in alarm. "It is time anyway for your medication. You must rest." She thought it just as well, for she was uncomfortable with the personal direction of their conversation.

The earl opened his eyes again. "My dear woman," he said, "by your account I have just spent something like seventy-two hours sleeping. I do not wish to rest any more right now. What I do desire is to sit up."

Phoebe hesitated. The doctor had emphasized the importance of rest. Furthermore, she doubted that the earl could sit up by himself. "I do not think that is a good idea, my lord."

"What kind of nurse refuses to assist her patient?" He raised himself up onto his elbows and glared balefully at her from under a dramatically lowered brow. She almost laughed.

"I see I shall be forced to exhaust myself doing this without your help." He raised himself higher and began to pull his body up beneath the sheets.

Phoebe could see the effort it cost him. His arms shook, and perspiration trickled down his temple. "If you would just wait, I can get Edward, or a footman."

"That is not necessary. Would you at least be kind enough to reposition my pillows?"

With a sigh of defeat, Phoebe closed the distance to the bed, depositing the cloth on the table that stood beside it. She reached rather stiffly for the earl's pillows and placed them up against the headboard. "All right, my lord. I will try to help you, but I have not the strength that is really required." She hesitated, her hands suspended, for she truly did not know quite how to begin.

"Do not try to pretend that you have been my nurse for three days without touching me," said the earl.

Phoebe was embarrassed to feel the betraying tingle of a blush creep up her cheeks for a second time, which of course only intensified her reaction. When the fever had been at its worst, she and Mullins had needed to bathe Devenham's entire upper body, clothed now so properly in a shirt. She knew all too well that the golden hair just visible in the earl's unfastened neck placket covered most of his well-muscled chest with downy softness. But touching him now while he was awake seemed quite different than touching him when he had not known she was there.

Lord Devenham grinned at her. "Don't pretend either that you are missish, for then you would never have been given the job of nursing me. I promise you it will require only a moment."

She nodded, biting her lip.

"All right then, just put your arms around me." He seemed to take great delight in her discomfort. "Put one arm behind my back, and the other around my chest. When I say the word, try to help me slide up. I will push with my good leg."

Phoebe did as he said, her face burning. Her breasts were pressed against his upper arm. The flame of her embarrassment seemed to race through the rest of her body. Thank God they would be done quickly.

She waited for his signal, but he said nothing. His eyes were closed. His face showed only a hint of a smile. Was he summoning his strength, or savoring their highly improper contact? Under any other circumstances she might have slapped him, but as she debated, he opened his eyes again. "Now," he said.

She pulled and he pushed and between them they managed to get him into a position that was close to sitting upright. She withdrew hastily.

"Your shirt is soaked," she observed, straightening the dampened sleeves of her chemisette.

"Yes, it is. I should like very much to change into a fresh one."

That was too much. "Well, I am afraid you will have to wait. Mullins sat up with you all night and he is sleeping now. I will not wake him before it is time."

"I see." The earl seemed to ponder this, and then he said, "I suppose it will do me no harm to take a chill while I sit here in wet clothing, waiting, while he sleeps."

"It is a warm day."

"Nevertheless, I feel chilled."

"Then perhaps you should lie down again." Really, the man was insufferable! "I am not your valet."

"No, but you are my nurse. Is not my welfare supposed to be your interest?"

"Not at the sacrifice of all modesty and propriety."

"I would be happy to debate that." Phoebe heard his reply, even though Devenham uttered the words softly under his breath. When she stiffened, he looked at her and smiled wickedly. "It seems to me the nursing relationship is a very intimate one. Would you not agree, Lady Brodfield?"

Phoebe marched indignantly toward the door. "My lord, you go too far. I will summon a footman to assist you with your shirt and sit with you until Mr. Mullins is awake." She knew it was all a game to the earl, but truly there were polite limits and he had most definitely exceeded them.

"Please stay." The contrite sound of his voice made her hesitate at the door. "I apologize." As she stood still, debating his sincerity, he went on. "I am sorry I was disrespectful. You have been nothing but kind and generous to me, and I am grateful. If you knew the high regard I have for Sir Edward, you would know this is true. You are his sister-in-law. I just have bad habits that are hard to break, especially in the presence of a beautiful woman. Apparently even illness such as I have been suffering is not enough to break them. Please say you forgive me?"

Phoebe turned and took a few wary steps back toward the bed. "Can we leave off playing this game?" Would she have to weigh the sincerity of everything he said?

"Perhaps you would be willing to read to me? That should be innocent enough."

"All right." Phoebe sighed with relief. A number of books were stacked on the bedside table next to the earl's bottles of medicine. Edward had selected them from the bookroom himself and brought them in only the previous evening. As she looked for a suitable choice, the earl said, "How long until Mullins returns to his duty?"

Phoebe glanced at him and realized from his hunched position and the way the sheets were drawn up around him that he really must feel cold. Perhaps she had been unfair, attributing motives to him that were not really there. Now she was the one feeling contrite. "I suppose your bed linens and everything are soaked, besides your shirt. But it is more than I can do to change them without help. Perhaps I can find a blanket to put around your shoulders."

"A dry shirt would suffice until Mullins gets up," Devenham said quietly. "But I will confess I fear a footman's rough hand in assisting me with the task. My shoulder is still quite stiff from being injured. I have aggravated it a little by sitting up."

Phoebe's first reaction was annoyance, like a parent confronted by a child who will not give up what he wants. Then she wondered again about her fairness. She had rather forgotten about his shoulder. She sighed, resigned to a second defeat. "Very well. But I hope to heaven no one comes in while we are doing this!"

Devenham chuckled, and she found the sound annoyingly pleasant. "It will look no worse than if they had come in before."

She found a clean shirt in the earl's trunks. Sitting gingerly on the edge of the bed, she proceeded to help him remove his wet one.

"You can close your eyes if you truly object to seeing me," he said as he eased his right arm out of its sleeve.

"That wouldn't be very helpful, would it?" she replied matter-of-factly. She had to lean closer to work off his other sleeve, for he could not raise his left arm high enough. When finally she was able to lift the shirt off over his head, she swallowed nervously at the fine display of his chest and broad shoulders. She fought the urge to touch the angry red scar below his left collarbone.

Surely she must be the most wanton-hearted woman who had ever borne her family name. This man had merely to show himself and she was already conquered, without his uttering a word. But she would die before she would ever let him find it out. Quickly she snatched up the fresh shirt from the bedclothes where it lay and pulled it over his head, reversing the process they had just completed. She was careful to slow down and proceed gently as she worked again with his arm and injured shoulder.

When they were finished, he lay back against his pillows, thoroughly spent. "Perhaps I will rest, after all," he said weakly. "Will you read to me later?" A huge yawn nearly enveloped his last words.

Phoebe rose from the bed quickly. "Of course." She noticed that despite his fatigue, his hands were restless. "After all this activity, will you have the laudanum now?"

He yawned again before he answered. "Yes, I will take it. I guess I am still too weak to go without it."

His remark puzzled her a little, but she got the spoon and bottle from the bedside and carefully measured out his dose. "You will be glad of this when Mullins comes, for he will have to change your dressing, and I'm sure you will find that uncomfortable enough, if you are still awake."

He swallowed the drug and rested against the pillows again, looking at her through half-closed eyes. "You could do it."

"What? No, I could not!" The very idea shocked her. His wound was quite far up his leg, almost to his hip, the doctor had said. The idea of any female other than a lover ever seeing. . . .

She stopped herself. He was doing it to her again, making her think the most improper thoughts! How could he know? Were other women as susceptible as she? Had he known so many?

Defiantly she met his eyes, and too late realized her mistake. His head was tilted provocatively to one side, and his brilliant blue gaze openly challenged her. The Devil himself was visible there. How on earth would she ever resist this man?

"Perhaps I should give you more laudanum," she growled. "I may have miscalculated the dose."

The earl was sound asleep within minutes. Watching him, Phoebe noted that his breathing came easily and his color was good, a far cry from the feverish paleness she had seen the day of his arrival. In sleep, his face bore no trace of insolence, no hint of mockery. Instead, he looked composed—peaceful and almost innocent, his shapely lips curved in a slight smile.

His expression reminded her of Stephen, on so many nights when she would lie awake beside him, watching him sleep. For an instant, an old, familiar tenderness welled within her, and she almost touched the earl's cheek. Then she pulled her hand back hastily. What was she thinking? Who knew better than she how deceiving such an appearance could be? What thoughts and feelings really turned in Devenham's mind? So many nights she had lain beside Stephen in the last months of their marriage, never guessing the torment he must have been hiding. No trace of it had ever shown in his face.

She set her chair at a distance from the bed so she would not keep looking at Devenham. She took up her needlework, but she was not able to stop thinking about the earl. Truly, she did not think that they could become friends. He was far too attractive, too dangerous, and she was far too vulnerable.

Needlework, while eminently respectable, was not an activity Phoebe found stimulating. Before long her head dropped and she dozed in her chair, victimized by the long hours and lost sleep of the past few days. Her rest was fitful and fragmented, as such stolen moments tend to be; she thought she was simply remembering as Stephen came to her, warm and real enough to touch. But when she reached her hands out to him, he turned away, and as her fingers connected with his flesh, he suddenly became Devenham. She awoke in alarm and confusion, to find no one there and nothing amiss save that her embroidery hoop had slid from her lap to the floor. All was silent except for the sound of the earl's deep, regular breathing, coming from the bed.

Clearly, the man was having an effect on her, just as she had feared. Phoebe got up and walked to the window, not willing to risk another lapse into sleep. How would she deal with Devenham now that he was beginning his recovery? Insensible with fever, he had been harmless enough. She had been able to bury the attraction she felt to him. Awake, he had been both provoking and manipulative. She was mortified that she had given in to his wishes so easily, and terrified by the physical response he had stirred in her. She did not know how she would get through the weeks ahead.

She was still at the window when Mullins presented himself and allowed her to make her escape while the earl still slept. She retreated up the stairs to the safety of the schoolroom and the part of her life she knew she could mange.

"Who would like to go to the park?" she called brightly to Lizzie and the children as she entered, knowing their response was guaranteed. She smiled at the expected chorus of affirmative replies.

She had assigned the children writing exercises to perform in her absence and now proceeded to check their work.

"Yours seem rather short, Thomas," she chided gently. "Even great soldiers must write reports, you know. Where would Wellington be without the dispatches he exchanges with his officers, or the reports he sends back to Prinny and to Parliament? How would anyone know what was expected of them?" With sudden inspiration she said, "How would you like to write me a make-believe sort of military report for later this week?"

The little boy was clearly delighted. "Oh, Aunt Phoebe, that's capital! Can it be whatever I want? Oh, I know you will like it!"

Dorrie made her opinion very clear. "I suppose I have to continue muddling along more lines of Caesar. Aunt Phoebe, why can I not have an assignment in something that is more interesting? Even Shakespeare would be better—at least he wrote plays."

"I promise I will consider it," Phoebe replied.

William had played an alphabet game with Lizzie, part of Phoebe's secret scheme to teach reading and writing to the young maid along with her charges. Now he stood by the long shelf near the windows where the children's small menagerie was kept. They had fish, a turtle, a frog, mice, and even a bird. William never ran out of questions. "Can we bring Mrs. Finchley with us to the park?"

David rolled his eyes with an older brother's typical intolerance, but Phoebe appeared to ponder William's question quite seriously. Mrs. Finchley was their pet bird.

"You could take her to the park, William, but let me ask you something. She is used to the schoolroom and her cage. How do you think she would feel when she saw all the open space in the park, and the clear blue sky overhead?"

William's round, brown eyes were full of childish innocence. "I think she'd like it!"

"Indeed, so do I. But do you think she would want to stay inside her cage?"

"No."

"Would she be happy when we brought her back to the schoolroom?"

"I guess not."

"Yet, would she be safe if we let her out? What do you think she would do?"

"Fly away?"

"And perhaps get into trouble. So, do you think it would be a good idea to take her?"

"No." The little lad's disappointment was clearly expressed in his deep, heart-rending sigh.

Phoebe's own soft heart was seldom proof against the children when they were disappointed in something. Casting about for something that would distract or appease William, Phoebe was struck with a sudden impulse. "How would you like it if I were to come with you?"

It suddenly seemed like the most logical thing in the world.

Five pairs of eyes turned on Phoebe in surprise. She had never accompanied them on excursions outside of the house, except in their own garden.

"Would you? Oh, would you?" The children clapped their hands in delight.

"Are you certain, my lady?" Lizzie's eyes were as big as William's at this sudden departure from normal routine.

Phoebe had rather surprised herself as much as the others, but the idea pleased her. She thought accompanying the children would be the perfect escape from her unsettling reactions to Devenham. How would she get her mind off the earl if she stayed in the house, staring at walls while the children went out? She loved being with them and would enjoy watching them play instead of study.

She knew she would be nervous and shaky, fearful of being recognized in public, but it could not be as disastrous as her first attempt to step out into the world, at her father-in-law's commemorative. Surely this would be a much easier test. The park did not carry all the emotional connections that plagued her at St. George's, and she would not be alone. She needed to get on with her life. She could not do that if she continued to hide inside this house. She would also find it much easier to avoid Lord Devenham if they were not both continually closeted under the same roof.

Chapter Four

Phoebe's initial enthusiasm for her decision to go out had begun to wane by the time she, Lizzie, the children, and the long-suffering footman carrying their hamper had walked as far as Oxford Street. She had declined Edward's offer of a carriage to take them to the park; in her disturbed state of mind she had thought she would welcome the exercise. She had not realized how quickly the warm, pleasant sun would become oppressively hot, nor had she counted on the busy pedestrian traffic along the streets, or the children's slow pace.

Dorrie stopped at every third shop window to ogle whatever was on display—shawls, toys, kid slippers, perfumed soap. David inspected and rated every rig that passed by in the street except for those he missed while distracted by Dorrie. Thomas appeared to be marching smartly but slowly to the beat of his own drummer, while William—well, William seemed to be accompanied by several invisible companions, all of whom required that no one step on any cracks or joints between paving stones, lest their magical powers be destroyed. Phoebe thought Hyde Park had never seemed so far away.

She thought that she ought not to mind. She had known she would feel self-conscious as their little procession made its way along the street. She had hoped the challenge of overcoming that discomfort would prove helpful in dispelling her thoughts of Devenham. Even so, she felt the glances, real or imagined, of people they passed.

She knew she was being foolish. Surely she was as anonymous as anyone else walking on Oxford Street this morning. She had chosen a bonnet with an especially deep brim, and thought that there was no reason why anyone should particularly take note of her. Yet she dreaded the possibility that she might suddenly run into someone who knew her.

Am I a coward? she asked herself. *What is the worst that could possibly happen?* She knew what she feared most was that someone would report having seen her and all the old, ugly gossip would start up again. *Am I not stronger now? What can they say now that was not already said a year and a half ago?* Besides, she did not feel alone now, as she had during those first awful days after Stephen's body had been found. She had a loving family to support her.

She looked ahead at the children enjoying the innocent pleasures of their walk, untroubled by the complexities of the adult world. As if they felt her gaze upon them, they all quite suddenly turned to her.

"I am all right," she said to the concerned little faces in front of her. "Do let's go on."

She had no sooner pushed aside one group of uncomfortable thoughts, however, than the other group came back to the fore. Devenham refused to stay out of her mind.

He definitely puzzled her. Here was a man the doctor had said did not care about living. Weakened as he was, he had nevertheless been deliberately provoking. But why? Was it truly out of habit, as he had said? The earl had not known who she was and clearly had no knowledge of her history. His baiting her had been nothing personal, which, she decided, made his behavior all the more reprehensible. Yet, if he was habitually so provoking, how had he managed to win the hearts of so many ladies of the *ton*, or such devoted loyalty as Mullins had shown in the past three days?

She could not answer these questions, although they turned slowly about in her mind like leaves caught in the outermost edge of a whirlpool. She wondered again if she might have misjudged him. Had he really said anything so shocking? Perhaps it had all been conjured up in her own wanton mind. How had he managed to ruffle her so much that she actually sought refuge on the streets of London? But when she closed her eyes and recalled his words and the look in his eyes, she knew the fault was not hers alone. He had manipulated her and enjoyed every minute of it. He had practically seduced her, not in body but in mind and will. She had not proved very resistant. When she thought of this, she felt ruffled all over again.

They had hardly gone another block before the children as one body halted abruptly in front of a haberdasher's shop.

"Aunt Phoebe! Aunt Phoebe! Oh, look, Aunt Phoebe!" they cried excitedly. Loudly.

Phoebe's heart sank. If she had merely imagined people noticing them before, such was surely not the case now. She couldn't imagine what could possibly be of such interest in a haberdasher's window, and hurried to catch up to and quiet the children.

"Lady Brodfield! Phoebe! How wonderful! It *is* you, isn't it?"

Phoebe had dreaded hearing those words for so long that now the actual sound seemed unreal. Yet two female figures on the other side of the street had detached themselves from the flow of traffic there and were hurrying across to her. She could not run, and there was no place to hide. She had no choice but to face them.

The slim young woman in lavender had fashionable ringlets even darker than Phoebe's peeking out from her bonnet and a voluminous shawl that slipped off one shoulder as she first embraced Phoebe and then held her at arm's length for inspection. She was Lucinda Follett, with whom Phoebe had once been quite friendly. Phoebe recognized the portly woman clad in elegant gray silk behind Lucinda as her mother. A young maid trailed in their wake and narrowly escaped being run over between a hackney and a landau passing each other in the street.

"Phoebe, how remarkable to run into you! I could hardly believe my ears and eyes. Where have you been keeping yourself all this time? It must be all of a year and a half since I've seen you. You simply disappeared!"

Phoebe paused awkwardly. What could she say? "Lucy, how well you look. Married life must agree with you."

Lucinda nodded happily, a faint tint coloring her cheeks, but she was not deterred. "When did you return to London? Can you imagine how much we missed you? What in heaven's name are you doing here at this time of year, although," she added with a giggle, "you might well ask us the same question. Imagine our meeting like this!"

Imagine, indeed, thought Phoebe wryly. The irony was almost too great to comprehend. If she had wanted to advertise her presence in London, Lucinda's mother would have been on her list of top ten candidates for the task, right next to the *Morning Post* and the *Chronicle*.

Still, Lucinda seemed genuinely pleased to see her. Phoebe knew the other young woman had always been friendly and kind, and she felt a pinprick of guilt at the way she had abruptly dropped all of the people she had once counted as friends.

She sighed. "I found that I just couldn't face people after what happened, Lucy. I hope you understand. I never meant to offend my friends. I have been living very quietly with my sister and her husband."

Lucinda bobbed her head sympathetically. "It was a terrible time, wasn't it?" She eyed Phoebe's black bonnet and dyed black muslin dress. "And poor thing, here you are in mourning again. I—of course. You are in Town because of Lord Tyneley's commemorative! I'm sorry, Phoebe. You know sometimes I am so feather-brained."

Phoebe thought there was no point to correcting Lucinda's conclusions about her presence in London. Whatever it was that had captivated the children was being shown to Lizzie and Goldie at the moment. The children were far too well-bred to interrupt their aunt's conversation, but Phoebe knew from looking at them that they were close to bursting with impatience.

"You remember my mother, Lady Shadwell?" said Lucinda, drawing the lady in question to her side.

"Of course," Phoebe responded politely, valiantly restraining her urge to make further comment. Lady Shadwell was a rather unforgettable figure.

"My dear," said Lady Shadwell, holding out her hand limply. "I can see that you are a bit occupied at the moment." She glanced significantly toward the children.

"Yes," answered Phoebe, well aware that the woman was fishing for information at the same time she was providing

Phoebe with a perfect way to end the conversation. How peculiar to feel annoyed and grateful at once! "I am with my young niece and nephews, on our way to the park."

Lucy graciously yielded. Grasping Phoebe's hand, she said, "This is of course no place to have a conversation, dear Phoebe. Will you be in Town long? Do say you will come for tea later this week. I will send 'round a note to remind you. Just tell me your direction."

Trapped, Phoebe thought. *So much for coming out slowly.* She thought she must feel rather like a snail who has just poked out its horns, only to be blinded by the light. She could not say she did not know if she would be in Town long enough, for certainly the word about Devenham would soon be making the rounds, and her prevarication would be obvious. She genuinely liked Lucinda. She would need allies when she began to circulate again. She would make herself go.

"I should be delighted, Lucy, thank you. You may recall my sister is Lady Allington, Sir Edward's wife. They are on Wigmore Street, near Portman Square."

Even as she spoke these last words, Phoebe felt a small hand slip into hers, and there was William, gazing up at her with an intense expression. She took her leave of the ladies and as they went on their way up the street, she allowed William to lead her rather indecorously the other way, toward the haberdasher's and the children bouncing about in front of it. "Yes, children. Now, what *is* it?"

An open crate sat in the window, displaying a quivering mass of brown and white fur that resolved itself into six separate spaniel puppies as she studied it. "Goodness! What a curious thing to find at a haberdasher's, to be sure," she said in a teasing voice.

"Oh, Aunt Phoebe, aren't they beautiful? Can't we get one? Aren't they adorable?"

The questions were predictable, and Phoebe knew what her answer had to be, despite the power of the puppies' considerable charm. She had to stiffen her backbone and will her sensible head to prevail over her soft heart. "What, pray tell, would you do with the poor thing, stuck here in the city as we are? Dogs need to be able to run in the fields. I'm afraid you are much better off with Mrs. Finchley, Tobias, the Mousekins, and Fremont, none of whom would appreciate the addition of a puppy to their number, I'm certain."

"That's true, the Mousekins might die of fright," Dorrie said reluctantly.

"They would not! They are braver than that," Thomas said, staunchly defending the honor of the pet mice.

"Anyway," David added thoughtfully, "the puppy wouldn't live in the schoolroom with the Menagerie. He could go everywhere we did."

"Nevertheless, there will be no puppy," Phoebe said firmly. "Come, let us continue walking, or we shall faint from hunger before we ever reach the park. Have you no interest in the nuncheon that Cook put up for us?" Phoebe knew that food was always a reliable distraction for her fast-growing charges.

They had to cross the carriage ride that circled the park, but at this hour of the day it was not busy. Phoebe thought that her courage might have failed her in the afternoon hours when riding in the park was *de rigeur* for the fashionable.

The trees and grass offered welcome relief from the late morning heat, and the children ran on ahead. "Here, right here!" called Thomas, choosing a shaded spot on the grassy sward. His siblings danced around him, echoing his cry.

Phoebe laughed. "Are you certain? This exact spot?"

Goldie spread the blanket for them and they settled down to consume the goodies in their basket. When they had finished, Phoebe and Lizzie laughed as they watched the young footman settle himself in position for a nap under the nearest tree.

"Such a great protector he'll be," Lizzie ventured scornfully, but Phoebe thought she could detect a hint of warmth beneath the maid's words.

"Ah, now Lizzie, I've no doubt he has a right to be tired," she responded generously. "The earl has robbed us of several nights' sleep."

Phoebe reflected on how tired she felt herself, and wondered whether she might have handled Lord Devenham better on another day, when she was better rested. Since his arrival, she had not only lost sleep keeping watch at his bedside, but she had also been troubled by recurring dreams of Stephen and fragments of memories, all painful to her now.

It seemed important that the earl should not know he had such an effect on her. Next time they met, she would do better. *Next time?* Well, she could not hope to escape him. It would be some time still before he would be well enough to finish his homeward journey, and in the meantime he would continue to need care. But she resolved to try as much as possible to avoid being with him when he was awake.

Dorrie was full of questions about the earl, but Phoebe tried to distract her by sounding her out on the subject of finishing schools. The three boys had taken William's ball out into the open grass where they raced about like demons in the midday sun. One by one their jackets collected in a pile on the edge of the blanket. Phoebe was not paying particular attention to them until she heard a shout of dismay issue from their direction.

That dratted ball again! thought Phoebe. This time the errant ball had escaped the players and rolled down a little slope into the middle of a game being played by a group of rather dirty urchins, to Phoebe and Lizzie's alarm. At this unfashionable time of day and equally unfashionable time of year, the park seemed to be given over largely to the city's poor.

Lizzie lost no time going to Goldie and trying to rouse him. Phoebe watched as her nephews bravely confronted the other boys. By the time the sleepy footman was headed in their direction, the children had sorted things out themselves with an odd exchange of assorted gestures and words Phoebe could not hear. David, Thomas, and William returned triumphantly with the ball as the other boys went peacefully back to their own business.

"What was that all about?" Phoebe asked.

The boys exchanged looks and replied innocently, "What? They're just some boys, and they gave us back William's ball."

"Lucky for them that they did," harumphed Goldie, apparently disappointed that no heroics had been called for.

"Why were they pointing off into the bushes?" Phoebe persevered.

"Oh, no reason."

"They were just showing us some places to watch out for— you know, if we lost the ball again."

Satisfied, Phoebe squinted up at the sun, and consulted the watch she always wore pinned to her bodice. "Well, I think it may be just as well you were interrupted," she said, "for it is getting to be time to head home."

She waited patiently through the chorus of protests that met her remark. "If we had spent the entire day here, you would still think it too soon to go home, you know," she pointed out reasonably. She supervised the process of packing up the assortment of things they had brought with them, and led the way as they left the park. She did not notice the boys looking back at the clump of shrubbery that had been the object of their earlier interest.

The significance of the escaped ball incident was not revealed to Phoebe until dinner. Contrary to the fashion, Judith and Edward often dined early with their children at table in the absence of guests. Judith staunchly maintained that there was no better opportunity for them to practice their manners free from the critical eyes of society. Phoebe wholeheartedly supported this practice, agreeing that the loving eyes of their parents were far more merciful, although watching little William trying to sip milk out of a crystal goblet sometimes lent an element of suspense to the proceedings.

The children had happily recounted their earlier adventures, detailing every item to be seen along Oxford Street quite as if neither they nor their parents had ever set foot there before. They lingered hopefully over their descriptions of the spaniel puppies, to no avail. Finally they had reached the point in their narrative where the straying ball had to be retrieved in the park.

"It rolled right into the midst of some rather rough-looking boys playing Fox and Geese," David announced, pausing with a dramatic flair worthy of Dorrie. As he surveyed his audience to let the tension build, William jumped into what he clearly took for a breach in the flow of the story.

"I was afraid they would not give it back," he said, his little face solemn. "They were *dirty*, and they looked mean. But David and Thomas weren't scared," he added with an appreciative look at his brothers. "They marched right up to the biggest boy. And he turned out to be nice. He gave us back the ball, and he even told us about the man in the—"

"Sh-h, idiot!" David rolled his eyes in despair. Thomas covered his face with his hands and very slowly shook his head. William clamped a hand over his own mouth and turned anxious eyes toward his mother.

"David, you will not call your brother an idiot."

"Sorry."

"We will not have our dining room mistaken for a nursery, children. No names, no games, and no secrets. Now, what is all this to-do about a man?"

The boys exchanged looks and silently appointed David spokesman, since he was the eldest of the three. He immediately looked at Judith. "Mamma, may I have a word with you in private—please?"

Judith might not have relented except for the agonized expression on David's face, and the unusual amount of emphasis he had managed to give the last word. When she nodded, the lad fairly bounded out of his chair to go to her.

Phoebe felt extremely uneasy. Obviously something had occurred at the park of which she had been entirely unaware. Had she been too distracted by her own thoughts to exercise appropriate vigilance? What bothered her most was that, whatever had happened, the children obviously had not felt they could confide in her. She felt far more shaken by that than anything else that had occurred all day, including her encounter with Lord Devenham.

"All right, I understand," Judith was saying as David finished whispering in her ear. "I am sure you thought you were being noble. But although your motives may have been the best, I have to tell you that in this case you did not do the right thing."

All three boys looked crestfallen at this and, for a moment, they did not seem to Phoebe all that far apart in age.

"David, please tell your father and Aunt Phoebe what you just explained to me." Judith looked very serious indeed.

"The boys told us there was a man over in the bushes who had been watching us ever since we had settled down in that spot in the park. We didn't believe them. I thought if there was somebody, he was probably just—you know, cup-shot."

Phoebe saw Judith cringe as she heard this comment from her ten-year-old, but she did not interrupt.

"We looked where they pointed, and sure enough, there was a man there, watching Dorrie and Aunt Phoebe. But when he saw us looking his way, real quick-like he slid out from the bushes and walked away fast. We decided not to tell, because he left, and we thought Aunt Phoebe and Dorrie would just get frightened."

Dorrie had remained most noticeably silent after her siblings' revelations at dinner. When the children were sent up to bed, Phoebe followed, and sought to give her niece some reassurance.

"You mustn't be alarmed about the man in the park, Dorrie. He was most likely just a secret admirer, embarrassed at being discovered. He did us no harm, and I'm sure he meant us none. We should feel flattered that he found us so worthy of his attention!" Perched casually on the edge of Dorrie's bed, she managed to achieve a light, reassuring tone. She only wished she could believe her own words as easily as she hoped Dorrie would.

When she stopped in the room that David and Thomas shared, the boys in turn assured her that they had sought merely to spare her feelings by not telling her about the unknown man. "There seemed to be no point in it," David finished, "once the man was already gone."

"I appreciate and thank you for your attempt to shield me from being upset," she said gently, observing their chastened spirits, "but I think somehow we have gotten things turned about. It is the adults who are supposed to shield the children, not the other way 'round."

She bid each of them good night with a kiss, and quietly headed for the stairs, lost in thought. Did the children see her as so fragile, so weak, that she needed even their protection? Did they think, perhaps, that she was cowardly? She had never stopped before to consider how they might perceive her in the light of her reclusive habits. If that was indeed what they thought of her, then it was far and away time to make a change. It was time to take back control of her life, and to stop hiding. For the first time all day, she felt glad that she had accepted Lucy's invitation to tea.

Mullins was waiting for her in the shadows of the first floor landing. He stepped forward just as she came down the last step.

"Oh, Mullins!" she exclaimed, putting her hand to her throat in an instinctive gesture. "I didn't think there was anyone here but Aristotle," she added, smiling as she regained her composure.

"Sorry to startle you, Lady Brodfield. I never meant to. It's just that his lordship has been askin' for you all day. Would you be kind enough to see him?"

Would she? Phoebe hesitated. She had spent the afternoon with the children and their lessons, and with Judith in her sitting room. She supposed she was not a very responsible nurse if she did not at least check on her patient, much as she might prefer not to. Hadn't she just resolved to stop hiding from things? "Very well," she agreed. "I'll stop in for just a moment."

As she entered the guest room, Phoebe was surprised to see by the soft light of the bedside lamp that Devenham's bed was quite empty.

"I believe you have been avoiding me since this morning," came his deep voice, startling her. How jumpy she was! Perhaps her nerves were more overset by old friends roaming Oxford Street and strange men lurking in bushes than she had thought. She took a breath to calm herself.

The earl was seated in the wing chair by the hearth, clad in a dressing gown with a blanket covering his legs. As Phoebe approached, she noted that the glow from the fire in the grate lit his face and emphasized the whiteness of his shirt collar against the deep blue of the brocaded silk wrapper.

"You should be in bed, my lord," Phoebe chided. "Whatever was Mullins thinking?"

"Nonsense," replied the earl in a dampening tone. "If you are any kind of a nurse, Lady Brodfield, you should know it is important for a patient to change his position whenever possible. Demmed if I'll suffer bedsores on top of everything else."

Phoebe ignored his language. "But you are so weak! You need to rest."

"I have been resting all day, waiting for you." He gave her an angelic smile. "I wanted to apologize."

Phoebe did not know whether to sit down or stay standing. She did not know whether he was being sincere, or starting a new game with her. She looked at him dubiously.

"You surprise me," Devenham said. "I thought you would deny avoiding me. Have I been punished sufficiently for my bad behavior? Please, Lady Brodfield, since you are here, sit down." He indicated the straight chair that was already so familiar to her, now drawn up by the hearth opposite the wing chair.

She perched uneasily on the edge of the seat. "Had you not considered the possibility that I am charged with other duties besides yourself?" she asked testily.

His attractively lopsided grin appeared, gleaming in the dim light. "Indeed, I had. But I am a man, with a man's vanity. I found that I preferred to think I was being punished, and that I was at least that much on your mind."

Disarmed by his candor, she stood up again and moved a few steps toward the fire. She could not possibly admit to him that he was so completely right, or that he had read her so well. What an aggravating man! Aggravating, yet at the same time dangerously charming.

The earl continued when she did not respond. "As I said, I wish to apologize to you for my behavior this morning. I often act the scoundrel without thinking—it is a role that comes easily to me. I am sorry I offended you. Especially you, of all people!"

She turned around at that, her question in her face. "Why me, of all people?"

"Mullins has told me how faithfully you attended me in the throes of my delirium. I am greatly in your debt. I am sure you must be tired, and I shall not detain you long. But I must make it clear to you how much I shall still need you, now that I appear to be recovering." He sighed, and suddenly looked as weary as Phoebe knew he must be.

"Shall I call Mullins?" she asked quickly, making a move toward the door.

Devenham waved a hand vaguely as if to detain her. "No, let me finish first." He interrupted himself, serving her with a penetrating stare. "*Will* you sit down, woman? You are very restless and unusually quiet tonight. I hope it is not on my account."

She shook her head and sat down again meekly. Her discomfort was not on his account alone, at least. But she was not about to confide her troubles to him.

"Better. Now, I will still be needing you as a nurse, I know, but I shall need a secretary while I am here, as well. Since I have not shown sense enough to die, there is a good deal of business that I must attend to. Mullins will have to serve as my legs and my presence about Town, temporarily. He will not always be able to spend entire days at my side as he did today." He lifted one eyebrow, managing to produce a mischievous expression despite his obvious fatigue.

Sobering again, he continued. "Mullins's handwriting resembles chicken scratches more than anything alphabetical in nature, and I will have letters that must be sent. So, after what happened today, I would like to arrange with you in advance for your services. Will you help me?"

Phoebe folded her hands in her lap and fought the impulse to get up again. Did she really have a choice?

She ventured a glance at Devenham, only to discover his blue eyes regarding her intently. She could feel his magnetism; indeed, she had been more than a little aware of it from the moment she stepped into the room. She decided it was inescapable and that she had better become accustomed to it. Some perverse fate seemed to have decreed that she must spend time with the earl.

"Do you promise to behave?" she asked.

"You have my word on it."

So much for her decision to avoid him. She closed her eyes, feeling that somehow, just when she had decided to take charge of her life, everything in it was spinning in different directions, out of control.

"You may call Mullins in now," Devenham said softly.

Chapter Five

The following days settled into a regular pattern. Phoebe divided her mornings and afternoons, spending part of each with the children at their lessons, and part with Lord Devenham, assisting him with correspondence or whatever else he required. Her hours with him passed quietly, measured more by the scratch of her pen on foolscap and the deep, regular cadences of his voice than by anything else, Phoebe thought.

She had not desired to deepen her acquaintance with the earl. His presence in her life, while unsettling, was temporary, and once he was gone she planned to get on with the business of building some sort of future for herself.

However, her role as his secretary had suddenly positioned her squarely, if uncomfortably, on intimate terms with his private affairs. Her elegantly rounded script spelled out seemingly endless instructions and queries to his bailiffs at three estates, and comforting reassurances to his mother in Rutland. She penned letters to his commander and to fellow officers in his regiment, and others to solicitors and bankers. She even wrote notes to several of his personal friends, whose names she recognized as among London's most notorious. She was relieved that these contained nothing even remotely out of the ordinary. And, he had not asked her to write to any women.

In truth, she found no evidence to support the dire reputation he was supposed to have. From what she could tell, he was nothing if not conscientious, dutiful, responsible, and courteous—just exactly what she had not expected. His demeanor toward her was businesslike, except for his occasional lapses in language and a tendency to ask her discomforting questions.

"Where did you get that God-awful stuff you've been passing off on me as tea?" he asked one afternoon when she had finally allowed him to indulge in a cup of the regular beverage.

He was ensconced in the wing chair, which had been pulled over to the window. She sat in the straight chair opposite him, with a small writing table between them. For the moment, it was burdened with tea things rather than papers.

"That was tea," she replied calmly, "just not of the Chinese variety. Milfoil, or yarrow as some call it, has been known for centuries as an aid to healing wounds and combating fevers. An old name for it is Soldier's Wort."

"Did you make it?"

"I instructed our kitchen help in making the tea. I grow the herbs right out there in the garden." She nodded toward the window.

"Ah that explains the scent."

"What do you mean?"

"The scent you wear. It has been haunting me ever since I arrived here."

Suddenly the conversation seemed to have become very personal. "It is a combination of rosemary and lemon verbena," Phoebe said in a flat, matter-of-fact voice. How ridiculous that such a small comment from him had set her pulse racing! She could feel it in her breast, her throat, and the palms of her hands.

"It lingers very pleasantly," he said. "I can smell it on the writing paper after you are finished each day, and sometimes on other things as well. Yet it is very delicate, very light." His voice was suddenly warm, and Phoebe realized with alarm that his gaze was, as well.

I mustn't appear flustered, she told herself firmly. Truly, the idea of him sniffing the paper after she left the room each day, of him *haunted* by her scent, was very unsettling indeed. "I—I make it myself." She felt a response was necessary and did not know what else to day.

"It is very seductive."

He was pushing her for a reaction, she knew. He must be very bored to be playing games with her after his promise to behave. "It isn't meant to be," she snapped. She reached for the rolled copy of the *Times* that lay on the tea tray and opened it with a loud rustling of pages. She scanned quickly for something that would distract him from this line of conversation.

"Did your husband like it?"

Her head jerked up at that. She couldn't help showing a reaction. "That is certainly none of your business!"

His voice was gentle, in contrast to her sharp tone. "I am not toying with you, Lady Brodfield. I only ask because I am interested in you. I want to know you, to understand you. You never speak about your late husband. It seems curious."

The pages of the newspaper were shaking. "I find it painful to talk about the past. Like most human beings, I prefer to avoid pain."

He was looking at her with sympathy now, and Phoebe was not sure she liked that any better than the hunger she had detected in his eyes just before.

"I am sure you must have some very happy memories of your husband," he said. "Sometimes it helps to share those with a caring friend."

Phoebe raised the pages of the newspaper like a barrier between herself and the inquisitive earl. He had managed to touch a chord in her—to reach through some infinitesimal crack in the wall she had built around her heart, to some loneliness and longing she did not want to admit existed there. She could not, would not acknowledge it.

"His Royal Highness, the Duke of York, has broken his arm," she announced, studying the small print and swallowing the lump in her throat. "It seems he slipped on the oilcloth while taking a showerbath at Oatlands."

Devenham sighed, and Phoebe took it as a sign of capitulation. After a pause he commented dryly, "How undignified, and how embarrassing to have it reported in the *Times*. His poor Highness, although certainly it is nothing compared to a juicy scandal. Will he be all right?"

She was relieved that he had accepted the change of topic. "It says his doctors have seen to him."

"I suppose that will keep him at home for several weeks to come. As far as I am concerned, that is all to the good. I should like to be mobile again before my presence is required at one of his military levees."

Their conversation was interrupted by the arrival of Maddocks, bearing mail for Phoebe.

"You look astonished," Devenham said as Phoebe broke the seal on the letter.

"I seldom receive mail," she answered absently, intent upon reading it. Her face cleared as she saw the note was from Lucinda Follett. "As it happens, however, I was told to expect this."

She smiled as she refolded Lucy's letter. There was a certain note of satisfaction in her voice as she informed him, "I am afraid you will have to do without me tomorrow afternoon, my lord. I am invited to take tea with an old friend."

It was Judith who convinced Phoebe to take Goldie instead of Mary Anne as her escort to tea at Lady Follett's. In the several days that had passed, Phoebe had rather forgotten about the lurker in the park, but Judith had not. Aware that her sister's fears were now mirrored in her own anxiety, Phoebe was inclined to dismiss as pure imagination her feeling that someone was following them when she and Goldie walked the short distance to Lucy's gracious town house in the heart of Mayfair.

Phoebe had taken extra pains with her appearance, ferreting out the best articles of mourning dress in her wardrobe for this occasion. She had made Mary Anne fuss with her hair quite uncharacteristically, and she knew it was from nervousness at the upcoming encounter.

Upstairs in Lucy's elegantly furnished drawing room, Phoebe felt awkward. How out of practice she was at making conversation! However, she had given some prior thought to the meeting, and had resolved to set things straight with her old acquaintance. Nurturing a friendship from a base that was tainted by misconceptions would be like trying to grow seedlings in soil filled with rock and weeds.

"Lucy, you were very kind to invite me to tea," she began politely. "It will surprise you to hear that I have not been in the habit of going out at all for some time now. I actually feel quite nervous. Please, you must not think it is on your account."

"Oh, my dear, I feel honored that you've come," Lucy responded sympathetically. She settled Phoebe into a chair beside the tea table and proceeded to pour, passing her guest a steaming cup made of the thinnest porcelain. Everything in Lucy's drawing room was of the latest style, as was Lucy's lemon-yellow muslin gown. "I had no idea. Of course, you are in mourning . . ."

Phoebe shook her head. "There is something I would like to clear up between us, Lucy. I am in mourning again, as you say. But I am not just arrived in London for my father-in-law's commemorative. I have been here through the entire Season."

"The entire Season?" Lucy was dumbfounded. "But no one knew! What a terrible waste! Why would you hide like that? You are so beautiful and charming; you would have been such a welcome guest. However did you manage to keep your presence such a secret? Your servants must be the rarest souls of discretion. I can scarcely credit it."

Phoebe smiled sadly. "Nonetheless, it is true. I have become a recluse. I appreciate your confidence that I would have been welcome everywhere, but I do not share it. Do you not remember all the scandalous things people were saying after Stephen's death? I doubt you have any idea the number of people who gave me the cut direct after all that."

Lucy set aside her tea and rose from her chair to come to Phoebe. She took Phoebe's hand between hers and looked earnestly into her eyes. "Phoebe Brodfield, have you no idea how short a memory the *ton* is subject to? You missed the entire Season after Stephen's death, when the scandal was fresh in their minds. By the time this year's Season began, all sorts of new scandals had occurred to take up their attention."

Lucy gave Phoebe's hand a little pat and released it, moving to the tea table to pass the plate of cakes.

"You may be right," Phoebe replied, sighing, "but I cannot help feeling that it is partly because I stayed out of sight. You know, out of sight, out of mind? I am afraid that will not continue to be the case, however. I am very grateful, despite the heat, that it is August and that most people are gone from Town."

"Heavens, Phoebe. Whatever do you mean?"

Phoebe took a deep breath. "The Earl of Devenham is stay-ing with us while he recuperates from his war wounds. If it is not already common knowledge, I am sure that it will be soon. I am afraid there is no way the rest of us will escape being no-ticed."

"But Phoebe," exclaimed Lucy, turning around to study her, "that is famous! What a wonderful way to re-emerge on the scene! You cannot have planned to hide forever. The Earl of Devenham, imagine!"

"I don't know that it is so wonderful, Lucy. He has a scan-dalous reputation. And I have most definitely put myself on the shelf. I had no desire to 're-emerge on the scene.'"

Lucy sat down again across from Phoebe. "My dear," she said, "forgive me for phrasing it so bluntly, but I thought Stephen was the one who was buried, not you. You must allow me to help you start circulating again." She lowered her voice then and said, "Now, tell me all about Lord Devenham."

The earl himself was fretful and bored in Phoebe's absence. After listening to Mullins's halting attempts to read him the day's news, he had snatched the paper from the poor fellow's hands and spent some time reading it for himself, thanks to the brand-new pair of spectacles Mullins had succeeded in procur-ing for him over the course of the past few days.

He soon wearied of this occupation, however, and set the precious spectacles back on the table beside him with a sigh. "Perhaps I will take a nap, Mullins. I am sick to death of being incapacitated. If I am not allowed out of this room soon, I think I shall go mad. At least there might be some entertain-ment value in that."

Mullins obligingly rose to his feet, but as he did, Devenham heard giggles outside his door. "I believe we have company," he said, grinning at the prospect of young visitors. Here was entertainment likely to at least approach the pleasure he got from Phoebe's company. He motioned Mullins toward the door with a quick nod.

All four of the older children stood outside in the hallway. They looked hopefully at Mullins and entered eagerly, if a bit shyly, at the earl's invitation.

Devenham studied them with interest, well aware that he was being studied in return. It seemed a fair exchange. He tried to recall the children's names, from the little information he had extracted from their aunt. She generally continued to rebuff his attempts to learn something of her life here.

Dorrie was the only girl, he recalled, except for a baby who ruled over the quite separate domain of the nursery. Dorrie was the eldest and the tallest, already showing signs of becoming pretty like her mother and her aunt, with glossy dark curls framing her young face. He could not remember the names of the middle two brothers, who were only a little apart in size. The taller one had brown hair almost as dark as his sister's, and the other's hair was a lighter brown, as if the sun had faded the color and warmed it at the same time. The smallest boy's hair was touched with red, and a sprinkling of freckles decorated his nose.

Clearly taking the earl into his confidence, William was the first to speak, with his typically engaging candor. "I don't think Aunt Phoebe wants us to be in here," he whispered, standing on tip-toe to reach the earl's ear.

"Indeed?" chuckled Devenham, making a mental note to add this restriction to his list of complaints. "Then, I propose we just don't tell her. Agreed?" He looked at Thomas, David, and Dorrie, including them all in his broad smile. "I am delighted that you have come to visit with me. I am Major John Allen Jameson, Earl of Devenham, although I suppose you are already quite aware of that. I am at your service." Seated in the wing chair, he could not exactly bow, but he nodded his head quite formally.

The children gave their names in turn and made their respective bows and curtsy, observing perfect manners with grave expressions on their small faces.

"Now that we have taken care of that business, shall we not all be friends?" Devenham invited.

With such encouragement, the children quickly settled onto the thick Turkish carpet and began to ply him with endless questions. He was happy to respond, relating various stories about his experiences with great relish despite the need for frequent editing. They heard about life in his regiment and a little about the war; they even heard a few stories about his childhood in Derbyshire.

In return, he soon learned a good deal about the children. Dorrie's unappreciated desire to be a stage actress was revealed, as was Thomas's fascination with all things military. William's incredible imaginings were described in some detail, along with David's interest in studying the various habits of natural creatures.

Diplomatically, Devenham tried to make certain each child had equal time and equal shares of his attention. He learned about the puppies on Oxford Street, the stray cats that Phoebe had tamed in the garden, and the menagerie whose home was the schoolroom. He was vastly entertained, and quite pleased to discover that, as the children's lives intertwined so thoroughly with their aunt's, he was learning something about her as well.

He even expressed polite enthusiasm when William offered to bring Fremont Frog down to visit the sickroom. "I should like to meet him," said the earl. "In fact, I have a special reason to want to make his acquaintance. Shall I tell you? I heard an interesting story while I was in Vienna for a short time last winter."

He delivered this introduction just as Mullins returned to the room with a new tea tray laden with treats for the children. He waited while they helped themselves, and then began his narration.

"The story is about a frog, but not just your ordinary sort of everyday frog, no indeed. This frog was in actuality a prince, who had been put under a spell by a wicked fairy."

The earl could see that he had the children's full attention. He had surprised himself by remembering the story, and he was not at all sure of how well he would retell it, but he was pleased to try, for he was enjoying the children's visit.

"Now, this frog lived in a well, and I am certain he lived in despair of ever being rescued from his terrible fate. But one day a beautiful young princess came by, playing with her ball. What do you suppose should happen but quite unexpectedly the ball fell into the well."

Devenham's enthusiasm for his task carried into his tale,

and he kept his small audience enthralled as he related the frog's persistence in getting the princess to keep her promise. "After all," he said, "she did give her word to allow him to eat at her table and sleep upon her bed, did she not? And he knew that somehow he must be able to do that for three nights in a row, or the spell would never be broken."

As if he and his listeners, including Mullins, were themselves under a spell, not one of them noticed Phoebe's arrival until the earl reached the end of the story. "So the frog prince kept his promise, and loved his bride as she loved him forevermore."

Phoebe was not quite certain what to make of the scene before her. "My lord, I do apologize," she said as soon as Devenham had pronounced the eternal happiness of the frog prince and his lady. "I had specifically instructed the children not to disturb you in any way while you are here. I never dreamed they would disobey."

Turning to the four downcast culprits in front of her she scolded, "And how long have you been in here, pestering Lord Devenham? I am very surprised. Had you quite forgotten what I told you?"

Devenham interrupted her. "Please, Lady Brodfield, I invited them. You may lay the responsibility on me." Suddenly he looked as sheepish as the children. "In truth, I have no idea how long we have been at this. They have been very entertaining company."

"I would have said you were entertaining them, not the other way 'round," Phoebe commented dryly, but her expression softened a little. He had, after all, been doing a very creditable job of it. "I am sure you are well and truly tired now. Of course, you deserve no less."

The children had scrambled up and gathered around Phoebe, undaunted by her reprimands. She touched their cheeks affectionately. "Come, children, off you go." She clapped her hands and shooed them out the door like a flock of reluctant pigeons.

Mullins began gathering up the tea things.

"I hope you will not be upset with them," Devenham said. "I truly enjoyed their visit and encouraged them to stay. Why had you instructed them not to come in here? Am I such an ogre?"

Phoebe busied herself with straightening his bed, for she was certain he had been up far too long. *No, not an ogre*, she thought. *I do not know what you are.*

She had experienced such a confusion of feelings when she and Lucy had begun to talk about him, she had surprised herself. She had felt a strong desire to protect his privacy when Lucy had first asked her to tell "all about the earl." When Lucy had pressed her, she had found herself defending his character, describing virtues she had only reluctantly admitted to herself that he possessed. When Lucy in turn had related with relish a number of scandalous stories about him, Phoebe had wanted to cover her ears and run away. She had been astonished to hear the names of some of the women Lucy said were rumored to have had affairs with him.

It is all nothing but rumor and innuendo, Phoebe reminded herself now, as she had at Lucy's. She had gone so far as to make that point to Lucy, for what little that was worth. But the conversation had resurrected her doubts, and made her realize that in the past few days she had relaxed her defenses. She must not allow herself to fall under Devenham's spell.

"I thought you might not care to be bothered by a parcel of inquisitive children," she answered carefully. "I knew you would not be used to them, and I also know very well how quickly they can tire someone who is quite healthy, let alone someone who has been very ill."

"I want them free to come in whenever they wish, especially if you are not available. They can save me from dying of boredom, a far worse death than any of the ones I have already escaped."

His commanding tone nettled Phoebe, as did his words. She had not seen herself as entertainment, saving him from boredom. "I do not believe anyone ever actually died from boredom, my lord," she said primly. "Moreover, I do not think it a good idea to allow the children to visit whenever they wish. I will allow them to come occasionally, however, at arranged times."

"Thank you. I am not used to children, but I found it very easy to talk with them."

I wonder what they talked about, Phoebe thought. A sudden pang of jealousy mixed with apprehension. She had only witnessed him telling them the story; she had not considered what might have transpired before that. "I had no idea you were such a *raconteur*," she said, pausing to look at him. "That was quite a charming story you told them."

She was surprised to see the look of apparently genuine pleasure that crossed his face. "Did you hear it, then? I did not know at what point you arrived."

She nodded. Goodness, his eyes were so incredibly blue, even at this distance. "I believe I came in just after the ball fell into the well."

"I spent a few weeks on furlough in Vienna last winter, and that is where I chanced to hear the story. In fact, if I can remember them, I heard several others I could tell the children besides that one. There was a scholarly fellow there for the Congress, part of the Hessian delegation, who collects these kinds of stories, and he had formed a little group in Vienna who delighted in exchanging them to pass the time."

Phoebe saw the wicked light that she had learned to recognize so well come into his eyes, and she quickly turned away to fluff his pillows. What could possibly be wicked about fairy tales? And where was Mullins? She realized suddenly that both he and the tea tray had disappeared.

"I must add that many of these stories had more than one version," Devenham continued. "I saw ladies far less reputable than you put to the blush. Some of the French and Italian stories I heard were enough to curl even my hair. Of course, I would never repeat those versions to children."

He chuckled, but to Phoebe it had a sinister sound. She could picture the devilish grin that was probably on his face, but she refused to look at him.

"Why, in The Frog Prince, the older versions call for the frog to sleep *in* the princess's bed," he continued. "In other words, to lay with her. No wonder the poor princess was so dismayed."

Phoebe's cheeks were positively burning. She opened her mouth, then closed it firmly. She smoothed a last wrinkle from the earl's bedcovers, then walked straight out the door without a word.

Chapter Six

The puppy arrived at noon on the following day. Mullins had gone out briefly in the morning and then returned, but Phoebe had given the incident no thought at all. She had refused to dance attendance on the earl, sending a message that she was indisposed.

She was in Judith's sitting room trying to explain why she was no longer willing to attend the earl when the new arrival was announced. It was a novelty to see Maddocks looking flustered.

"Your ladyship," said the red-faced butler with a formal bow to Judith, "we have a rather unprecedented situation downstairs. It concerns a delivery that, uh, no one seems to have been expecting."

"What is it, Maddocks?" asked Judith, obviously intrigued. She exchanged a wary glance with Phoebe.

"A puppy, madam."

"A puppy? Oh, no." Both sisters rose to their feet in dismay, the same thought running through their minds. Who could have . . . ?

"Surely not Edward," Judith said aloud, the question never needing to be voiced. "He was very clear at dinner the other evening that he agreed it was impractical. And I don't see any way the children could have . . ."

Phoebe had a sinking feeling. "I think I may know who," she said ominously. "Lord Devenham."

"But how? And why?" asked the astonished Judith.

"The children spent some time with him yesterday—perhaps as much as the entire time I was gone to Lucy's. He was quite taken with them. They might have mentioned it. And now that I stop to consider, Mullins did go out this morning."

"I do not think my children would ask a guest of ours to buy them a puppy, or anything else for that matter," Judith said slowly, "especially when Edward and I had already refused our permission." She sat down again. Her small frown of puzzlement did not quite mask her obvious pleasure in the idea that her children might have charmed someone like the high-living earl.

"Oh, I quite agree," Phoebe hastened to reassure her sister. "I rather expect it is something Lord Devenham thought up all on his own after talking with them." She could not prevent the stormy state of her emotions from showing on her face. This time the earl had definitely gone too far, and this time his bad behavior had extended to other people besides her—very special people at that. It was too much to overlook.

"How extremely awkward," Judith lamented. "How can we refuse the puppy without seeming extremely ungracious? If only he had checked with us first!"

Phoebe did not sit down again, but rather began to pace in a circle around her chair.

"As his hostess, *you* may be in an extremely awkward position," she declared, "but *I* am not. In truth, I am in a perfect position to intervene on your behalf, Judith. Someone needs to set Lord Devenham in his place."

"Oh, now, Phoebe, please don't say anything rash," Judith began, but at just that moment the three boys came tumbling into the sitting room in a dither of excitement, followed by Dorrie at a slightly more decorous pace. In their haste they nearly bowled over poor Maddocks, still waiting patiently for his instructions. David held clutched in his arms a small, wriggling mass of brown and white fur.

"Mamma, oh *look* Mamma!" they all cried in a chorus. "Isn't he wonderful? Did you ever see anything so adorable?"

The puppy was promptly deposited in Judith's lap. Watching her sister's hand stroke its soft fur a moment later, Phoebe knew all was lost. The puppy would stay. But that did not mean Lord Devenham should escape her indignation.

"Well, Maddocks, I believe we have a new member of the household," Judith told the butler with a resigned sigh.

As the older man started out the door he nearly bumped into

Goldie, who had been just about to knock. "Visitor for Lady Brodfield," the young footman whispered. Maddocks did an abrupt about-face and re-entered the room he had just left.

"I am informed you have a visitor, Lady Brodfield," he announced in his usual grand manner. Apparently realizing that he had left out an important piece of information, he wheeled around again to consult Goldie.

The effect was quite comical, really, but Phoebe was too surprised to be amused by it. Who could be calling on her? Perhaps Lucy, although it was quite early in the day for a purely social call, and it was not usually the thing to repay a visit so soon as the day after it was made. Yet as far as she knew, Lucy and her mother were the only people outside of this house who knew she was here, not counting Dr. Fortens. Surely word could not have spread this fast!

Maddocks faced the room again, his official blank expression fixed firmly in place. "It is Lord Brodfield's brother, my lady, Mr. Richard Brodfield."

Phoebe felt as if she had been turned to stone; she sincerely doubted whether her feet would be capable of moving in any direction at all. Amazingly, her mouth opened and the words "I'll see in him the drawing room" came out quite calmly.

How had Richard known she was here? When had Richard arrived in London? Would she never be free of her ties to Stephen's family? Stephen was gone, and Lord Tyneley was gone, and she desired nothing so much as to make a clean break with Lady Tyneley and Richard.

She dreaded the prospect of facing him alone. She looked at Judith, still surrounded by her delighted children and anchored firmly by the puppy in her lap. There was no help there; she could not ask her sister to leave them. Edward was no doubt buried in papers in his study. She had no choice. Squaring her shoulders, she followed Maddocks out of the room.

In the drawing room, Phoebe surveyed Judith's fashionable scroll-backed sofa, the Sheraton chairs arranged neatly near the octagonal center table, and the reasonably comfortable armchairs flanking the marble fireplace. She decided to receive her visitor standing. Her palms were damp; caught so unexpectedly at home, she wore no gloves. She was not even wearing black, as she certainly would have been in public—she was dressed in a gown of brown pique trimmed with bands of black grosgrain. She decided to stand in front of the hearth, and wet her lips nervously, watching the door.

Even braced as she was, Phoebe was still shocked by the sight of Richard when Maddocks showed him in. For that brief moment as he came toward her, he looked for all the world like Stephen. Then he smiled, shattering the illusion.

Phoebe had never found the resemblance between the two as strong as other people were wont to claim, but she had to admit that she was probably more sensitive to their marked difference in expression than to their actual features. Both men had favored their father, Lord Tyneley, who had been a handsome, distinguished man. Stephen's face had always been kind and open, a quality that had attracted her to him from the very first. Richard's face, however, usually wore an expression of disdain and aloofness that was so like his mother's Phoebe had often wondered how anyone could ever have confused the two half brothers. Yet seeing Richard now stabbed her with pain as unbearable as if Stephen himself were standing before her.

She wondered if she could manage to unclasp her hands long enough to offer one to Richard. That fraction of a moment's hesitation cost her, for Richard moved quickly to envelop her in an embrace instead. It was so typical of Richard, she thought afterward, that his hands lingered just a little too long, and what should have been a chaste, brotherly kiss on her cheek somehow ended up on her jawbone, in the sensitive spot close to her ear. A little tremor of distaste ran through her when he released her, and she wondered if he noticed.

"Ah, Phoebe," he said with what she had always thought of as his sly look, "ever the prim and proper, eh? Poor sister Phoebe, how are you bearing up?" With a finger, he tilted her chin up, but she refused to meet his eyes. She twisted her head to the side and then slipped away from him, sinking gratefully into the nearest straight chair.

"Won't you have a seat, Richard?" she asked pointedly. She felt relieved when he did so.

"It has been a difficult time, hasn't it, my dear," he began, "although I see you have lost no time in putting off full mourning. My father has been in his grave, what, two weeks at best? Of course, you were in blacks a full year for my brother, were you not, dear Phoebe?"

He had chosen the straight chair opposite her, and sat sprawled in it with a practiced nonchalance, one leg crossed over the other. His gaze swept her from head to toe and back up again, resting on her face. Phoebe tried to will away the flush she felt creep across her cheeks.

"I was not expecting company," she responded faintly.

"I suppose I am hardly in a position to criticize, having missed both the funeral itself and even the memorial service. It is infamous, is it not? Such an amazing thing, the military."

"I thought you were still in France."

Richard laughed. "Surprised to see me? Yes, I'd wager Prinny's royal throne on that."

"How did you know where to find me?" Phoebe was quickly tiring of trying to maintain a polite front for him.

He paused to look at her, a malicious amusement dancing in his eyes. "It was kind of you to attend my father's commemorative. I understand the place was packed to the roofbeams. It was also extremely helpful. I thought if you were in London you would not stay away. The rest was easy. The Allingtons are your only relatives in Town."

Phoebe stared at him, thinking now of the man in the park, and the suspicions she'd had that someone had followed her to Lucy's. "You have been spying on me!"

"I have found it useful to have eyes and ears in Town when I am not able to be here myself. My friends thought you a pleasant subject for surveillance, although they were devastatingly disappointed and quite bored when they discovered how little you go out. You live like a cloistered nun, my dear!"

"Why are you here, Richard?" Phoebe's voice was tight with her growing impatience.

"Why else but to see to your welfare, sweet Phoebe? I feel a certain responsibility for my poor dead brother's widow. Did you think I would just let you disappear from my life? Are you going to live here with your sister forever?"

"Yes. No. I don't see that it is any of your business." She struggled to keep her composure. Richard was the kind of person who made ferreting out other people's weaknesses a well-refined art, and she was still working to overcome so many! Her uncertainty about her future and her need to establish some sort of independence were only one.

He smiled his sly smile again, the one she hated. "It has become my business more than either of us would have imagined," he said smoothly. "I sought your whereabouts purely out of my own concern, I assure you, but I was quite glad that I had when I met with my family's solicitors. It seems they had no idea where to find you. My dear departed father made you a bequest in his will."

With this astonishing pronouncement, he reached into his coat and produced a letter, which he handed across to Phoebe. She read it in silence, aware that he was watching her intently.

The letter's contents filled her with hope. *Bless Lord Tyneley!* He had left her an annuity of two thousand pounds a year, and a modest property outside of London, which he had occasionally used as a hunting box. She was to contact his solicitors regarding the details. Mindful of Richard's interest, she schooled her features to remain calm, despite her wildly beating pulse.

She had never expected any remembrance from her father-in-law, much less a gift of such magnitude. Figuring quickly in her head, she estimated that the annuity he had left her together with the income she already had would be enough to maintain her in comfort on the estate. Here was the key to independence, dropped generously into her lap! Tears of gratitude welled in her eyes, despite her resolve to show nothing. She was even ready to bless Richard for bringing her this news.

"I can scarcely believe it," she said, lifting her eyes from the paper at last. "Beau Chatain, to be mine!"

Richard laughed, but there was no amusement in his eyes now. He got up and paced away from his chair. "I could scarcely believe it myself," he agreed. "I have been using Beau Chatain in season for several years now, and I am certain my father was aware of it. Do you want to know what he left me?" The bitterness in his voice warned Phoebe that perhaps she did not, but the question was rhetorical.

"He left me everything in the farthest corners of the country that was not entailed. Of course the title, and everything attached to it, go now to a cousin in Hampshire I've never even met! I have a tin mine in Cornwall, a country seat in Northumberland, for God's sake, a tract of fenland in Norfolk and a farm in the Lake District. If I were to spend any time at any of them, I would never get to be in London at all!"

Phoebe was not quite certain how to respond. Secretly, she suspected that keeping Richard out of London might have been his father's goal. Richard ran with a notorious group and lost great sums of money gaming. When he drank with his friends he was prone to very foul tempers. She was just enough afraid of him not to dare say so to his face.

"They should provide you with a reasonable income, should they not, Richard?" she ventured cautiously.

"Oh, aye. The income's there, but I want Beau Chatain. I'm prepared to offer you twenty thousand pounds for it."

Was her bright future so quickly gained and lost again? Oh, *why* did Richard have to want Beau Chatain? How would she know if what he offered was a fair price for the property? What if it was worth fifty or a hundred thousand pounds? Yet, perhaps she would be better off to sell to him and buy another property of her own elsewhere.

It was easy enough for him to offer, but did Richard have the ready available? Could she buy another property if he paid her in portions? As a woman, she might not even be considered a viable buyer without actual cash to wave in someone's face. Richard was frequently under the hatches, and she doubted his inheritance would change that. The tin mine in Cornwall or the estate in Northumberland could vanish on the turn of a card. She would have to ask Edward to act as her agent. She needed time to think and to consult with advisors.

"I am sorry, Richard. This is so sudden! I hardly know what to say. Give me time to think on it, and allow me to meet with your father's solicitors."

A quick movement brought Richard to stand right in front of Phoebe. "You don't need to think, woman, and I can take care of my father's solicitors. I've made you a fair offer." He reached down suddenly and grasped her wrist, pulling her to her feet. He loomed over her, standing just inches away. "If you don't like that offer, consider this. I occupy Beau Chatain lock, stock, and barrel. Every horse in the stable and every servant on the premises at this moment is mine. You'd have a devil of a time getting me out of there."

He paused thoughtfully. Phoebe used the moment to try to release her wrist from his grip.

"On the other hand, perhaps there is another alternative," Richard said, ignoring her struggle. "While I was never my brother's keeper, I think I could enjoy keeping his lovely wife. Perhaps we could share." He raised Phoebe's hand to his lips and kissed it.

Phoebe jerked away with a savage motion that caught him by surprise. "How *dare* you," she hissed, rubbing the back of her hand against her skirt. "Is that your idea of a jest? I think your battles overseas must have addled your wits. Leave this house at once. If I need to communicate with you, I will do so by letter."

"I will leave you now, madam," he said, stalking toward the door, "but you would do well to consider my offer." He gave her a sweeping bow that made a mockery of the act. "Either of them."

Phoebe was so angry that she could not sit down for several minutes. She paced the carpet furiously, waiting for the rage that surged through her to cool.

"He is insidious! Hateful! Odious! Repulsive!" Not one of the adjectives seemed adequate to express her feelings. She could not remember when she had felt so insulted. Gradually, the urge to throw something waned and her pacing slowed. She sank onto the sofa, only to discover that she was shaking.

Had she forgotten how nasty Richard could be? She had known it well enough when she had lived under the same roof. She had learned to avoid encountering him in hallways or being alone in any room with him. . . . His vile joke went far beyond vulgarity; it was far worse than any of the provocative remarks Lord Devenham was wont to make.

Black as his reputation might paint him, the earl was nothing like the scoundrel Richard was. She knew instinctively that there was really no comparison. Lord Devenham's remarks might be just as deliberate, but she knew they were meant to tease, not insult. She might feel wary and on her guard in the earl's presence, but the feeling came not from a sense of alarm, a sense of danger, as she felt with Richard, but more likely from an awareness of her own attraction to him.

Richard's visit and his unexpected news had pushed the earl momentarily from her mind. He had slipped back in quickly enough, but even thoughts of him could not overcome her reaction to Richard. It was not until she heard the yipping of the new puppy from the sitting room down the hall that she recalled that she still had a bone to pick with Lord Devenham.

His purchase of the puppy went beyond mere remarks. His high-handed behavior had gone too far this time, and the remnants of her anger regrouped around that thought. She jumped to her feet again, her hands balled into fists. She stalked to the drawing room door, pulling it open with more force than was required. It very nearly crashed into Edward's prized Chinese porcelain umbrella stand before she pulled it shut again behind her.

Devenham was sitting in the wing chair engrossed in a book when Phoebe's knock came on the door. He recognized it as hers at once, although it sounded a bit more forceful than usual.

He snatched off his spectacles and tucked them out of sight between the books on the table beside him before he bid her enter. He was surprised to note how his spirits lifted at the prospect of her company.

Phoebe came in looking more like a storm cloud than a ray of sunshine, however.

"Should we think that we have made you so comfortable here that you feel quite at home, Lord Devenham? Or do you always do exactly as you please, no matter where you are?"

She spoke in a cutting tone he had never heard her use before. Something had upset her deeply, but what? He masked his concern with a display of arrogance. "Dear me, what can I have done this time? Did I refuse to take my medicine again? I can't seem to remember. It must be something more than that to have put you so out of countenance."

Phoebe positively bristled. Her anger brought color to her cheeks and a notable brightness to her eyes, confirming his suspicion that there was passion hidden behind her usual gentle manner. He found it quite becoming, although he would have preferred to see it sparked by an altogether different cause.

"You have more than overstepped your authority this time, my lord, interfering in matters that are not your concern," she accused him. "You have upset the order of things in this household, and undermined Edward and Judith's authority in their own home."

"How exceedingly thoughtless of me. Exactly how have I managed to accomplish all that?"

"You purchased a puppy for children who had already been told they were not to have one. It is at this moment cavorting in Judith's sitting room."

"Oh, it's the puppy, is it? Who told you I bought it for them?" She looked so angry that he could see where the expression "looking daggers" came from. He wondered if he should duck.

"It was not difficult to deduce. There is no one else who could have done it. Do you deny it?"

"Not precisely. I *did* buy the puppy." He saw no need to mention that he had in fact bought all four of the remaining pups in the litter at the haberdasher's shop. If his instructions were being followed, the other three were en route to his estates in Rutland and Derbyshire even as he and Phoebe spoke. "But given that I am such a dastardly fellow, why would you think that I bought the dog for anyone but myself?"

"Well, I—" She stopped.

Aha. I have you there. He could not help smiling as she looked at him.

"Perhaps you thought you could bribe your way into the children's affections."

"As I have not been able to do with you? I see." He never could seem to stop himself from goading her. "Is it not possible that I thought the pup would amuse me and help to pass the time? Provide me with some companionship?" he challenged her.

She turned away and paced a few steps. He noticed she was rubbing her wrist. "If that is so," she said slowly, "then you have compounded your error. The dog has already secured its place in the children's hearts, and Judith's as well." She turned to him, her expression pleading. "They will be devastated if you tell them now that the pup is not theirs."

"Ah, Lady Brodfield. Your compassion is always for others," he responded. His voice had become rather husky. "I suppose you yourself are quite immune to the charms of a small puppy."

"No, I am not," she admitted in a very small voice. He saw the tears spring into her eyes before she spun away from him again.

Damn! He had never meant to make her cry. "I am a bloody thoughtless beast," he muttered.

He watched her raise a hand to her averted face, presumably to dash away the moisture from her cheeks. As she did, he noticed the red marks on the pale skin of her wrist, which until that moment had been concealed by the edge of her sleeve. Rather shakily he got to his feet and took a step toward her with his weight on his good leg. "What have you done to your wrist?" he demanded sharply.

Both his movement and his question clearly caught her by surprise. For a stunned moment she stood looking at her wrist, then she quickly came to his side.

"What are you doing?" she cried with a little gasp. "You could fall!"

He allowed her to assist him back into his chair, savoring the small pleasure her touch gave him. She did not know he had been working with Mullins to improve his mobility. As she started to withdraw, he caught her hand by the fingertips and drew it toward him.

How easily he could have put it to his lips just then! But he knew instinctively that the time was not right. He did not want to do anything to jeopardize what little trust he might have managed to achieve with her. Gently he pushed back the edge of her sleeve and turned her wrist to reveal the marks he had seen there. "What is this?" he asked again.

"It is nothing. It is none of your concern." She pulled her hand away and smoothed down her sleeve.

"I am making it my concern," he said with a note of insistence he hoped was unmistakable. "Apparently I am not the only thoughtless beast you have had to deal with today."

He locked his eyes on hers. All the anger seemed to have gone out of those gray pools, and now he thought he saw pain, wariness, and uncertainty there instead. "Who did that to you?"

Her gaze slid to the window. She was obviously uncomfortable, but he would not let go of the question until he had an answer. "I will only keep asking," he said softly.

Her ever-erect posture seemed to give way a little, as if some tight knot inside her had suddenly loosened. "I had an interview with my brother-in-law just before I came in here," she finally admitted.

"Edward?" Devenham could not believe it.

"Not Edward. Richard Brodfield. He is my late husband's half brother."

"I gather the interview did not go altogether smoothly." *Would she tell him anything more?*

"There is a business arrangement at stake. He became a little emotional, but there is nothing to be concerned over. He did not hurt me, despite how it may look. That is all." She gave him a level stare that told him more clearly than words that the subject was now closed.

Chapter Seven

The doctor had come to check on the earl's progress, and had pronounced him improved enough to come downstairs each day for dinner. Devenham was delighted. His release allowed him a much closer glimpse of the family activities, which he found entertaining, and ensured at least one occasion each day when Phoebe could not avoid his company. It also afforded him exactly the opportunity he wanted to learn more about Phoebe's connections when he and Edward were left alone to indulge in the ritual of after-dinner port.

Devenham was aware that not all of the Brodfields were held in as high esteem as Lord Tyneley had been. The earl vaguely recollected some sort of unsavory rumors, but he couldn't remember what they were, or even specifically who they were about. Had Phoebe been married to a bounder? Was the half brother one also? Or something worse? A painful marriage of that sort might have been enough to make a young, attractive widow retreat from the world. Especially if she had loved the fellow. He did not know any of the Brodfields personally, nor did he know what opinion Edward held of them, so he proceeded with tactful caution.

"I imagine you are chafing at the bit to get outside of these walls, Devenham," Edward said cordially on the second night. The two men had adjourned to the room that served as study and library combined. Edward occupied a carved mahogany and velvet armchair in a comfortably sprawled position, alternately swirling the port in his glass as he spoke and drawing puffs from an old-fashioned clay pipe. "It must be a great relief to at least have the run of the house now after your confinement, although I'm certain you find our style here very tame compared to your usual. I'm afraid we live rather quietly."

"Allington, my friend, the quiet here has been exactly what I needed. I have felt quite reluctant to advertise my whereabouts or stir up any activity among my friends, and while I am certainly glad to be up and about a bit now, I have no complaints of being bored. Your sister-in-law, Lady Brodfield, has been quite diverting company for me." The earl sat adjacent to his host in a rather more upright position. He held his glass before him with both hands and peered down into it curiously as if the drink, rather than his recent behavior, merited intense study.

"Enjoyed Phoebe's company, did you? Well, I'm glad of it," came Edward's hearty response. "I have no doubt you did her some good as well—reminded her what it's like to be around a sociable single man. She is too young to lock herself away in this house forever.

"I doubt the peace and quiet you have found here will last much longer, unfortunately," he added. "Town gets emptier every day, and as it does, we who remain here move closer and closer to the center of that powerful microscope, the public eye. I was approached by someone at my club who wanted to know if you were staying with us—it seems your disappearance from the Clarendon has put you in the betting books. I said I knew where you were, but was not at liberty to say. I don't expect that answer will serve very long. I also heard that the Duke of York wants to see you at the Horse Guards once his arm mends and he returns from Oatlands. Something about confirming a field promotion?"

Devenham sighed. Steering his host's conversation was proving more difficult than he expected. His first opportunity to talk about Phoebe had come and gone again in the space of a single breath. He supposed he owed Edward the courtesy of discussing his promotion from major to brevet lieutenant-colonel at Waterloo, but it was the last thing he wanted to talk about.

"I would like one person in London to know the real truth about that business, Allington, and I am choosing you," he said wearily. "I am no hero. I did nothing more at Waterloo than any other man would have done in my place, or as many other men did do. I would refuse the promotion if I could do so without mortally offending those who mean well toward me by offering it. I swear, military politics are as complicated as pleasing a woman."

"Ho, you are right on that score," Edward agreed, laughing. "Military politics, or any other kind, and the rewards are often not nearly so satisfactory."

Devenham drained the last drop of port from his glass and held up the empty vessel with a questioning look at the baronet.

Edward answered with a nod toward the glass decanter on the corner of his desk, and the earl got up and proceeded to pour himself another drink. "You certainly seem satisfied with your married life," he commented guardedly.

Edward straightened in his chair, almost visibly puffing up with pride. "There's nothing can touch it, if you ask my opinion. You ought to consider settling down, Devenham."

The earl was dubious. "Have you never felt shackled by the responsibility? Has your wife never been jealous when you strayed from her bed to another's?"

Devenham's host fixed a very serious eye on his guest. "I have never strayed from Judith's bed since we've been married," he answered distinctly. "That's over twelve years."

"Your wife is charming, but can you really tell me one woman is sufficient to meet all your needs, Allington? Have you never tired of her?" Devenham was amazed.

"I know it sounds incredible, but it's true."

"You think I should give up chasing lightskirts and offer myself up for matrimony? Have pity! Once I do, I shall be nothing more than another piece of meat for the marriage mart." The earl resumed his seat. "The prospect of all those society matrons flinging their daughters at me horrifies me more than a charge by a battalion of French lancers."

"If you have survived one, you can survive the other," Edward replied, chuckling. "I assure you, there is much to be said in favor of the married state."

"How long was Lady Brodfield married, if I may ask?"

Devenham posed the question casually. He hoped Edward
would not find it odd.

"Two years—almost two years exactly. Her husband died a
year ago last February."

"Then she's stayed in seclusion a year and a half?"

"Yes." Edward sighed. "God knows we tried to get her out
into company again. It was a devil of a thing, very hard on
her."

Devenham held his glass very still. "She doesn't talk about
it."

Edward exhaled a little cloud of smoke from his pipe. "I
know. I suppose a thing like that is hard to get over, but sometimes I think it would help if she would let her feelings out.
She isn't at all like my wife, Judith, in that respect. My wife
may go a trifle too far the other way, I sometimes think, but
don't get me wrong. My Judith is the light of my life. I have
never been happier than I am now as a married man and a father."

Devenham accepted the turn in the conversation. He did not
want to make his questions about Phoebe too obvious. "I suspect some of us are better suited to those roles than others,
Allington. You must admit you enjoy the significant advantage
of having achieved a love match. I wouldn't expect to be so
fortunate."

"And why not?"

"I was taught from an early age that love is for fools and
weaker men than the Earls of Devenham. Please don't think I
am putting you in that class, Allington—I have never truly believed that. But at the same time, I find I know very little about
it. Sexual liaisons, yes—I could be classed, *am* classed, an expert. But not love. When I see you with your wife, I feel as if
you share some foreign language of which I know nothing."

Edward held up his glass in a salute to his friend. "It is a
language that can only be taught by the heart, I'm afraid. If
you ever fall in love, you will start to hear and understand it."

Devenham laughed a short, bitter laugh. "I doubt one
woman will ever hold me long enough for that." He paused
then, considering the subject. Phoebe seemed to speak that language fluently, even though her partner was gone. Her loving

warmth seemed to touch everyone in the house—even, if only occasionally, himself.

"Your sister-in-law must have loved her husband deeply," he speculated.

"Phoebe? Indeed she must have, to grieve so much after all she went through. Certainly we all thought she and Stephen were the perfect match."

The earl thought he heard a note of regret in Edward's voice. "Another love match?"

"Positively. I swear Lord Brodfield was smitten the first time he saw her, and so was she. She had eyes for no one else. It was only her first Season, you know. She had been declared a diamond and had flocks of admirers—we were so proud of her! Judith and I sponsored her come-out."

Edward's pipe wanted refilling and he looked at it thoughtfully, as if trying to decide if the conversation would continue long enough to warrant the effort. He set the pipe aside, apparently concluding that it would not. "She was a great success," he continued, his voice soft with memories. "And she would be as welcome now at Almack's as she was before. But she will have none of it." He shrugged. "Soon we will be dragging you out instead, Devenham, if you continue to improve so rapidly. The theaters and the Opera House will stay open till the end of the month. By then you should be well enough to travel home. And, please God, we will head for the country, too. The harvest waits for no one, not to mention the start of shooting season."

Judith and Phoebe were waiting for the men to join them, however, and it would not do to keep them at it too long. Devenham realized that he had learned as much as he could for one evening, and let his inquiries go. He was tired, but he managed to play a hand of whist with the others before retiring. Phoebe was his partner and he played badly, distracted by his own thoughts and his fascination with her deep gray eyes.

Something unusual had occurred in Phoebe's marriage—of that he felt certain. What had Edward said? That she must have loved Brodfield to grieve so "after all she went through," and that she would be as welcome now at Almack's as she had been before. Before what? Her marriage? Or had there been some kind of scandal? That did seem to fit, although he could not picture the gentle creature he had come to know at the center of some major brew. He wanted to know now more than ever. He would enlist Mullins to help him find out.

Devenham's increased mobility allowed him greater participation in the daily routines of the household, and he began to learn its rhythms and the patterns of each of its members. He discovered that Phoebe was an early riser who would usually go into the garden first thing each day to inspect her beloved plants and feed the stray cats she had tamed.

One morning he awakened early enough to be groomed and dressed, and still catch her there. He made his way slowly down to the dining room, whose glass-paned French doors opened onto steps down to the garden. He hesitated on the threshold, taking in the sun-washed image of Phoebe with her cats.

She was crouched upon the gravel walkway, her skirts gathered about her in a way that emphasized the roundness of her form quite nicely. She was not attired in mourning clothes as was her usual habit—instead, she wore a simple morning dress of thin white muslin, figured with some kind of tiny pattern. Her head was uncovered, allowing the sun to bounce joyfully off her glossy dark curls. Her broad-brimmed straw hat lay discarded on a bench nearby. Three cats sallied around her like officers on parade, and she reached out to pet each one in turn. The sight of her hand stroking their soft fur warmed his blood.

He was quite content to stay where he was, admiring the picture. He must have made some unconscious movement or slight sound, however, for the cats noticed him suddenly and scattered in an instant. He saw annoyance cloud Phoebe's face before her polite mask slipped into place. Sighing, he came down the steps, leaning heavily on the ebony cane Mullins had purchased for him in Bond Street.

"I apologize for scaring them away," he began sincerely. "I did not mean to." He gave her a stiff but dignified bow. "You have every right to be annoyed with me."

"I am not annoyed with you, Lord Devenham," she said,

straightening up and brushing off her skirt. "You need not concern yourself. They run away from everyone."

As she turned to retrieve her hat, he risked another step closer. "Why do you not allow yourself to be annoyed with me? It is a perfectly natural reaction, and I am certain I deserve it. And it is not true that they run from everyone—they clearly have great affection for *you*." *As does everyone who meets you,* he wanted to add.

She moved away from him and scooped up the basket she had left on the path. "It is only because I feed them," she answered. She seemed poised for flight, but hesitated as if she could not decide how best to escape him.

"Why do *you* always run away?" he asked gently.

He had clearly caught her off-balance with that. She looked at him for a moment, her eyes wide with surprise, and then she stared down into her basket as betraying color flushed her cheeks. She managed an almost convincing laugh.

"I do not always run away, my lord! Do you think I am frightened like the cats? I think you are imagining it."

"Indeed? I hope so. You can prove it by walking with me, and allowing me to carry your basket. We can engage in polite conversation."

She raised her head and looked up at him with a challenge in her eyes. "I recall very few exchanges where we have managed to engage in polite conversation, Lord Devenham. It will be interesting to see if we are able to do so."

Smiling, he reached for her basket. "I promise I will be a veritable pattern card of courtesy." He offered his left arm, and she had no proper choice but to take it.

"I think perhaps it is you who is more like the cats," she said, glancing sideways at him as they began to walk slowly down the nearest path, away from the house. "They watch and lie in wait for unwitting birds, deceiving them by their quiet study."

"Ah, but the birds can escape quite easily by simply taking flight. It is only the unwary who get caught. You cannot blame the cats for something that is only their given nature."

He stopped, taking a moment to settle his weight on his good leg and his cane. He knew he should probably leave his defense at that. Most women were titillated by the idea of the chase and preferred casting him in the role of the predator. But Phoebe was different. It bothered him somehow that she should think of him that way.

"I would be wounded to think that you hold such an opinion of me, except that I am so accustomed to it. My reputation precedes me wherever I go. Yet I would ask your honest answer. You have been both my nurse and my secretary. Have I seemed like such a ruthless blackguard to you?"

He looked for her answer in her eyes even before she spoke. What he saw there was uncertainty, and that wounded him more than anything she might say. He was surprised to realize how much her opinion meant to him. He had always followed his own inclinations with total disregard for what other people might think.

"Never mind," he said, suddenly not wanting to hear the words that were coming. "Perhaps you would show me your herbs? There is a wonderful mixture of fragrances in the air this morning." He did not add that her own particular scent gave him pleasure above all the others. He began to walk again.

Phoebe was not put off, however. "I do not know what kind of man you are," she said slowly, matching her steps to his. "I have been your nurse, and your secretary, but all I have learned is that you are fond of playing games. I have not learned how to tell when you are not doing so."

Now, right now, he wanted to say, but he could not bring himself to do it. He had learned to protect himself by playing roles at too early an age, and the habit ran too deeply. *I am a greater coward than anyone would believe,* he berated himself. *I am afraid to show my true self to a woman.*

Outwardly, he laughed. "That is the highest compliment you could pay to a gamesman and strategist, and perhaps in the end that is all I truly am. Please forget that I even asked. Let us proceed with the tour."

Their progress down the path was painfully slow and awkward. At length Phoebe said, "I think your attempt at courtesy undoes you, Lord Devenham. You would fare better without these added appendages." She attempted to reclaim her hand from the crook of his elbow and her basket from his hand.

Devenham stopped instantly and tightened both his grip on the basket and his arm against his side to prevent her withdrawal. "You do me a disfavor by trying to escape," he said. "I have not the use of my other hand to forestall you. I know it is awkward, but I had hoped you would bear with me. It makes me feel more like a whole man again to escort a lady and carry her basket. Is it so much to ask?"

The momentary hesitation before she replied, "No, I suppose not," spoke volumes to him, but he was determined to proceed. He laughed to take away the sting. "That is not the most gracious acceptance I have ever heard, but it will serve."

They moved carefully down the garden walk, the earl with a pronounced limp and Phoebe with a hesitant step. Devenham thought Phoebe's hand trembled on his arm. As they reached the shade of the hawthorn tree at the bottom of the garden, he cast his eyes gratefully upon the two stone benches that flanked the path.

"Would you still bear with me if I sat for a moment? I fear I may have overreached myself."

She looked at him as if weighing his words. *She doesn't trust me at all,* he realized, *not even enough to sit on this bench.*

"Really, my lord, you press me too much," came her answer, but at least her voice was gentle, almost sympathetic. "If you are truly so weary, however, indeed you must sit. I will go into the house and find you some assistance."

"No." The last thing he wanted was to give her an excuse to leave. He lowered himself onto the bench. "I will be all right if I rest but a moment. I suppose you would not join me?"

"I shall stand until you are ready."

He sighed. *Such slow progress.* With her, with his injured leg. He knew if he pushed for any more than her simple company at this moment she would turn on her heel and leave him there.

When Devenham had appeared in the garden, Phoebe's first instinct had been to flee, just as he had challenged her. By denying it, she had cut off her own escape. Why had she not simply admitted her cowardice and fled anyway? He had looked so handsome in his perfectly fitted dark blue coat and tan buckskins. She had felt his magnetic power over her from the moment she saw him framed in the doorway. Being with him here, in the garden that served as her private retreat, somehow felt unbearably intimate.

He seemed vulnerable and full of pain this morning, and she saw how easily her heart could go out to him. He was attractive and dangerous. When she had seen how heavily he set himself on the bench, she knew that he was truly tired, but she still dared not give in to her own impulses. What a stubborn man! Would he never give up? *Male pride*, she thought with a pang. So like Stephen, or even more like Judith's boys. Men were such children sometimes!

The thought of Stephen sent ice through her veins, reinforcing her intended aloofness. She could not afford to relax her guard around this man, for he could break down her barriers too easily. She realized that her resistance itself might be the reason for his interest in her, but if she persevered long enough, she believed he would lose patience and seek amusement elsewhere.

She could not bring herself to look at him, so she contented herself by gazing about the garden, focusing her thoughts on the precious growing things around her and trying to draw strength from them. She inhaled, savoring the early morning scents that he had noticed. She was genuinely impressed that he had done so, for she assumed that most men would not notice such things. But thoughts like that were dangerous to allow.

"You are right about the fragrance of the garden in the early morning," she said to break the awkward silence that had fallen on them. "If you close your eyes to block out your other perceptions, you can sort out the different scents, like finding familiar faces in a crowd."

She risked a glance at him to see if he would try it. She discovered she had looked too soon, for her eyes met his intensely blue ones and locked there until she managed to pull her gaze away again. She turned away and closed her own eyes, concentrating on what she could smell. She tried not to be distracted by the tension she could sense in her body; she felt like a harp string vibrating at the mere possibility of being touched.

"I can smell the earth, the roses, and especially the lavender, where we have brushed against it along the path," she recited. This was a game she often played with the children as a way to make them more aware of their surroundings. She heard a deep chuckle behind her.

"It is difficult to identify the faces in the crowd if one doesn't know the friends they belong to. I smell something so sweet I can almost taste it—what would that be?"

Why did his words always seem so suggestive? There was nothing in his tone this time to indicate he meant anything other than the simple question he had asked. The suggestiveness had to be all in her own mind, and that realization appalled her.

"That would be the lilies," she answered numbly.

"Ah. 'Consider the lilies, how they grow.' The lavender I recognize—it is so popular with ladies. I smell something spicy, also."

She moved a few steps down the path and reached into the border, breaking a stem from a blossoming pink. "The pinks are spicy," she began, returning to her position and holding the flower out to him like a peace offering. "The thyme is spicy, too. Bees love it."

Before either of them could say another word, the scrabbling sound of several small feet running down the gravel walk toward them interrupted them.

"Aunt Phoebe! Aunt Phoebe! Come quick! Mrs. Finchley got loose in the schoolroom. We don't know what to do!"

Chapter Eight

"Dear heaven above, how did Mrs. Finchley get out?" Phoebe asked in surprise as she was quickly surrounded by four distressed children. "Never mind, you can tell me on the way upstairs."

She turned to Devenham with an apologetic look. "My lord, I never intended to abandon you here at the bottom of the garden. Will you forgive me if I do so? Shall I send someone to assist you?"

"Who is Mrs. Finchley?" asked the bewildered earl.

Phoebe sighed. "She is the children's pet bird, part of their so-called menagerie. I am more afraid that she will hurt herself as she flies about in the room than I am that she will escape. I am sure you see the need for me to act quickly."

He nodded and gestured toward the house with his hand. "Please. I understand completely. And you need not take time to send someone out to me. I can manage quite well."

This assurance was enough for Phoebe. With the two older children racing ahead of her, she hastened toward the house with the younger two close on her heels. By the time they had ascended all the stairs to the top of the house and arrived at the schoolroom, Phoebe's heart was racing and she was quite out of breath.

"Let us open the door cautiously," she warned the children, "and see where Mrs. Finchley has gotten to. We don't want her to escape from the room, else we may never catch her."

Phoebe opened the door a crack and ascertained that Mrs. Finchley was perched quietly on the back of one of the school desk chairs, preening her feathers with an air of satisfaction. Phoebe and the children slipped in through the door one at a time and closed it carefully behind them.

"I think it best if only one of us approaches her," Phoebe cautioned. "David, you get her cage and be ready. Dorrie, you see if you can coax Mrs. Finchley onto your finger."

It was a reasonable plan, and might have worked if Mrs. Finchley had been at all cooperative. The little bird, however, had other ideas. She sat quietly until Dorrie was within an arm's reach of her, then she flew up and circled around the schoolroom twice before perching on the window ledge. The long table with the other contained members of the menagerie was in the way of reaching her conveniently, although Thomas tried. The other small creatures were becoming a bit restless from all the excitement around them.

"I never meant to let her out," a greatly subdued William explained. "We wanted to clean her cage in case we were going to show her to Lord Devenham today. We promised to bring Fremont down to visit him, and I thought Mrs. Finchley might like to go, too. She never tried to get out before."

Mrs. Finchley seemed to be enjoying herself, leading her people on a merry chase. She had finally flown up to the top of the door frame, and Phoebe was in the process of dragging over a chair on which she intended to stand. "I just hope she doesn't take it into her little brain to fly at the windows," she said. "David, be ready with her cage in case I get her."

Standing on the chair on tiptoes, Phoebe stretched her arm up as high as she could reach and held her breath as she offered her finger hopefully to the errant bird. Mrs. Finchley hopped once and then dispatched herself to the top of the tall bookcases at the far end of the room.

Phoebe exhaled in disgust. "I may wring your little neck when I catch you if you keep this up," she muttered just as the door opened a crack and one very blue eye peered through the aperture.

"Mercy, I beg you! I only came to see if I might help," Devenham said, laughing.

Phoebe was quite surprised to see him. He had never ventured into the top reaches of the house, and to do so must have required an excruciating effort on his part. It took her a moment to realize that while he could see very little of the room beyond her, he had a very close view of her own form raised

up on the chair just inches from his nose. She got down
quickly and moved the chair out of the way.

"The fugitive is still at large?" the earl asked as he opened
the door just enough to admit his broad shoulders turned sideways. He eased himself in, quickly pulling the door shut again
behind him. "I had hoped to bring you better reinforcements,
but your brother-in-law and sister have not yet emerged from
their rooms this morning, and Mrs. Hunnicutt had just sent
Goldie out on an errand. I did not dare to ask Maddocks—
chasing escaped birds does not seem quite in his line."

"I'm not sure how much help they would have been,"
Phoebe admitted. "Mrs. Finchley seems not at all inclined to
return to her cage."

"Where is she?"

Phoebe thought Devenham looked apprehensive as his gaze
swept the room.

"She is up there, on top of the bookcase." She pointed, for
the tiny finch was not very noticeable in the shadows.

Devenham looked, and for several moments said and did
nothing. He seemed locked into position, staring at the small
source of all the uproar. Phoebe was standing so close to him,
she sensed his tension, and heard him swallow. Then he
seemed to shake himself out of the spell. She might have
thought he was afraid, except that the notion was so entirely il-
logical.

"What have you already tried to do?" he asked quietly. He
nodded as she explained the antics that had preceded his arrival. "You have been leaving the choice up to your opponent,
which is never a wise policy in battle. We must plot our strategy like commanders in the field."

He motioned to the children, who collected around him de-
lightedly. "I will be the general, and each of you will be my
field units. Our objective is to force Mrs. Finchley to go into
her cage. The way to achieve that is to make all other options
unattractive to her, so she will choose to do exactly what we
want." He paused, casting a wary glance toward the bookcase.
Mrs. Finchley had not moved.

"Thomas, as my second-in-command, I wish you to dispose
our troops around this room, spaced in such a way as to cover

the most likely positions our opponent would wish to occupy. Do you understand the assignment?"

Thomas nodded eagerly, his face glowing with the excitement of the game. "Yes, sir! You want us to spread out around the room."

"As the commanding officer, and the tallest person here, it falls to me to flush Mrs. Finchley from her present post. I am afraid the most effective way to get her back into her cage is to frighten her away from landing anywhere else. If that is not successful, we will have no choice but to capture her."

The earl looked at Phoebe. "Have you a cloth or a towel I might use?" He was making a delightful game out of the operation, yet Phoebe noticed his face looked grim, as if the military maneuver was quite real. His mouth was set in a narrow line.

She looked about the room quickly, noticing a shawl she had left on one chair the day before. She was surprised that Lizzie had not given it to Mary Anne to return to her wardrobe, but she was grateful at this moment for the oversight. "There is my shawl. Would that serve?"

"Admirably."

She retrieved it and gave it to Devenham.

Thomas stationed his siblings around the perimeter of the room and asked his aunt to position herself at the opposite end from the bookcase.

Devenham nodded in approval. "An excellent job, young sir. I see you have taken into account the varying strengths of your units, which in this case has mostly to do with how tall they are."

Using his cane, the earl limped resolutely toward the bookcase, dragging a chair with his free hand. When Phoebe realized he intended to climb up on the chair in the same manner as she so recently had done, she protested vigorously.

"Lord Devenham, you must not be thinking to climb upon that chair with your injury? I can never let you do so. Oh, please. If someone is going to climb up, it will have to be me. You will do yourself damage."

"What is this, woman? Insubordination is a punishable offense. Follow your given orders."

As far as Phoebe was concerned, the game had stopped. "No, I will not." She left her post and walked quickly between the desks to join him by the bookcase. She held out her hand. "Please give me the shawl."

"Aunt Phoebe! What are you doing?" came the dismayed cries of the children.

"Trying to save Major Lord Devenham from his own destructive impulses. The shawl, my lord, please." She would stand her ground no matter what he said.

"My dear," said the earl, "you are not tall enough for this assignment." He moved to stand quite closely in front of her, gazing down at her as if to emphasize his point.

Phoebe caught her breath and held it, hoping the sudden racing of her heart would stop. Devenham was an impressive man at any distance, but this close he was devastating. She struggled for control over the excited reactions that were rippling through her. "I will use the shawl to extend my reach. I need merely flip the end of it toward her, and she will take flight. Is that not what you intended?"

He exhaled, as if he, too, had been holding his breath. What was happening between them?

"All right," he agreed, "but you will have to accept my assistance."

They repositioned the children around the room, and set the chair as nearly underneath Mrs. Finchley's perch as possible. Phoebe was mortified when she realized what a fine view of her ankles and perhaps more the earl would have when she climbed onto the chair. There was nothing for it but to proceed, however. He handed her up like a perfect gentleman and betrayed no hint of any improper thoughts.

"Everyone ready?" she asked. When they all nodded, she gathered the shawl as much as she could into a ball, and flung it at the little bird huddled on the bookcase, keeping hold of one end. For an awful moment she tottered off-balance on the chair. Then she felt the earl's strong hands at her waist, righting her.

Mrs. Finchley flew excitedly around the schoolroom, looking for a new perch. The children raised their arms and shooed her away from each potential landing place as she circled the room repeatedly. In the meantime, Devenham and Phoebe seemed frozen in place, she on the chair and he beside her, his hands still upon her.

Phoebe felt as if bolts of lightning had been let loose inside her body. She could not breathe and she could not move. She was astonished by the force of her reaction. She was even more astonished that Devenham did not immediately remove his hands. As the frozen moment lingered, she looked down at his hands. Strong and warm and masculine, they seemed to burn right through the thin fabric of her dress and her chemise, as if they touched her bare flesh. But she realized something else through her shock—his hands were trembling. When her eyes finally went to his face, she discovered that his eyes were closed and that he was apparently even more paralyzed than she was.

Mrs. Finchley flapped past them on one more circuit, and finally landed on the school desk beside her open cage. Devenham opened his eyes. "Is she done, then?" He seemed to suddenly become aware of his hands still on Phoebe's waist and quickly removed them. "Forgive me, Lady Brodfield," he said in a scandalized tone. "I just did not want you to fall."

She nodded, quite unable to form words although he seemed even more shaken than she was. The entire incident struck her as bizarre, not to mention confusing.

"Do not move in on the bird too quickly," the earl cautioned the children. "Let her decide to go into her cage on her own. I suspect she may be tired now."

Mrs. Finchley hopped about on the desktop briefly, tilting her head and looking around her out of bright, curious eyes. Then at long last, she hopped up into her cage, quite as if she had planned to do so all along and had done nothing remotely out of the ordinary. Dorrie approached quietly and snapped the door shut as everyone heaved a collective sigh of relief. This was immediately followed by cheers and applause. Devenham offered Phoebe his hand and helped her down from the chair.

"However did you know what to do?" she asked him admiringly. "I'm certain we would never have recaptured her without your help."

"Ah, yes, you would have, in time," he answered modestly.

"But you might have had to leave her closed up in the school-room until nightfall."

"I was so afraid she would escape into the rest of the house, or hurt herself. How can I thank you?"

He was pale and still appeared quite shaken. As she looked at him, however, she saw the irreverent twinkle come into his blue eyes and the too-familiar wicked grin light up his face.

"I can think of several ways that would be delightful," he said in a seductively low voice. "Unfortunately, I am so greatly in your debt, no thanks are owed. I am pleased to be able to perform some service of use to you."

He paused, looking at her sincerely for a moment.

"You must be exhausted," she said apologetically. "This was far more activity than you should have had for one morning. We must get you back downstairs to your room so you can rest."

"I will agree on one condition."

"Which is?"

"That you will promise to spend some time visiting with me this afternoon. You lavish all your attention on children, invalids, and helpless creatures. Now that I am so much improved, you have been avoiding my company. Am I so disagreeable? It is almost enough to remove my incentive to get well."

"Oh dear, we can't allow that," she said quite seriously. *You must get well, so you can leave—the sooner the better for both of us.* She had not asked to feel this attraction between them. Like the earl himself, it seemed to grow stronger every day. Avoiding him had been the easiest way to deal with it. "You leave me no choice but to come."

On the whole, Devenham found life itself was improving. His strength was coming back a little more each day, although he still limped and used the cane. His shoulder seldom bothered him anymore. Phoebe seemed resigned to keeping him company, and he had come to believe that she was in actuality a good deal more fond of him than she let on.

Mullins had proved to be as good a detective as he had hoped, piecing together an account of Phoebe's history that disturbed the earl whenever he thought about it. He had not given Phoebe any indication that he knew, hoping that one day she would feel comfortable enough with him to confide it on her own.

Devenham had been in his room, resting as he frequently did in the wing chair by the window, on the day Mullins finally came to him. Mullins had wisely engaged the vast company of backstairs humanity in his quest for information, casually dropping a remark or a question or a few shillings here or there, pulling information from servants in the Allingtons' own household as well as the Brodfields', and a good many more who merely had good memories for gossip as he traveled about Town on the earl's mission.

"Married for two years they was, without the slightest sign of trouble," he reported. "Supposed to have been a love match made in heaven. It was a shock to everyone when he was found dead. It was a clear case of suicide—apparently the pistol he used was still in his hand."

"Suicide!" Devenham had risen from his chair and paced to the fireplace and back, placing his cane with exaggerated care. Suicides were scandalous indeed, although not terribly uncommon, yet it was not at all what he had expected. "Was he deeply in debt? I would have thought his father . . ."

"Apparently no one knew. They say even his creditors did not realize the extent of his folly; not one knew of the others. But that is not all. It gets worse."

"Worse?" Devenham thought of the gentle spirit he had come to know, and of how greatly she must have suffered at such a sudden and very final parting from the man she had loved so much.

"They found him in an alley behind a Covent Garden nunnery. The abbess swore he had used to be a regular there, until he set up one of the doxies as his mistress. She said he had come back that night, drunk and swearing, looking for the woman and claiming that she was his wife."

"He must have been mad!"

"This all came out after they found him dead. Then it seems some marriage papers were found among his things that

showed he did marry the woman, even though he was already
married to Lady Brodfield."

"Dear God! Bigamy!" Devenham sank back into his chair.
"Is that all?" he asked faintly.

Mullins nodded.

Devenham could see now why Phoebe had been so devastated. The scandal had to have been enormous. He had been in
the south of France with Wellington at that time—February of
1814. He was surprised that they had heard no word of it, for
usually the mails were full of London's latest gossip.

Yet he found the whole story hard to fathom. "Was there an
investigation?" he asked Mullins. He simply could not believe
that any man married to Phoebe would have conducted himself
in such a manner.

"There was the usual inquest, but the ruling of suicide was
never considered much in question."

Devenham shook his head in disbelief. "Why would anyone . . . It makes no sense." The story had deeply shocked him.

Still, his brain worked, trying to grapple with it. The rumors
about the Brodfields that he couldn't quite recall had nothing
to do with this tragedy, he was certain. For one thing, they pre-
dated the episode, as the last time he had been in London had
been during the Season of the preceding year. A sudden
thought occurred to him, although he disliked it.

"They had no children, in two years of marriage?"

"No, sir."

"What of the other so-called marriage? The one to the
doxy?"

"I don't know."

"All right, Mullins. You've done well. Find out who this
other woman was, and what happened to her. I want to know
when that false marriage took place, and if there were any
children. Can you find that out?"

"I'll try my best, sir."

Mullins was looking at him with a peculiar expression almost like sympathy. Why? Was he behaving strangely? He
didn't think so. He just wanted to know more. "Thank you,
Mullins. I know you will. I will try to dig up some information, also."

He let his gaze fall absently on the writing table where Phoebe had helped to write his letters. *How could she have mourned so for a man who had put her through hell?* Did love make people completely irrational?

Still, Mullins was looking at him with that odd expression. A strange sensation crept along his pine. "Blast and confound it, man! You can stop looking at me like that! I just find the whole story hard to accept," he blustered impatiently. "My interest in it does not mean that I am in love with Lady Brodfield."

Chapter Nine

Phoebe thought Devenham seemed to treat her a little differently in the days that followed, although she could not quite say how, or why. His health continued to improve. He had insisted on gradually reducing his reliance on the laudanum, and had grown increasingly restless.

He began to go out, sometimes accompanying Edward to White's or Brooks's, sometimes hiring a hackney to take him to Hatchard's or Weston's or to dine with army friends at Stephen's Hotel. He seldom stayed out long, for he still tired easily, and always when he returned he would seem anxious to see her.

The volume of mail delivered to the Allington house tripled with the invitations and notes that began to arrive once the earl's presence there became generally known. On several occasions he asked Phoebe if she would not care to attend some affair or another, and Edward and Judith asked her also, but she always refused. She did not feel ready to face what still seemed to her like an ordeal.

One day an invitation arrived from Lucinda Follett, with a note especially addressed to Phoebe inside. The Folletts were sponsoring a musicale, and Lucy urged Phoebe to attend. "I know you will be disinclined to come, my dear, but I promise I will arrive on your doorstep to choose your dress for you if you refuse. You must make a start, and a musicale is easy, for you will hardly have to speak two words of conversation to anyone."

Phoebe had been sitting alone in the drawing room as she sorted the mail. She sighed and refolded the letter, tapping it against her lips as she thought about how she should answer. Lucy was right—she *did* need to make a start, and a musicale would be easier than almost any other type of event she could think of. At the theater a prodigious amount of socializing went on during the intermissions, and even during the performances. Dinners were taken up entirely with talking, as were card parties, routs, even balls. But if the earl would go to Lucy's with them, she could sit with Judith and Edward on one side of her, and Lord Devenham on the other, protected from dealing with other people almost entirely.

As if she had conjured him up with her thoughts, she suddenly heard Devenham's deep voice. "I hope that isn't bad news."

"What?" She turned toward the door, so surprised that the letter in her hand slipped from her fingers.

He stood there, handsomely framed by the fluted columns of the doorway. He was dressed immaculately in a coat of rust brown superfine over a blue waistcoat and cream pantaloons that looked so perfect she suspected they were being worn for the first time.

"I beg your pardon. I didn't intend to startle you. Maddocks informed me that you were here, and apparently you did not hear my knock. Shall I go out and begin again?"

She could not help smiling. She shook her head.

"You appeared to be lost in your thoughts, and those not particularly happy, judging by your frown. I hope your mail did not contain bad news," he repeated.

"You are welcome to take a seat," she offered. "I was just getting ready to deliver this mail to Judith. She is upstairs visiting with Nurse and the baby."

"Ah. So I am welcome to my own company, and you are already running away again."

"Not exactly." Then what was she doing? She made herself take a deep breath, and bent to retrieve the fallen note. "Actually, you might be pleased to know that, rather than bad news, this is something you might view as positive," she said, holding up Lucy's letter. "We have actually received an invitation to something that I cannot refuse."

"I am astounded! What enterprising hostess has brought about this change of heart, and what sort of invitation has she offered?" He advanced from the doorway at last, as if satisfied that they would at least share a conversation before she tried to escape. He surveyed the assortment of chairs arranged about the room and selected the most comfortable one to sit on.

"How do you feel about musicales? A woman with whom I used to be quite friendly has invited us all to one two nights hence. Do you know Lady Follett?"

"Follett, Follett . . . is she not the friend with whom you had tea recently? Her name rings a bell, but I can't match a face to it. Musicale, eh? I'm actually quite fond of music. That is enough to instill in me a natural dread for those kinds of affairs, since the performers are too often amateur friends of the hostess who do their best to murder the music they purport to perform."

Before the sinking feeling in her breast crystallized into true disappointment, he went on. "I could, however, be persuaded to attend on the basis of enjoying your pleasant company, Lady Brodfield. Perhaps your friend has happened across some true musicians. In that case, her event would be a rare delight I should enjoy sharing."

"Lady Follett has exquisite taste in most things," Phoebe hastened to reassure him, amazed at how much lighter her heart felt already at the prospect of his company. "I am certain she would not subject us to a painful evening." *At least, not musically painful,* she added to herself.

"I shall look forward to it, then."

She stood up, clutching the pile of mail she intended to deliver to Judith.

He stood up, too. "I came seeking you because I had something I wished to ask you," he said with a slight lift of an eyebrow.

Phoebe had quite overlooked the point that he had particularly asked Maddocks where she was. "I'm sorry. You were right that I was preoccupied. It has been a long time since I attended anything even so modest as a musicale. I have shunned company for so long, I do not expect it to be easy. What did you wish to ask me?"

"I wanted to invite you to go with me to the park this afternoon. I have promised to accompany the children and Henrietta, and thought perhaps you would be brave enough to come along. Are you?"

Henrietta was the unlikely name the children had given the new puppy. Friendly and affectionate to a fault, she had attached herself devotedly to everyone in the household including the earl.

Devenham himself had won the affections of not only the pup but the children and even Judith, who had held her judgment of him in reserve. Phoebe wondered how all of them would deal with it when the time came for him to leave. She did not dare to contemplate her own feelings.

She had not returned to the park since the day she had gone with the children and been spied upon by Richard Brodfield's agent. She had explained the mystery to the children, to make sure they would not be afraid to go there, but had declined to go with them on all subsequent expeditions. She did not feel very brave at the moment. There stood Lord Devenham, however, watching her expectantly, having all but dared her.

She looked down, fidgeting with the mail distractedly. "I suppose you think me a great coward, hiding away here in this house, refusing to go out." She had not realized until this moment how much she wished him not to think that.

She also did not realize that he had moved closer to her until she suddenly felt the tips of his fingers touching her chin, raising her head to make her gaze meet his.

"I believe I ought to answer yes, so you would feel challenged to prove me wrong," he said softly, his fingers lingering. The blue of his eyes seemed to blaze with intensity. "However, I will be honest with you, Lady Brodfield. I myself have been judged and misjudged so many times by so many people, I try not to indulge in the habit."

He snatched his fingers away abruptly. "I will only say that a good general recognizes the strategic value of both the advance and the retreat, and has the wisdom to know when each is appropriate."

Phoebe could not seem to pull her eyes away from his. Was he telling her now was the time to advance? Certainly Lucy was. "All right," she conceded, "I will go with you and the children to the park." After all, it was not the same as if she were going there with him alone.

"I'm putting a visit to Tattersall's at the top of my list for next week," Devenham groaned as the Allingtons' overfilled landau made its way toward Hyde Park that afternoon. "I'll not go another week without at least a curricle and pair of my own in this city."

Henrietta was in the earl's lap, shedding white and brown dog hair all over his impeccable new ensemble. Phoebe had William in her lap, for although he was heavier than the pup, he had made it clear that familiarity won out over his fondness for his new friend, the earl. Dorrie sat beside her aunt without complaint, and facing them sat Lizzie with Thomas and David.

"I wish I could go with you," David said enviously. "When I am old enough, I'm going to be a regular there."

"It surprises me that you have no Town residence and keep no stable here of your own, Lord Devenham," Phoebe observed. "I would have thought it almost a requirement for a man of your station."

"My Town residence is leased out, Lady Brodfield, since I had no expectations of spending time in London. I am at heart still a military man, with simple tastes. For that matter, I never had any expectations of becoming Earl of Devenham. It always seemed much more likely that I would die than my brother. I was the one who went overseas to face Napoleon's armies. Who would have guessed that my fool brother would break his neck in a hunting accident? Consequently, I have not the accouterments one might expect."

He paused, and Phoebe did not know what to say. She thought she detected traces of both bitterness and regret in his voice.

"I suppose my campaigning days are over now," he continued. "I have had to give some thought to what my life should be from now on. I must say I have had ample time in which to reflect upon it." He did not expand upon his topic, however, for the carriage had reached the park, and John Coachman desired instructions as to how they wished to proceed.

"We have come to give Henrietta a bit of exercise," Devenham said, scratching the pup's ears affectionately. "Not to mention the children," he added with a teasing look at them. "I believe we will get out and walk a bit. You might as well take the horses for a turn or two around the park, and we'll keep a look-out for you when we are ready to go back."

The servant nodded and climbed down from his perch to hold the horses while the little party descended. The earl handed Henrietta to David and got down first to assist the rest of them. "Keep a tight hold on her leash," he cautioned the children. "All this space and fresh air is likely to go to her head."

As he handed Phoebe down, he allowed his hand to linger and bent his head close to her. "I must keep a close watch to make sure that it does not do the same to you."

Caught off-guard, she pulled away to look at him. She saw the familiar wicked twinkle in his eye. *Oh, dear,* she thought. *I did not expect things to go in this direction.*

As it happened, however, the children had already raced off ahead with the dog, with Lizzie trailing in their wake, doing her best to keep them in sight. Devenham tucked Phoebe's hand under his elbow and began to walk slowly in the same direction. His limp was much less pronounced now than it had been, and his use of the cane could at first glance have been attributed to mere fashion. Phoebe thought he walked a good deal more slowly than was necessary.

To mask her discomfort, she laughed a little and nodded her head toward the spectacle of the children running about in the grass with the puppy. "I am always of two minds when I see Dorrie go running off with the boys in such a fashion. She is really at an age when she should be practicing more decorous behavior. In just a few short years she will be old enough to make her come-out. Then I think of how short those years will be until the time she must put such behavior forever behind her, and I feel more inclined to let her run."

"You sound regretful," Devenham said. He seemed to be aiming for a bench in the meager shade offered by an ancient pollarded oak. "How old were you when you made your come-out?"

She brushed an imaginary speck of dust from the deep gray

skirt of her pelisse. The day was warm and she was glad she had changed out of the black bombazine she had worn in the morning to the light muslin dress she wore now beneath the crepe overdress. "I was eighteen," she answered. "More than ready. Some girls come out sooner."

"Ah yes," he said with a chuckle that reminded her of how much she liked the sound. "Some families find that they cannot wait. I have always found that the age of the chit directly correlates to her family's financial need—the younger they are, the worse off their parents."

"That is not a fair statement!" Phoebe exclaimed. "I thought you were the one who tried not to judge people. Sometimes a young girl is desperate to be married, and she all but bullies her parents into giving her an early come-out."

"Or sometimes she is too hard to handle, and the parents are desperate to palm her off onto someone else."

"Really! I can see you are quite embittered on the subject."

"I apologize if my remarks distress you. I have had too many young chits launched at my head, I suppose. I have grown weary of ducking them."

He gave her such a sheepish look that she had to laugh. "You make them sound like artillery missiles."

"They can be just as explosive and far more dangerous if they are truly determined," he answered soberly. "What about you? Were you eager for your come-out? What sort of a husband did you hope to find?"

"Well, I . . ." Phoebe hesitated, remembering a joyful, carefree young girl who had delighted in the beautiful swirl of social activity during her first Season. It all seemed such a long time ago, so far removed from present realities. That girl had been innocent and utterly, tragically blind. What could she say about it now? "I suppose I was—eager, that is," she began woodenly. "I don't think I had formed any particular expectations, however, about a husband. Then I met Stephen and nothing else mattered."

"You were married after a single Season?"

"We announced our engagement at the end of it, and were married the following February."

He looked at her with an oddly triumphant glint in his wide, not-so-innocent blue eyes. "You must be all of twenty-two, then."

She didn't know what she had expected him to say, but it was hardly that. She was indignant and her voice rose a note or two. "Don't you know it is highly improper to ask a lady her age?"

He laughed. "I never asked you. I will admit that I outmaneuvered you, however. You should play more chess, so you will learn to anticipate other people's strategy. You need to look farther ahead than simply one move at a time."

She wondered if their conversation was part of a larger strategy of his, and if it were, what his objectives could possibly be. She did not dare to ask him that. "I believe my chess game is passable," she retorted instead. "I do not see life as a game between myself and a world full of adversaries, despite what you may think."

"A pity. I was going to offer to teach you."

"Are you such a skilled tutor, then?"

He smiled rather coldly. "The Earls of Devenham and all their close relations are weaned on maneuvering other people." He did not sound especially proud of the fact.

They had long since reached the bench under the oak tree, and had been standing in front of it continuing their conversation without sitting down. Devenham gestured now to Phoebe, asking her if she cared to sit. She guessed that he might need to, but she did not particularly wish to sit there beside him, so close. Pretending that she was not attracted to him was too difficult.

She was just starting to shake her head when she heard the children's cries of distress.

"Henrietta! Oh, no, Henrietta! Come back!"

With a sinking heart, Phoebe looked in their direction and saw just what she somehow had known she would see. Henrietta had escaped from the children and was running pell-mell toward her and Lord Devenham, the leash dragging crazily over the grass behind her.

"I'll get her," the earl volunteered. He set his hat carefully on the bench.

"But your leg!"

"She's naught but a fat little puppy," he said with mock disdain. "On those little legs she shouldn't be a match for even a lame man, especially when she's already headed our way."

He went nobly forward to meet the little dog, but at the last minute Henrietta veered off and struck out in a new direction to Devenham's left. Unfortunately for the earl, Henrietta had seen what he had not. A huge flock of birds had been feeding and resting on the grass in the area just beyond where he and Phoebe had stopped, and Henrietta was apparently convinced they were there just for her. Sounding joyful puppy barks as loudly as she could, she dashed into the midst of them, setting off a maelstrom of panicked fluttering. The noise was deafening as the birds cried in alarm and rose into the air.

Phoebe did not hear Devenham's own cry of alarm. She was alerted to his distress by what she saw. As he was enveloped in the swirling cloud of frightened birds, he dropped to his knees with his head bent, his hands covering his ears.

"Lord Devenham! Oh, dear! What is the matter?" Phoebe shooed a few straggling birds out of her way as she hurried toward him.

Most of the birds had taken shelter in the nearby trees where their continued cries and chatter could still be heard. Thoroughly disappointed, Henrietta had turned around and now intercepted Phoebe, bouncing up to her shamelessly and wagging her tail anew, quite unaware that she had done anything even slightly objectionable.

"David, come and take her," called Phoebe in exasperation as she captured the dog's leash. To Henrietta she said sternly, "Go with David. Go!" She pointed to the approaching lad, hoping the dog would take the meaning. It was too late to scold the pup now. She all but threw the leash to David in her haste to turn back to the earl.

She saw that he had not moved at all. "Lord Devenham, are you all right?" Clearly he was not. "Is it your leg?" She didn't see how his leg, so much stronger now than it had been, could suddenly have given out on him. She realized that she was wasting her voice as she approached him, for he still had his hands over his ears, apparently frozen in place.

Frozen. She suddenly remembered the morning in the

schoolroom when he had helped to rescue Mrs. Finchley. He had frozen in place with his hands on her waist. She hadn't understood then, but she thought she was beginning to now. She moved to him quickly and gently pulled his hands away from his head. "Lord Devenham," she said in a voice that was warm with compassion.

She did not quite know what to do with his hands this time. It would have been so simple if he were a child—she could have put his hands around her and given him the comfort of an embrace. As his head lifted and his eyes locked with hers, she did the only thing she could. She gave his fingers a reassuring squeeze and let them drop. "It isn't your leg, is it? 'Tis the birds. I never guessed."

She noted that the color was slowly returning to his face, and that the children and Lizzie were quickly approaching with guilt, concern, and curiosity etched on theirs. "Everything is all right now," she said, reassuring him gently as if he were a child. "Here come the others. We'll let them think it was your leg. You can explain it to me later."

He nodded, a hopeful sign that he was recovering. "I don't believe I can get up without assistance," he said with a rueful expression.

She smiled with relief. That seemed more like Devenham. As the others joined them she said, "Here, Lizzie, you must help me. He can't get up." She crouched down by his side and allowed him to place his arm over her shoulders. She motioned for the young nursery maid to do the same, and as they levered him up from the ground he managed to get his feet back beneath him and stand.

"Ladies, I thank you," he said, sketching a bow. "How often do you have the opportunity to aid a gentleman in distress?"

Despite his attempt to achieve a teasing tone, Phoebe could hear in his voice that he was still terribly shaken.

The children were all full of apologies as the little group made their way back to the carriage ride and waited for their landau to come in sight.

"What do *you* have to apologize for?" a miserable David snapped at his siblings. "*I'm* the one who let go of the leash."

"But we all wanted to bring Henrietta to the park," Dorrie

said, determined to be equally miserable. "It's all of our faults."

"And we all of us were playing with her. Maybe we made her too excited," Thomas added.

William stood silently, listening to the others, until suddenly tears started to run down his small cheeks. "It's my fault," he declared between sobs. "I was the one who most wanted a puppy."

Phoebe had heard enough. "Stop it, all four of you. What happened was no one's fault, except possibly Henrietta's, and we're not blaming her either. She is only a puppy who doesn't know any better than to go chasing birds. Lord Devenham is fine, and no harm was done—you can see for yourselves if you will only stop feeling guilty long enough to look about you." She gave William a hug and fished in her reticule for a handkerchief.

Devenham chimed in as if on cue. "That little episode was something of a surprise, but as your Aunt Phoebe says, you can see that I'm perfectly fit."

To illustrate his point, he set the tip of his cane carefully in the gravel and walked a tight circle around it. He doffed his hat and bowed nicely. It was a convincing performance, and only when he raised his eyes to meet Phoebe's did she see that there was still something lingering there—a haunted, desperate look she would have described as a bleakness of expression if she had been pressed to name it. She smiled at him in gratitude for his support, hoping some of her warmth might help to dispel whatever it was.

The ride back to Wigmore Street in the landau was accomplished for the most part in silence, punctuated by occasional snatches of conversation centered primarily on Henrietta. Phoebe's mind was on Devenham, and since she could not easily look into his face, she focused on his hands.

As his eyes had, they told her he was still shaken by what had happened. One clutched the silver knob at the top of his cane with unnecessary force, while the other maintained a tense grip on the edge of the squabs. His buff-colored cotton gloves fit like a second skin and did nothing to hide either the strength or the tension in those long, masculine fingers.

Phoebe thought she had certainly misjudged him. After what she had seen today, she was convinced that the earl was not only unselfish but quite heroic. For some unknown reason, he had a fear of birds, yet he had climbed all those stairs to the schoolroom that day to help her and the children with Mrs. Finchley. She flinched from the memory of her angry words when she had determined he had bought Henrietta and had her delivered. She had actually accused him of trying to bribe his way into the children's hearts. He hadn't needed to, she reflected now, for they had taken to him naturally.

He cared about others, whether he admitted it or not. She found that she could readily believe he had been a hero at Waterloo, despite his denials. And now she was curious to know why he worked so hard to make it seem otherwise. For it was surely his reputation more than his behavior that had made her distrustful of him.

Upon arrival, Phoebe sent the children with Henrietta and Lizzie off into the upper reaches of the house with some vague instructions to get clean and change into fresh clothes. She exchanged a glance with the earl, thinking that they could both benefit by the same treatment after their outing, but she was afraid the chance to speak with him in private would be gone. She suggested they go into the drawing room.

"So," he said with a twisted half-smile, "we shall end our afternoon's adventure in the same room where we began it." He was standing by the window, next to the gaming table that was laid out for chess.

"I did not realize it would be quite so much of an adventure," Phoebe replied. "I have only ventured into the park twice in a year and a half, and both times something extraordinary has happened. I don't know whether it is enough to convince me to continue staying home, or to entice me to go more often, on the theory that I am missing a great deal." She smiled to take away any possible sting he might find in her words. "Shall I ring for tea?"

He shook his head. "I must apologize to you for what happened." As if he found discussing it difficult, he moved away from the table and began to pace. His gaze was directed downward to the invisible path he followed back and forth.

Phoebe sat down in the carved armchair near the fireplace. "You need not apologize," she assured him. "As I told the children, what happened was no one's fault." She hesitated, wondering if she was right to push him to explain. "Have you always been afraid of birds?"

A moment passed with no other sound than his footfalls across the patterned Turkey carpet onto the polished wood floor and back again. Finally, he began to speak in anguished tones.

"I am sorry that you had to witness such idiocy. I have had a problem with that since I was a small boy."

"Something must have happened."

He stopped, and lifted his gaze to the window, as if he could see through it back into his past. "Yes."

For a moment she thought he was not going to tell her. He fidgeted with his cane, rubbing the palm of his free hand over the smooth, round surface of its silver knob over and over again.

"I don't know how old I was when this happened, but I was quite young," he said slowly. "I had followed my brother Jeremy up into the limestone hills behind our estate in Derbyshire. There are many caves, and we were exploring. I don't think we had permission to be there, for we had no servants with us. Some of the caves we already knew well—some are even used by the locals for storage. But we went into one we did not know as well, or at least one *I* did not know.

"We came to a place where the cave floor dropped down abruptly. Jeremy, being older, was big enough to climb back up, but I was not. Jeremy, being who he was, would not help me. 'If you can't climb back up by yourself, you'll just have to stay there,' he said, and he left me there.

"We were far enough from the cave entrance that when he left with the lantern it was very dark. I was frightened, but I believed he would at least tell someone I was there."

A tone of bitterness had crept into Devenham's voice. Instead of rubbing his cane knob, he now slapped his palm against it. "I was there for hours, and no one came. My dear brother told no one. If I was missed, no one knew where to look for me. I did not know if it was night or day, but it began to get very cold, and I began to hear noises around me that I knew I had not made. I had left off crying a while before that."

Phoebe shivered, horrified by the tale. She felt the cold as acutely as if she had been there, and she heard the coldness in Devenham's voice.

"To make a long story short, there were bats in the cave. There must have been hundreds—it seemed like thousands. As evening came on, of course, they awakened, and began to fly about. In the darkness I was not sure what they were. They never touched me, naturally, but I did not know they would not. The sounds were terrifying to me. When I felt the air brush my skin as one flew especially near to me, I let out a scream that would have waked the dead."

He shrugged, and turned finally to look at her. "That had both good and bad results."

Phoebe could not have said a word. There was a huge lump of sympathy stuck in her throat. She blinked back tears and put one hand to her mouth to stop its trembling.

"The bad result was that, not surprisingly, my sudden loud noise disturbed all the rest of the bats that had not stirred yet. The sound of their shrieking and flapping wings was magnified in the cave, and still haunts my worst nightmares. The sound of wings flapping reaches back through all the years that have passed and revives the terror of that little boy who still lives inside me somewhere.

"The good result was that one of our tenant farmers who was taking a shortcut home from the local pub, heard me scream. He was terrified, of course, but he went racing to the big house, and informed my father that a hideous monster had taken up residence in one of the caves—that he had heard it with his own ears. My parents put two and two together, and confronted my brother. They sent up a rescue party to fetch me home."

Phoebe stood up and went to the earl. Not to offer him comfort at such a time went against everything in her nature, and she had already denied her first impulse at the park.

He was standing absolutely still, one hand clutching his cane and the other at his side, clenched into a fist. Phoebe reached for the fisted hand and slipped her own hands around it. It was so much larger than her own that she needed both of hers to cover it.

Devenham unclenched his fist and took one of Phoebe's hands in his. He let the cane drop to the floor and put his other arm around Phoebe, easing her against his chest. They stood there quietly embracing, drawing warmth and comfort from each other's nearness. Their hearts seemed to beat in unison.

"Your parents did not come themselves to find you and comfort you?" Phoebe whispered.

"Ah. My parents both believed that any son of theirs should be man enough to weather such an event without complaint."

"And did you?"

"As best I could."

"Was your brother punished?"

"Yes, for causing the tenant farmer to be frightened."

"That is terrible!"

"Is it?" He pulled away from her a little and released her hand so that he could turn her face to look up at him. His hand slid up to cradle her cheek.

Phoebe closed her eyes for a moment, savoring his touch. How good it felt to have a man holding her again! When she opened her eyes she felt the sudden flood of something much stronger than sympathy flow through her veins as she gazed into the depths of his blue eyes. Her rapid pulse seemed to have risen into her ears.

In the next moment she felt his lips on hers, touching gently and tentatively at first, then pressing harder, as if they had found reassurance in her response. She felt drunk—dizzy and out of control. An inner voice screamed at her that this was wrong, all wrong, yet another one screamed with equal force that nothing had ever been more right. She slid her arms around him and kissed him back, almost in relief at giving in at last to something she had been fighting from the first time she'd seen him.

The kiss escalated and Phoebe began to tremble with the force of her denied passion. Then Devenham broke it off, pulling his head back.

"God help us," he said, looking down at her.

Chapter Ten

"I must be mad." Devenham looked at Phoebe in shock, thoroughly appalled at what he had done. He stepped back from her, still staring.

She stood absolutely still, apparently frozen in horror. Never in his whole life had he so regretted a kiss; he was not certain he had *ever* regretted one before now. "If I offered a thousand apologies, it would not be enough," he said miserably. "After all that you and Allington and Lady Allington have done for me—this, this is how I repay you!"

He continued to stare at her, as if somehow he might discover an explanation for what had happened in the stricken expression on her face. He pushed away the lingering sense of the intense pleasure he had felt while kissing her, and he also pushed away his recognition of her warm response.

He was the one to blame. He was the one who had stepped so far out of bounds. He was the one who had jeopardized the fragile bonds of trust and friendship that he thought had begun to form between him and Lady Brodfield. He was the fool.

He uttered a brief, sharp laugh and turned away, moving toward the window. "You see? I am every bit the blackguard you took me for at first." He stared out into the garden. "There are many people who would have warned you what to expect from me—nothing but the most reprehensible behavior. They would only be surprised to learn that I had not attempted to take advantage of you sooner. Edward gave no thought to your reputation when he allowed me to come under this roof."

"Stop!"

The sharpness of her tone made him turn back to her in surprise.

She had buried her face in her hands and was shaking her

head. "It was my fault—*mine*. You did not take advantage of me, and nothing you try to say now will alter the fact."

"How can you say so?"

She raised her head again and let her hands drop. "Think on it. I was the one who asked you to come in here, and I was the one who went to you. You may try now to take refuge behind that black reputation you seem so unaccountably proud of, but I have seen what sort of man you really are, and I tell you, that pretense will not fadge with me, not anymore. I have seen you to be kind, generous, thoughtful, and courageous. If you were the blackguard you claim to be, you would not be trying to apologize, nor would you be accusing yourself of any wrongdoing. You are a fraud, sir."

He hardly knew how to respond. "I have been called worse, although not without repercussions. But I will not challenge you to 'grass before breakfast.' You are generous and softhearted; you offered me comfort, and instead I took my pleasure. Now you try to spare me from my own villainous actions. That I see them clearly does not change their nature. I apologize for this entire day—for making you come to the park, for forcing you to witness my cowardice, and for compounding these efforts with what can only be the greatest insult!" He turned away again, shaking his head in despair.

"You did not make me come to the park; I chose to go. And I am not insulted by what happened here." She spoke very softly. "You know nothing of me or my history, sir. If you did, you would see very easily that the fault is mine. I pray you give it no further thought. What passed between us meant nothing. If you wish to pretend, then pretend that it never happened. We must simply forget it."

She turned on her heel as she finished and hurried from the room.

Devenham stared after her, still in shock after the events of the day. *What passed between us meant nothing?* He did not think so. Nor was he about to forget it. He had never told anyone about his fearful experience with the bats, yet Phoebe had gotten him to confide in her. She seemed to have magical, curative powers over both the ills of his body and those of his heart. She had responded to his kiss like a wilting flower given water. But he did not know what to do about it. He definitely had a good deal of thinking to do.

Despite her strict intentions, Phoebe did not manage to treat Devenham quite as if nothing had happened between them. She had been appalled that he had blamed himself for what happened, and was relieved that he seemed to have listened to her arguments. But she realized now how fragile was her control over her own yearnings. The easy comaraderie that she had so gradually begun to enjoy with the earl was a pleasure she could no longer afford; when she was with him she fought a constant battle against her longing to feel his touch again. A relationship between them was impossible. For both their sakes she needed to put distance between them; it was the only way she could keep up the pretense that she felt nothing.

Late in the afternoon of the second day after the incident, Edward asked her to join him in the study/library. She guessed that he had something to report about Beau Chatain, for she had spoken to him about her visit from Richard and had asked him to look into the value and status of the property.

"Do take a seat, Phoebe my dear," Edward said cordially.

The shadows of the house had overtaken the garden outside the windows at this hour of the day, and the room was rapidly losing what was left of the natural daylight. Edward lit the lamp on his desk and sat down.

"You and Lord Devenham do not seem to be rubbing along together as nicely as you were, I have noticed," he began, to her surprise. He was looking rather longingly at his collection of pipes, it seemed to Phoebe, instead of at her.

"What makes you say that?" she asked, trying to match his casual tone.

"Ahem! Er, well, to be honest, Judith, actually. Not to say that I didn't notice, for I did. But Judith was the one who wanted me to speak to you about it. I say, you and Devenham haven't had a disagreement, have you? As the one who invited him under our roof, I do feel responsible. I hope nothing untoward has occurred. I felt certain that you would have told me if it had."

Phoebe sighed. There was nothing to be gained by burden-

ing Edward and Judith with the trials of her heart, or by causing any ill-feeling between them and the earl. "No, dearest Edward," she said, "rest assured that I would tell you if Lord
Devenham behaved with any disrespect. If I have seemed distant, perhaps it is just that I am preoccupied. I have been thinking a good deal about Beau Chatain and what it could mean
for my future."

Edward seemed only partially mollified. He leaned forward,
interlacing his fingers and setting them in front of him on the
desk. "I have been thinking about your future, too, my dear. I
shall speak of Beau Chatain in a moment, for I do have information for you. But Judith and I were hoping, frankly, that you
might begin to consider the idea of remarriage."

Phoebe watched Edward's fingers unlace themselves and
begin to trace invisible patterns on the leather desktop.

"Lord Devenham is a handsome and charming man. I will
confess that we had hoped that, at the very least, being with
him would awaken you to the fact that you are still young and
attractive and there are many who might jump at the chance to
be your husband. This recent increase in your fortune can only
make the prospect even sweeter. I hope you'll forgive me for
speaking so bluntly."

Poor Edward was obviously uncomfortable, and Phoebe
knew he had only her best interests at heart. "What is there to
forgive?" she asked softly. "I could never hold it against you
that you are looking out for me as my father would if he were
alive, even though it is a job you never asked for, Edward.
You have always been better to me than any brother by blood
could possibly have been. I am sorry if I have disappointed
you and Judith." She lifted her chin and added more force-
fully, "Lord Devenham is indeed handsome and charming; he
is even kind. I just have no interest in him. I have no interest in
remarrying."

Edward did not reply for a moment but sat as he was, eyeing
her thoughtfully.

I cannot tell him the truth, Phoebe thought in near panic. *He
must believe me. It will be far easier if he and Judith and all
the world with them simply believe that I choose to live my life
alone. If they think I am grieving for my lost love, so be it. I*

could not bear it if they knew how I all but smothered Stephen
with a blind, barren love that drove him to take his own life! I
could not bear it if I lost their love, too.

"We can only offer our advice," Edward said with a note of
sadness in his voice. "You must do as you see fit, of course."

"You said you had information for me about Beau Chatain?
What have you learned?" She settled back in her chair, trying
to appear unperturbed. It was a relief to change the subject so
easily.

"I drove out there to see the property and to check on what
Richard told you about the horses and servants. It is a small
but very attractive estate—one in which I think you could live
comfortably, although not luxuriously, given your supplemen-
tal income. However, Richard told you the truth about his having disposed of the stables and hired his own servants. The
cattle we saw seem to be his own, not the earl's. Apparently he
has been using the place regularly for several years, and not
only in hunting season. He seems well established there, and
given his interest in keeping it, I think you would do better to
sell it to him than to incur his ill-will by opposing him."

"Has he made me a fair offer?"

"That still remains to be seen. I took a friend with me who
is more experienced at evaluating properties, but there are several matters he says he must look into before he can arrive at
an overall valuation."

"Edward, I hope you know how much I do appreciate your
help with this matter." Phoebe bit her lip, thinking. "How do
you suppose Richard has managed to spend so much time
there in these past few years, when he has been serving with
his regiment overseas?"

The evening of Lucinda Follett's musicale was warm and
clear, with a sky full of stars that began to show even before
the last traces of sunset had disappeared. The beauty of the
evening seemed an encouraging sign to Phoebe. Her dismay
over attending had been doubled by the new awkwardness
with Devenham. How she wished she had never encouraged
him to come along! She had thought she would feel safe sitting
beside him for an evening, but how her heart had betrayed her!

She had summoned all her courage as she dressed before dinner and now faced the hours ahead with a reserved smile that was fixed rigidly in place.

She was dressed in an evening gown of black crepe over a black sarcenet slip which had resided in her wardrobe untouched for a year and a half. Mary Anne had spent considerable hours pressing it and freshening the trimmings of black *gros de Naples* and black crepe roses. Phoebe knew that it was not cut as low in front as might be fashionable, but the neckline was wide and exposed her smooth shoulders quite satisfactorily. Her hair was dressed with a black lacquered hair comb trimmed with jet that had been her mother's and some black crepe roses she had borrowed from Judith.

She had had a chance to admire Lord Devenham as the little party assembled in the entrance hall awaiting their carriage. He wore a perfectly fitted silk evening coat of deepest corbeau, with the obligatory white waistcoat and black pantaloons. An ornate silver watch fob covered his pocket and he leaned on his silver-headed walking stick. His brown hair seemed especially glossy, and his eyes seemed to dance with a lively spirit. He looked outrageously handsome. Phoebe could not stop her smile from broadening a little with genuine pleasure when he bowed elegantly and offered her his arm for the walk to the carriage outside.

There was little traffic at this hour in the West End, and the few blocks to Lucinda's home were covered quickly. There was a line of carriages waiting to discharge their passengers at the door, however, so several minutes were spent waiting. The occupants of the Allington landau were all surprised to see such a large number of guests arriving.

"I had the impression that this was to be a small musicale, not a major rout," Judith said with some concern. "I had no idea there were this many people left in Town this late! Where do you suppose they have all come from?"

"I could be wrong, my dear, but is that not Princess Esterhazy being helped from her carriage?" Edward was seated where he could observe the progress of the arrivals from the carriage window.

Judith twisted in her seat and tried to see out her window

without actually being so gauche as to stick her head out. "I can't tell. Oh, dear. Who would have thought that *she* would be coming?" The imposing wife of the Austrian ambassador and patroness of Almack's was notoriously high-in-the-instep.

"Come now, pet, don't get all in a fluster," Edward added in his gruff, kindly way. "We are all handsomely decked out and I'm sure every bit as respectable as we would have been if we'd known she was invited."

That Lucy had gone to considerable expense and trouble to put on her musicale was obvious from the moment her guests entered the house. Fresh flowers and ribbon streamers bedecked the main staircase that led to the first floor, and more of the same had been attached to the ornate ceiling cornice in her generously sized drawing room. A bank of candles on the marble fireplace mantel and another on the pianoforte, which had been drawn into the center of the room, supplemented the bright glow from the room's chandelier and wall sconces.

Beside the mahogany and satinwood piano stood a harp, two music stands, and chairs for five performers. Seating for the guests had been artfully arranged in several circular rows surrounding these. Lucy had obviously hired chairs for the occasion, for these were no hodgepodge of assorted sofas and arm chairs scavenged from other rooms in the house, but a regular and for the most part matching collection of black-and-gold painted side chairs with caned seats.

"I see that your friend Lady Follett does have an idea how to do a thing right," Devenham whispered intimately in Phoebe's ear as they entered the room.

She hoped no one noticed. She ignored the shiver that ran through her and nodded her head very slightly to acknowledge that she had heard him. What if he decided to be mischievous and improper, as she knew well he could be? He would not do so in public, would he? They waited quietly behind Edward and Judith as the guests ahead of them greeted their host and hostess and selected seats. Maybe there would not be four seats together by the time it was their turn. Maybe the earl would have to sit elsewhere.

"There you are, my dear Phoebe, and Lord Devenham, too.

I am so delighted you could come tonight," gushed a radiant Lucy, holding out her hands to both of them at once.

Phoebe wished Lucy would not make it seem so obvious that she and Lord Devenham had come together. Nevertheless, she managed to produce a sincere smile. "Everything is so beautiful, Lucy. What a lovely job you have done!" In a lower voice she added, "Although this is a much more elaborate affair than you led me to believe."

"I'm so glad you approve." Lucy laughed with a wicked twinkle in her eye. Under her breath she replied, "Would you still have come if you had known?"

Phoebe had to concede the point. She made the formal introductions between the earl and Lucy and Lord Follett, a job she wished Edward had lingered long enough to perform, but she did not wait while Devenham made his appropriate polite remarks. She attempted to catch up to Edward and Judith, who were heading for chairs across the room.

"Lady Brodfield, as I live and breathe!" exclaimed a male voice by her elbow. "Thought I saw you on the stairs, but I could scarcely credit it."

She turned to see Lord Lyndgreen, a young dandy who had openly declared himself her admirer even after her marriage to Stephen.

"It's like seeing a vision," he asserted warmly. "Whoever would have guessed that after you have been absent from us for two entire Seasons, you would suddenly appear at an obscure affair here in August? You are as lovely as ever, if I may be so bold as to say so."

Phoebe thought she had no choice but to be gracious and try to pass on as quickly as possible. "Lord Lyndgreen, what a pleasant surprise. Yes, imagine meeting like this. Would you ever have thought there would still be so much distinguished company in Town this late? I think Lady Follett has been quite adventurous in holding a musicale at this time of year."

"It has been an unusual summer, but Wellington has truly put Boney out of business this time. Doubtless we'll all be gone by the first of September. I think it is going to prove quite warm in this room with so many people, don't you? I hope the musicians will be competent at least." He fidgeted with his neckcloth, as if he found the room already grown too warm, but he also showed no indication of closing the conversation.

Phoebe sighed. She would have to do it herself, but gracefully. Just as she opened her mouth to speak, Devenham appeared, claiming her elbow with a proprietary air.

"Lord Lyndgreen, is it not?" he asked in a top-lofty tone she had never heard him use before. The young man seemed to shrink in size and his eyes became very round.

"Wh-why, yes, it is, Lord Devenham, sir." His tongue seemed to have become knotted after that much response.

"Good lad, I see you know who I am."

"I saw you spar at Gentleman Jackson's a few years ago, sir."

"I would also like you to know that Lady Brodfield is sitting with me."

"Yes, sir. Ahem. I was just telling her what a pleasure it it to see her again after such a long time." He bowed. "Lady Brodfield, I hope you enjoy the concert. My lord."

Bowing again, Lord Lyndgreen disappeared, and Phoebe turned to Devenham. "I am not sitting with you," she hissed. "I am sitting with Judith and Edward. If you choose to sit with us also, I hope you will behave! There was no need to scare the wits out of the poor fellow. He had not even asked about where or with whom I might be sitting." She snapped open her fan in annoyance and began to use it vigorously.

Devenham just smiled. He nodded toward Edward and Judith, who were attempting to keep clear the two chairs beside them. "I think we had best take our seats, while we still have our choice open to us."

The program began with a lively Mozart minuet and a song by Gluck played by the pianist and the harpist. Lady Follett had also brought in a violinist and two vocalists, one a baritone and the other a rather statuesque soprano. This last mentioned lady struggled through a melodramatic version of the ancient tragic ballad of "Fair Rosemund" before she launched into an enthusiastic rendering of several Italian and French folk songs accompanied by the instruments and the baritone.

"She must not be English," Judith whispered to Phoebe, leaning across Edward to do so.

The gentleman singer offered a selection from opera, which was followed by one of Dr. Haydn's piano sonatas in honor of Princess Esterhazy.

"Which one is she?" Phoebe asked Devenham softly. "You must have met or at least seen her in Vienna."

"Over there—see, she is nodding to acknowledge the compliment. Her husband's relatives in Austria kept Dr. Haydn employed for almost thirty years."

Devenham's knowledge about the music being performed surprised and impressed Phoebe. He was quiet, only offering an occasional comment, but he answered her questions with what she thought was admirable patience. When the last piece of the evening was announced to be a Beethoven sonata for violin and piano, he became quite visibly excited.

"This ought to stir some people up," he said with enthusiasm. "I chanced to hear some of his newer work last winter in Vienna, and he is beginning to strike out in some very unconventional directions. I will be interested to see what you think of it."

The piece that followed was indeed quite different from the rather restrained and dignified standard fare, and even from earlier Beethoven work with which she was familiar. The sudden changes in dynamic levels and the strong and varied emotion of the piece captured the attention of everyone in the room despite the soporific effect of the heat. The occasional dissonant harmony and irregular rhythm were not at all what anyone was used to hearing.

"Is that really how it is written?" Phoebe asked the earl in admiring disbelief.

When the piece was finished, there was no reaction at all from the surprised audience for several seconds save the continued motion of ladies' fans all around the room. The silent fluttering made Phoebe think of butterflies.

Then Devenham began to applaud loudly, getting to his feet. Others quickly followed suit, building the enthusiasm in the crowded room to a crescendo. The performers acknowledged the accolade, and then escaped the overheated chamber with what Phoebe suspected was gratitude. It took a good deal longer for the collected guests to exit and make their way downstairs to the dining room, where the Folletts had provided a cold supper buffet.

"I could tell you enjoyed the Beethoven by the look of rapture on your face," Devenham told Phoebe as they moved along with the crowd.

"I did not realize I was so transparent," she answered, wishing she would not blush so easily as she felt the tingling in her face. "It *was* very different, as you said. Very emotional."

"Passionate," the earl declared. He lifted one eyebrow at her suggestively.

Distracted by her concern about Devenham's behavior and delighted by the music, Phoebe had quite forgotten to be nervous or self-conscious during the concert. Her anxieties returned in full force when she reached Lucy's dining room and saw the milling crowd engaged in eating and conversation. Her steps must have faltered, for Devenham squeezed her hand and said, "Courage in the face of battle is the true test of a good soldier, dear madam."

"Let us find Judith and Edward," she begged. In the crush, her sister and brother-in-law had become separated from them.

Devenham spotted them quickly with his advantage of greater height. "There they are, near the windows," he said, steering her toward them. "Once you have joined them, I will get you some of the sliced chicken and pastries."

"Thank you," Phoebe said, trying to sound appreciative. "I think lemonade would go down more easily, however." Her throat felt too tight to admit solid food. Just then she saw Sir Charles Mortimer making his way toward them. If she had to converse with someone, she would prefer it to be him.

"Sir Charles," she acknowledged with a nod.

"Lady Brodfield! And Lord Devenham. How delightful to see you! My dear Lady Brodfield, my condolences on the loss of your father-in-law. I thought I caught a glimpse of you at his commemorative. I am simply glad to see you getting out and about again. Lord Tyneley was such a fine example of a man; his death is a great loss to all of us."

Turning to Devenham, the older mad added. "Having this

fellow back from the war is a great gain, however." The two men shook hands heartily.

"How nice that you are already acquainted," Phoebe murmured faintly.

"Welcome home, you rascal. Although I understand you haven't managed yet to get all the way home. You are looking well, I must say, if not yet quite hale and hearty."

"I have had the most excellent care in all of London, I believe," the earl responded, looking pointedly at Phoebe.

She blushed, feeling both embarrassed and annoyed.

"I would be on my way home already, I don't doubt, except for a small matter to clear up at the Horse Guards."

Sir Charles laughed. "Yes, I heard something about that matter, I believe. Something about heroic behavior while under fire, and a promotion to lieutenant-colonel?" He cast a teasing glance at Phoebe and added, "There always are other charming distractions to delay one in London, are there not?"

He forestalled her protest with another quick laugh. "I only tease you to see that lovely smile, my dear. I happen to know of your skill as a nurse, for there were times a few years back when you tended Lord Tyneley quite devotedly and gave him considerable comfort." Sir Charles smiled now a bit sadly. "I'm certain he never guessed that his bequest to you would turn out to be problematical. I know he held you in great esteem."

Phoebe glanced around her uncomfortably. Was there anything Sir Charles did *not* know? Was there anything he would consider private enough not to broadcast for all to hear in a public gathering? She thought it providential that at that moment Lucy interrupted them.

"Gentlemen, you must excuse us," Lucy said with an angelic smile. "I have been granted permission to present Lady Brodfield to Her Highness, the princess. I know you would not want me to keep a lady waiting."

Rescued from wolves to be cast to the lion, thought Phoebe in despair. Her face must have betrayed her, for Lucy squeezed her hand reassuringly and said, "Put that smile you had back on, my dear. The princess will be charmed with you, and her approval will help to hobble a good number of wagging tongues I know. Did I not tell you to trust your second come-out to me?"

As they walked away from the gentlemen, Phoebe heard Sir Charles resume his conversation with the earl.

"Devenham, you must join me for dinner at Watier's while you are still in Town, so I can congratulate you on your survival more properly."

"I would be pleased to do so. Just name the day; I am at your disposal."

Phoebe was too far away to hear Sir Charles answer with some urgency, "Good, then. Let's make it tomorrow."

Chapter Eleven

Devenham was quite conscious of the change in Phoebe's manner toward him. He had spent many hours pondering what had happened between them, examining his own feelings and trying to understand hers. Another man might have accepted defeat, convinced by her claim that she had no interest in him. But Devenham believed in the response he had sensed in their kiss.

He smiled as he maneuvered the Allingtons' gig through the traffic along Bond Street toward Piccadilly. She had been annoyed with him through much of the previous evening at the Folletts'. Annoyance was better than cold formality and wariness. He had also caught glimpses of something warmer in her eyes when she thought he was not paying heed to her. She had looked stunning in her black evening dress, with her dark hair caught up to expose her neck and her shoulders exposed by the cut of her gown. He had been hard-pressed to behave himself.

He was smitten, there was no question. He should have been grateful that she was trying so hard not to return his sentiments. He doubted he was either capable of or ready for the only type of relationship that was possible with a respectably widowed sister-in-law of a friend. Yet he was not grateful, and that in itself told him he had never felt this way about anyone before. He found, in fact, that his own needs seemed quite irrelevant. Gentle, loving, generous Lady Brodfield had begun to show him what love could be, yet was herself starved for love. He wanted to help her open her heart, even if she never accepted his.

"Your pardon, sir, but if you keep smiling and frowning in quite that way, I don't doubt you'll find yourself admitted to

Bedlam instead of the Horse Guards this afternoon." Mullins's voice cut into Devenham's wayward thoughts.

"What? Sorry."

"There's Piccadilly just ahead."

The earl put his mind temporarily back on his driving. He had not yet made good on his promise to visit Tattersall's, so he had been forced to rely upon Sir Edward's generosity in allowing him the use of the Allingtons' gig for the day. He had not been quite able to bring himself so low as to arrive for his appointment at the Horse Guards in a hackney. Mullins had been conscripted to act as his groom, for the earl still needed assistance getting up and down from high carriages.

Devenham made the turn onto Piccadilly and the second turn onto St. James Street. He had two goals to accomplish at the Horse Guards. The first was to make one last effort to stop the promotion he did not want, and the other was to learn something about Richard Brodfield.

He had listened with interest to Sir Charles Mortimer's reference to Phoebe's "problematical" inheritance, and had only managed to learn the details of this by later relating the odd conversation to Sir Edward. But what Edward told him had not shed any light on Phoebe's past.

The earl was convinced that Phoebe's resistance to him and, according to Edward, to the whole idea of remarriage was tangled up with what had happened after her marriage to Stephen Brodfield. Mullins had ferreted out the scandalous story of Lord Brodfield's death, but Devenham did not believe the story was straight. There were too many questions, too many things that didn't add up, not to mention the basic disbelief he felt deep in his gut. He was too much a soldier to ignore that kind of instinct. It made sense to him to get what information he could on the other players in the piece. That meant Richard Brodfield, and also his mother, Lord Tyneley's recently bereaved widow.

The gig proceeded down the length of Pall Mall and eventually turned onto Whitehall, bringing Devenham to his destination a full ten minutes early for his appointment with Sir Henry Torrens, secretary to the Duke of York as Commander-in-Chief. Devenham counted himself lucky to have obtained this appointment before the Duke's return to London, which was expected within days.

"Mr. Wilcocks," he said, addressing a young clerk to the secretary's under-secretary, who was scribbling away at some papers in the outer room where he waited. "Is there some service I might be able to render you in return for a small favor?"

"I suppose that depends, my lord," the young man answered with what Devenham thought was admirable caution. "What service can I perform for you?"

"You could find a few spare minutes to look up some information for me. Nothing that is not a matter of public record, rest assured."

The wrinkles of anxiety that had marred the young fellow's forehead disappeared. "I believe I could do that for you anyway, Lord Devenham, without obligation on your part. What was it you needed to know?"

"I would like to know the service record and status of Richard Brodfield, Lord Tyneley's son."

"Which regiment, sir?"

Devenham paused uncertainly. To his surprise, another voice answered for him.

"The 23rd Light Dragons, Wilcocks. And never mind looking it up—I can supply Lord Devenham with the particulars he wishes to know." It was Sir Henry, standing in the open doorway to his inner office.

"Sir Henry, good afternoon." Devenham felt a bit like a child caught sneaking tarts from the kitchen.

"Come in, sir, come in. We are ready for each other a few minutes early, which is to both our credits. I should be well pleased if the rest of my day would proceed so smoothly." Sir Henry bade the earl sit in a leather-upholstered wing chair which faced his massive, paper-strewn desk. He closed the door and moved behind the desk, regarding Devenham with a raised eyebrow.

"I did not think it was to check on Mr. Brodfield that we had arranged this interview. Am I mistaken?"

Devenham sighed. "Not at all, Sir Henry. I had not meant to bother you with that business."

To his surprise, Sir Henry laughed. "Ah, Lord Devenham, I

believe I know what brings you here, and to be sure, I think I also know why you are suddenly interested in Richard Brodfield. Word travels so quickly in this town, don't you agree?"

He leaned back in his chair, which creaked in protest. "On the first matter, the official one, I don't know that I can be of any help, but I am willing to listen. Why would anyone object to being retired as a lieutenant-colonel, I ask myself.

"Now the other matter, I think, has to do with a certain lady whose acquaintance you have recently made. You realize, of course, what the *beau monde* would make of it if they got wind you were checking out the lady's relations. However, I promise you that I will tell no one."

Sir Henry had been smiling and speaking in a light tone, but now he sobered. "The reason I do not need to look up this particular case is that it has very recently been under my attention. Richard Brodfield sold out his commission as a captain in the 23rd as soon as he could after Waterloo. I will tell you in confidence between us as gentlemen, Lord Devenham, that Captain Brodfield did so in some haste, as the procedures to have him cashiered out of service had already been set in motion by his superior officers."

"Cashiered!" exclaimed Devenham. "That is a serious business, indeed. Are you at liberty to say on what grounds?"

"I am not at liberty to tell you any of this, for it will not be in his record, but you are a good man and a good officer, and I think you should know. There were several charges made against him, including unauthorized absence and some rather ugly morals charges. You never heard this from me, however, you understand?"

"Completely, Sir Henry. And I am extremely grateful."

"Grateful enough not to stir up trouble over a promotion His Royal Highness is determined to confirm?"

Devenham exhaled. Then his lips turned up in a small smile of begrudging admiration. He had been outmaneuvered by an expert. "Could you not at least drop a word to him that I am not in favor of it?" he asked a bit helplessly. "Tell him the accounts of my behavior were greatly exaggerated, and the brevet rank bestowed upon me was given in haste at the peak of an action where other men were equally or more deserving."

"Do you question the judgment of your own superior officers?" Sir Henry asked pointedly. "Did you not lead the men under your care once the responsibility of the rank was put upon you?"

Then in a gentler voice he added, "I admire your modesty, Lieutenant-Colonel, and your concern for the men who stood beside you does you credit. My advice is this: Accept what is offered to you, and if it bothers you so much, when the day comes that you actually see the extra shillings in your pocket, take them and give them to those who need them more."

Sir Henry rose from his chair, signaling to Devenham that the interview was over. The earl rose as well, and the two men walked to the door together.

"Still giving you a bit of trouble?" Sir Henry asked, pointing to Devenham's leg and cane.

"Just a trifle," the earl responded offhandedly. "A touch of the laudanum still helps." He and Sir Henry exchanged a look that acknowledged the brotherhood between war veterans who have survived the ordeal of being wounded.

"Let me give you another piece of advice while I am at it, Lord Devenham," offered Sir Henry, his hand resting flat against the closed door. "If you wish to protect the reputation of the lady we have taken care not to mention here today, you should consider moving back to the Clarendon or somewhere now that you are so much improved and are getting about Town. You know how tongues will wag. I just mention it in case the thought had not already occurred to you."

"Thank you, Sir Henry. I am in your debt."

Young Wilcocks looked up questioningly as Sir Henry escorted Devenham to the outer door. The look on his face must have triggered something in Sir Henry's memory, for that good gentleman suddenly exclaimed, "By Jove, I nearly forgot to say! His Highness the Duke will be holding a reception on the twenty-ninth, to honor the Waterloo officers who were not yet returned in the middle of July. There are a good number of you, and what with all the other attendant guests, His Highness the Prince Regent has most graciously offered Carlton House for the event. The invitations go out tomorrow."

"That ought to keep the rest of us anchored here through the end of the month," Devenham said dryly. "In some places the partridges may remain safe for even an extra day!"

Sir Henry sighed. "Yes, the next week and a half will be busy. His Highness the Duke of Cumberland is due to arrive back with his new bride, as well. I wouldn't mind some time off to go shoot a few brace of partridge after this month is done! Be careful of that leg, sir. I shall look forward to seeing you again on the twenty-ninth."

After Mullins had helped Devenham into the carriage, the earl handed him the ribbons and directed him to drive to the park. He wanted to think, and the park seemed the best place to be undisturbed, as it was a little before the fashionable hour to be there.

Sir Henry was right about protecting Phoebe's reputation; it was time to give up the Allingtons' hospitality. He no longer had the excuse of convalescing to explain his presence at their home, and Phoebe's presence there would be common knowledge now after her attendance at Lady Follett's last night. Apparently it had already begun to be known around Town, or Sir Henry would not have been aware of it.

The idea that he should go home had actually been in the back of his mind, where he had rather guiltily been trying to ignore it. His mother had not yet seen him, although he had written her several letters. In all honesty, he did not want to leave London just now. Lady Brodfield certainly had something to do with that. But now he had the perfect excuse. He could not fail to attend the Duke's reception. He had an idea he'd like Lady Brodfield to go with him.

The other information he had learned from Sir Henry bothered him a good deal. He wished Phoebe did not have to have any dealings with a blackguard like Richard Brodfield. Sir Henry had given no specifics, but Brodfield had to have indulged in some extremely disreputable activities and been indiscreet about them as well to be called into question on morals. Unauthorized absence was also a curious but very serious charge. If Brodfield had not been Lord Tyneley's son, the whole matter would not have been allowed to slip under the carpet so easily, Devenham was certain.

Sir Henry had told him the information in confidence; he could not divulge what he had learned to Sir Charles Mortimer this evening when he met him for dinner. But he had no doubt he would be able to learn quite a bit else from Sir Charles, for it was clear he had been a good friend of Lord Tyneley's, and Phoebe had later confirmed that fact. He wondered at Sir Charles's haste to set up their engagement.

"Sir, we are being hailed by a lady in a phaeton over there," announced Mullins, interrupting Devenham's ruminations.

"Where? Oh, I see her, Mullins. Damn! Don't you know who that is? It is Sophia Legere. Too late to pretend we did not see her, eh?"

The spankingly stylish high-perch phaeton approached them even as he spoke, and its occupant blew Devenham a kiss in greeting. The woman was a stunning auburn-haired beauty, as stylishly turned out as her equipage. Only the smallest details of her appearance—the faintest enhancement of the natural color in her cheeks, a single button of her dark green spencer left unfastened—suggested that she was anything other than the fashionable young lady she seemed.

"Lord Devenham," she cried, apparently close to fainting from delight, "I have heard such tales since your arrival in London! How wonderful to see you are recovered from your illness enough to be out! 'He is too ill to come and see me,' I told myself over and over, wondering when I would hear something from you! If you only knew how I longed to be by your side to comfort you!"

She accompanied the last remark with a peculiar little twist of her shoulders that Devenham knew was meant to be sexually suggestive. He knew Sophia well—all too well. She had a wonderfully expressive body, a talent that had advanced her career on the stage as well as in bed. As she smiled at him now, however, he wondered why he had never before noticed that her teeth, while admirably straight, were quite a bit too large for her otherwise perfectly proportioned face.

"How are you, Sophia? You look as sleek and happy as ever. Someone's been keeping the cat in cream, I'm pleased to see."

Her face darkened slightly before she responded. "You

needn't be as pleased as all that, my lord. You do not sound as if you missed me at all. And *I* missed *you* dreadfully."

Devenham sighed. He had absolutely no wish to hurt the lady's feelings, but neither did he wish to encourage her. Apparently she was not as satisfied with her current protector as she had been with him. He had been congratulating himself that so far he had not run into any of his former flames in London, of the respectable variety or otherwise. He supposed it was inevitable that his luck should run out.

"Of course there were times when I missed you," he said diplomatically. "A soldier's life can get quite lonely." But never the way he missed Phoebe. He missed Phoebe now if he was gone from her for even a few hours. Seeing Sophia was merely making him wish to head back to Wigmore Street, where Phoebe was no doubt spending a quiet afternoon. He would do so, he decided, although first he would have to stop at the Clarendon to make arrangements to move back there, and he also needed to stop at the apothecary's on Oxford Street to replenish his supply of laudanum. He had not yet managed to accustom his body to doing without the drug. He found he was beginning to require regular doses of Lady Brodfield's company in a shockingly similar manner.

"Apparently you are not so lonely now," Sophia said, assuming a petulant expression. "I am quite devastated that you are out around Town and I have heard nothing from you. It must be that the rumors I'm hearing are true."

"What rumors?"

She glanced at him sideways with a mischievous pout. "Perhaps I shan't tell you. You have been naughty—you don't deserve to know."

He was tiring quickly of her childish games. "Then I will bid you good day, madam. I wish you well." He signaled Mullins to move on.

Sophia tossed her head and threw back her shoulders in annoyance, thrusting out her bosom rather dramatically. "I heard, Devenham, that you found your extended convalescence quite enjoyable, thanks to the ministrations of your nurse. Frankly, I was surprised to find I had competition in such highly respectable circles." She laughed as she slapped the ribbons to start her own pair. "If you tire of her, my lord, I would still take you back."

Devenham thought it was just as well that their carriages had already begun to draw apart then, for the surge of anger that went through him was quite violent. Several moments passed before he was calm enough again to direct Mullins to drive to the Clarendon.

Phoebe had indeed been spending a quiet afternoon in Wigmore Street. Judith and Edward had taken the children to Greenwich for a picnic, and even Nanny and the baby had gone with them. Phoebe had seen the perfect opportunity to do some work in her garden. She was fully engrossed in removing some unwelcome thistles when she heard a small commotion at the French doors that opened from the dining room. She glanced up and with a sinking feeling saw Richard Brodfield approaching, trailed by Maddocks absolutely looking daggers at him.

"I'm sorry, my lady," Maddocks apologized in obvious distress. "I told Mr. Brodfield I would present his card, but he positively brushed me aside." It was clear the dignified servant was highly insulted.

Phoebe stood up, brushing bits of dirt and greenery from her apron and stripping her soiled gloves from her fingers. "Richard, as you can see I am not receiving callers this afternoon."

"If I waited for you to be receiving callers, I could be cold and in my grave," Richard said. "Besides, I am not an ordinary caller, I am a family member. There is no need to stand on ceremony." He gave the butler a significant look, holding out his hat and gloves.

Phoebe sighed. "It is all right, Maddocks. I suppose there is no point in arguing, since he is already here. Thank you."

For a telling moment Maddocks looked as if he might disagree with her dismissal, but then he turned and disappeared back into the house.

"I told you I would communicate with you by letter once I had made a decision about Beau Chatain," Phoebe said to Richard coldly.

"I thought perhaps I could save you the trouble," Richard replied smoothly. "I had not heard anything from you yet."

"You did not indicate that there was any deadline on your offer. It is taking me some time to gather the information I wish to know."

Richard took a step closer to her, and she instinctively stepped back. She stopped herself there, for she did not want to appear as if she feared him.

"I have certain matters pressing me for resolution," he said vaguely. "I would find it very helpful to get this one cleared up." He did not meet her eyes.

"I have asked Edward to act for me—" she began, but he cut her off.

"Yes, I know that your dear Sir Edward has been out there snooping around." Now he was looking at her intently, and took another step toward her. "He does not seem to be the only one. Someone else has been around asking questions as well. Whom do you suppose that could be?"

She was genuinely puzzled by that, but it was the intensity of Richard's gaze that was starting to stir up the first flutterings of alarm inside her. She shook her head. "I have no idea."

He seemed satisfied, staring at her. "No, you probably do not. Dear little sweet Phoebe. I expect it is nothing." There was something very predatory in the way Richard was looking at her, and all of Phoebe's instincts screamed at her now to step away from him. But she could not understand why, and she felt rather as if she were suddenly rooted in the spot where she stood facing him.

"Now you know that I told you the truth—that I am technically in possession of the place. You will have to accept what I've offered, *one way or the other.*"

He moved suddenly with lightning speed and captured her hands. As she gasped in surprise, he raised one to his lips, keeping his eyes locked with hers. His hands were hot and moist, her own like ice. She tried to pull them away, but he would not release them. She wished they could freeze him to the bone.

"So cold," he said softly, putting her hands together and beginning to rub them gently with his fingers, as if to warm them. But then his rubbing slowed and began to be a very erotic, sensual exploration. "Cold hands, warm heart," he whispered, quoting the old adage.

She tried again to pull her hands away. He tightened his grip and pulled in response, bringing her hard up against his chest.

"No!"

"Yes!" There was a savage note in his voice. "There's only one way to warm these hands—that's the fire inside you." He lowered his head to her mouth. She struggled, turning her face away, and he buried his face in her neck. She felt his teeth grazing her tender skin.

A tremendous shudder ran through her.

"Ah," growled Richard. He stepped back from her with a triumphant gleam of satisfaction in his eye. "A year and a half is a long time to leave that fire banked, my dear. I thought I'd find a spark if I just reached in and stirred a little."

Phoebe gaped at him, speechless. She was certain she had reacted in revulsion.

"Just think of the blaze we could start if I stirred a little more."

Finally she found her tongue.

"Get out! Now, Richard! Do not ever try to set foot in this house again!"

"I don't think I will need to, my dear. You'll find in the end that you'll come seeking me."

She was not quite sure what he meant by that, but she was too angry and insulted to care. "Go!" she cried, pointing toward the house. She was astonished to see Devenham coming down the steps.

"You had better do as the lady says," the earl warned Richard. He looked at that moment quite capable of murder.

Phoebe stared in horrified fascination as the two men squared off, clearly taking each other's measure through narrowed eyes.

"You must be Devenham." Richard's tone was ugly as he faced the earl. "What are you, her watchdog? Or did you just think you had exclusive rights to her?"

"I have no 'rights' to Lady Brodfield whatsoever," Devenham answered with a calm so icy it made Phoebe shiver. "Nor,

I would add, do you. I certainly hope that you meant no disre-spect to her, just as I hope I did not hear you call me a dog just now. I will give you approximately ten seconds to comply with her wish that you leave, however, or my hearing may improve and you will certainly rue the consequences."

"You dare to threaten me?"

"I dare to, and I believe I just did."

"Lady Brodfield and I have unfinished business."

"Not according to what I just heard. I distinctly heard her tell you to leave, sir. Now do so."

For a moment there was nothing but highly charged silence. Richard glared at Lord Devenham, and then at Phoebe. The look on his face frightened her.

"You may be the ones to rue consequences," Richard muttered, his face white and his fists clenched. He spun on his heel and stalked back toward the house.

Chapter Twelve

Phoebe stood where she was, her face covered with her hands. Devenham was unsure whether to go to her and offer comfort or to wait for some sign of acknowledgment from her.

He could not blame her for being upset. He definitely had not liked the last look on Richard Brodfield's face. He was not sure he had ever made an enemy so quickly or seen hatred in so pure a form. The two men were about equal in size, and Devenham had judged Brodfield to be reasonably fit, but the earl had not felt intimidated. What he had felt was anger so overwhelming that he dared not let it out.

He looked down at his right hand, which still gripped his cane with a white-knuckled force fit to break the ebony shaft. He let out his breath slowly, as if releasing his anger with it. Very deliberately he set the tip of his cane back down on the gravel walk, shifting his hand to rest loosely on its silver head.

"Thank you, Lord Devenham."

He looked up. Phoebe was pale and obviously shaken, but she seemed to have collected herself.

"Your timing was impeccable—and appreciated. I am not at all sure Richard would have left without your persuasion. He—he can be somewhat unreasonable at times."

"Unreasonable!" He took a step toward her and was dismayed to see her flinch and retreat a step in response.

He sighed. So that was how it would be. He tried to speak in a gentler tone. "That seems a mild term to apply to his behavior. I must admit that the terms that come to my mind are not fit to be spoken in your presence." He gave her a concerned glance. "Perhaps you should sit down?"

She shook her head. "I am all right." She looked down at

her hands and then at the apron that covered her dark gray dress. "I was just . . ." She spread her hands apart in a helpless gesture, then let them drop. Shaking her head again, she turned away from him and stooped to begin gathering the small tools she had been using in the garden. She placed them in her basket with unsteady hands.

"I don't suppose you want to talk about what happened?" Devenham thought he had to try, at least.

She shook her head, not looking at him. *So intent upon her business,* he thought. He studied her, taking in her bowed head and hunched shoulders. He suddenly realized those shoulders were trembling. She was crying.

"Please let me help you," he said softly, moving beside her. He held out the neatly pressed handkerchief he had managed to retrieve from one of his pockets. She accepted it but still would not turn to him.

She wiped her cheeks and held the cloth pressed to her eyes for a moment. Then she drew a deep, shuddering breath. "Thank you. You have already helped me. There is nothing more to be done." She turned her face up to the patch of sky above the garden. "I will sell Beau Chatain to him, and that will be the end of it."

"Will it?" he asked. "Will he be satisfied to leave you alone then? And what will you do? Go on living with the Allingtons forever?"

She acted as if she did not hear him. She wrapped her arms around her as though she felt chilled. "Why, why did he have to come out here to the garden? It feels defiled, as if he was some rotten thing whose smell has overtaken all the flowers." She stood up with her basket, looking very distraught. Before Devenham could think of what to do or say, she gathered her skirts and ran toward the house.

He could only follow slowly.

Upstairs in the guest bedroom, the earl fidgeted while Mullins tried to make him presentable for dinner at Watier's.

"Blast and confound it, man, I don't care if you achieve the perfect 'Mathematical,' I would rather be able to turn my head. And I'm in danger of being impaled upon these collar points. Too much starch—I don't give a damn what Brummel said."

"My lord," remonstrated the patient Mullins, "if I can do nothing to improve your temper, the least I can do is to take some pains over your appearance. After inviting you to be his guest, Sir Charles does not deserve to find you lacking in both departments."

Devenham closed his eyes and attempted to rein in his anger and frustration. Poor Mullins had done nothing to deserve the brunt of it. If anyone had, it was Richard Brodfield, or at the very least himself. How he wished he had arrived back from his errands just a few minutes sooner! Or if only he had been able to walk faster through the house once he had learned from Maddocks whose hat and gloves were on the hall table.

He was not exactly sure what had passed between Brodfield and Phoebe in the garden, or exactly what had made him so certain that he should intrude upon them. He had not been able to hear their words until he had started through the door and heard her ordering Brodfield to leave. But he had seen the man release Phoebe and step back, and he had seen the look of utter shock on her face. Just the memory of it made his blood boil. He had desired enough women himself to recognize—even smell—that desire in another man.

No, Brodfield would not be content with Phoebe's inheritance alone. He wanted Phoebe, too, and the law forbade him to achieve his ends by marriage, as she had been his brother's wife. The very idea made Devenham sick as well as angry. How the hell was he supposed to eat a civilized dinner at Watier's?

When he arrived at the club at the appointed hour, he found Sir Charles Mortimer awaiting him. Sir Charles smiled pleasantly enough, but there was a certain air of gravity about him that alerted Devenham that this was not merely a social dinner.

What could be on Sir Charles's mind? He had proposed the dinner so quickly last night, it had made the earl wonder. What could be so urgent that they needed to meet less than twenty-four hours later?

"You are unfashionably prompt, Devenham," said the older man with obvious approval. He led the way into the club's dining room. "Have you dined here before? The food is infinitely superior to White's or Brooks's."

"That is not difficult to achieve," Devenham replied, "although I confess I have not had the pleasure."

They settled at their table and gave their order to the server who was hovering at their elbows.

"I believe the last time we shared a table was playing macao at Brooks's—it must have been more than two years ago," Sir Charles observed. "Young Lord Hadley lost ten thousand pounds that night. Have you been in London since?"

"No, I have not." Devenham was impressed by Sir Charles's memory.

"That was Lady Brodfield's second Season as a married woman. I don't believe she and Lord Brodfield were much in evidence that year. Did you ever meet them?"

"I am certain I did not." *If this was to be the topic, Sir Charles wasted no time getting to it.* "I would indeed have remembered Lady Brodfield if I had ever met her before this visit." The earl smiled a bit self-consciously. He had not intended his reply to sound quite so warm.

"They made a charming couple. Everyone thought so. Lady Brodfield is a very special young woman—a treasure, in my opinion. I would have been very proud to have had a daughter like her."

Sir Charles paused as the server brought their wine. When the glasses were filled and the fellow had again retired, the baronet continued. "You struck me as rather taken with her, Devenham, if you'll forgive my saying so. That is the reason we are sitting here at dinner, quite frankly."

A little chill ran through Devenham. "I see." *I should have known,* he thought. *What was I expecting?* He hid his disappointment behind an air of cold civility. "You thought this might be the most gentlemanly way to warn me off. Has my mere presence already had such a bad effect on her reputation?"

He was surprised when Sir Charles laughed.

"I say! I'm not displeased to see you are awake to that possibility. However, you misunderstand me. I have no right to 'warn you off' as you call it, nor have I any desire to do so. I happen to like you, Devenham. Because of that, I wanted to give you a little of the lady's history, before some scandal-monger comes along and gives you a shocker. I doubted whether Sir Edward would or even could give you full details. He and Lady Allington had not yet arrived in Town when the worst of it happened."

"You are referring, of course, to Lord Brodfield's death. Allington did tell me something about how Lady Brodfield and her husband first met, fell in love, and married. I could only guess at his references to the tragic way it all ended. I will confess that, being the persistent sort of fellow that I am, I was not content to remain in the dark, and I arranged to have some inquiries made. It did not take long to learn the story of what happened."

"I see." Sir Charles seemed uncomfortable, and the earl guessed he was wondering how much of the story had come out. Devenham waited while the soup was served, then took up the topic again.

"I must admit that I was shocked by the unsavory story that I heard. I find it hard to believe any man married to such an exquisite creature as Lady Brodfield would behave as Lord Brodfield apparently did. Nor do I see how he could have done the things reported without anyone's knowledge." He shook his head slowly. "The shock to Lady Brodfield must have been devastating."

"Indeed it was, to her and to Lord Tyneley as well. To all of us who knew Stephen. It all seemed most out of character. The Stephen Brodfield we all knew was a respectable, responsible young man, devoted to his wife."

Devenham leaned forward, more than a little interested. This was exactly the kind of thing he wanted to learn. "Had he always been that way?"

"Yes, from childhood. We concluded that he had been lead-ing a double life—that there was another entire side to his na-ture that he had concealed from everyone. It seemed ironic, and somehow worse, in contrast to his half brother Richard's openly deplorable character. At least Richard Brodfield does not pretend to be anything other than what he is."

"Lord Tyneley must have been broken-hearted to think that both of his sons turned out so badly."

"He was not ready to give up on Richard. He truly hoped that service in the military would turn Richard around. After Stephen's death, he clung to that hope even harder. That really seemed to be when his illness began to get a greater hold on him. He was never again as strong as he had been."

"What illness did he suffer?"

"A bilious stomach; some think it was cancer. His trouble seemed to come and go. Lady Brodfield was a great comfort to him, as I think I mentioned last night."

"She must have visited him often?"

"She and Lord Brodfield lived in the house on Charles Street with the rest of the family. It is a sizeable residence."

"What of Lady Tyneley?" Devenham felt he had stumbled upon a gold mine. He could ask Sir Charles questions to which Mullins might never have found answers. He ate his dinner mechanically, scarcely noticing the food in front of him.

"Ah. Lady Tyneley is a hard person to categorize," Sir Charles said, pausing to refill his plate with another slice of the tender veal. "She is very cool, very contained, and not given to showing her emotions. She was and still is an attractive woman; certainly Lord Tyneley was happy with her."

"Did she get along well with Lord Brodfield?"

"Being the second wife, it is not surprising that she tended to favor her own son over her predecessor's. I think that unfortunate circumstance combined with jealousy of Stephen to make Richard what he is."

"And what would you say that is?"

Sir Charles lowered his voice. "He is a libertine and a ruthless man. I believe I see him more clearly than his father ever did. That is the other reason I wanted to meet with you. I think it very unfortunate that Lady Brodfield must have any dealings with him over the property Lord Tyneley left her. I just wanted to warn you of his character, as you seem likely to be in her company a good deal."

Too late, thought Devenham. He dipped his fingers in the finger bowl and dried them on the serviette provided. The level of noise in the various game rooms of the club was increasing as the evening drew on. He looked across at Sir Charles, wondering if he should confide in him.

"I am not likely to be in her company as much as I might wish," he said tentatively. "Since I am sufficiently recovered now to do so, I have made arrangements to move back to the Clarendon where I stayed on first arriving, and Lady Brodfield seems quite resistant to my interest in her."

Sir Charles did not appear the least surprised. "Yes, I can think of any number of reasons why she would resist. She might feel that an attraction to you would be disloyal to Stephen's memory, for one. I've known some widows who were plagued by such ghosts of their own devising. I think her reasons may go much deeper, however, given the devastating experience she went through. The scandal was terrible on top of the pain I know she felt. Some of the things people said were extremely cruel. Some laid the blame at her feet for what happened, can you believe it?"

"No, I cannot. On what grounds?"

"All sorts of rumors flew about—you know how these things go. Infidelity on her part was one, without so much as a shred of evidence, I might add. All manner of wifely failings were speculated, not the least of which was that she gave him no children."

Devenham shook his head again. How cruel people could be! But then, he knew that himself. "You don't think that she holds herself responsible for what happened?"

"I don't know, Devenham. All I will say is that I don't think she is as averse to your company as she pretends, judging by what I saw last night. I would support your efforts to wear her down, sir, as long as your intentions are honorable, and I believe they are."

"Why? Most people would not think so."

"I fancy myself a good judge of character. I have also been around these parts a long time. I know something of your family, Devenham. I suspect it is difficult to live with a reputation you've been saddled with from the cradle. People always see what they want to see, eh? And perhaps sometimes it is just easier to oblige their expectations than to fight them."

Devenham was amazed by the older man's perceptiveness,

even if his words were nothing more than a shrewd guess. This sentiment must have been apparent in his face, for Sir Charles laughed.

"I've surprised you tonight, have I not? I'll wager you didn't think such an old cannon could still be loaded with so much shot."

"It has indeed been an enlightening dinner," the earl responded warmly. "I have to thank you for a good deal more than this elegant meal." He hesitated, then plunged ahead. "I will tell you in confidence, sir, that I am making inquiries into the whole business about Lord Brodfield's death, simply because I cannot accept it. I know it is probably a waste of my time, but if I found even one thing that would help Lady Brodfield, it would be worth the trouble to me."

"I applaud your efforts. If I can be of any help at all, please do not hesitate to call on me, Devenham."

"You have already helped, sir. Thank you."

Devenham declined the opportunity to stay at Watier's and gamble on macao or hazard or any of the other games. He preferred to try his chances with Lady Brodfield at the Allingtons' on Wigmore Street.

Phoebe was settled quietly with her needlework in Judith's sitting room by the time the Allingtons returned en masse from their expedition to Greenwich. She hoped there was no outward sign that anything was amiss. She had decided not to tell anyone about her unwelcome visitor, and she hoped Lord Devenham would say nothing of it if she did not.

She had felt even more violated by Richard's advance than she thought the garden had been, and for a little while had the horrible sensation that she was spreading the foulness of his touch from her own hands to everything that she subsequently touched. She had washed and changed into fresh clothes, and had finally washed her hands several more times before she was able to conquer the irrational feeling.

Richard frightened her. She had decided to sell him Beau Chatain as quickly as possible, at whatever price he would pay. If that was exactly what he had intended, she did not care. She would not put stubborn pride ahead of common sense.

Common sense said to get him out of her life as quickly and completely as possible.

Henrietta heralded the arrival of the rest of the Allington brood. The scrabble of her hastening feet was muffled by the carpet in the passage, but Phoebe managed to set aside her embroidery before a furry missile launched itself into her lap. The puppy was trying to climb her, licking her cheeks and chin with enthusiasm, when the children burst in upon her.

"Aunt Phoebe! Aunt Phoebe!" came the familiar chorus.

"We fed deer in the park."

"We went on board a ship in the dockyard."

"We saw the Royal Observatory!"

Each of the children wanted to be first to relate what they had seen and done. The resulting confusion created noise without conveying much meaning at all. It took several minutes for Phoebe to establish order and finally hear about the pleasures she had missed. By that time, Judith and Edward had also joined them.

"Oh, Phoebe, it is really too bad that you did not come," Judith lamented. "The park was so green and cool, I know you would have enjoyed it. We had a delightful picnic. And I think you would have found the Royal Observatory most interesting."

"We climbed to the very top!"

"There were all kinds of astro-nom-i-cal instruments."

"They had clocks! Lots of clocks."

"Chron-o-meters, William."

Phoebe listened patiently until the children were sent off to prepare for dinner. Judith and Edward had accepted an invitation to join friends for dinner and the theater at Drury Lane, so Judith excused herself to consult with the cook.

"You are certain you won't join us tonight?" Edward asked Phoebe. He had not sat down again after Judith left the room. "Last night was not such an ordeal, now, was it? I do not think our friends would mind." He seemed to be regarding Phoebe rather thoughtfully.

She forced a smile. "Last night was not nearly as difficult as I had expected. For the most part, I actually enjoyed it. But I do not feel inclined to go out again tonight, Edward, thank you. Perhaps on another night, soon. You should just go along and enjoy the company of your friends. I will enjoy the peace and quiet of an evening alone." As if to prove her point, she bent her head over the embroidery on which she had resumed work.

Her brother-in-law cleared his throat and hooked his thumbs into his waistcoat pockets. He looked at the carpet and then looked back up at her. "I have the distinct feeling you were not going to tell me Richard Brodfield called this afternoon."

Phoebe dropped her needle in surprise. "Oh, dear," she said, hunting about for the implement, shaking her skirts and searching the seat cushion of her chair.

"Maddocks told me that Brodfield appeared to be quite angry when he left here, and that you have requested he not be allowed admittance to the house from now on. Does this mean you have decided not to sell Beau Chatain to him?"

Phoebe stopped hunting for a moment. Now what could she say? She should have known Maddocks would inform Edward of her visitor. "I—actually, no, I mean to say, I had not made up my mind when he was here the first time. I had told him I would inform him by letter when I had decided what to do, but he was too impatient to wait. He—well, I guess he was angry to find I still had not come to a decision." Certainly, that much was true. "I have thought some more since he left, and I have decided that I will sell. That is all."

"Are you certain that is what you wish to do, Phoebe? You must not allow him to push you into a hasty decision. You know we have not quite finished with our evaluation of the property."

Phoebe went back to her search and found the needle when it stuck into her hand. "Yes, I am certain."

She joined the children for her evening meal rather than dine in solitary splendor, and passed the time with them playing spillikins and the Mansion of Happiness. She went up to kiss them goodnight after they retired for bed under Lizzie and Nanny's supervision.

"Were you lonesome here without us all day?" asked William in a sleepy voice as she bent over him.

"No, I spent the time in the garden, love. But of course I missed you. Hush now, and go to sleep."

Ironically, she had not been alone enough to be lonesome, she thought as she descended the stairs again. She wished she had been. But William's question, coming so soon after the ones Devenham had asked her in the garden, made her reflective. She had ignored the earl, but she had heard his words. Would she spend the rest of her life living with Judith and Edward? What function would she have as the children grew older? David was old enough now to be sent off to Harrow or Winchester or Eaton. Thomas would soon follow. She supposed she would have to take any amount Richard paid her for Beau Chatain and buy whatever sort of modest property she could get. Then she could live there for as long as her income would allow, receiving occasional visits from the children or Judith and Edward.

Maddocks surprised her when she reached the first floor landing.

"Madam, Lord Devenham has returned. He is in the drawing room."

Phoebe felt the conflict within her as clearly as if she saw it acted out in front of her. First there was a spark, a little thrill of excited anticipation, and then there was a thick blanket of denial that rolled down over it to snuff it out. Devenham! Everyone had assumed that he would spend his entire evening at Watier's. Conscious of her duties as hostess, Phoebe forced her steps toward the drawing room. Perhaps he would be content to entertain himself with the day's newspapers in Edward's study. Somehow, she did not think he would.

When Phoebe entered, Devenham was standing by the fireplace with one casually placed elbow resting on the mantel shelf. His back was to the door and he appeared to be examining the Meissen porcelain figures that invariably made their home on the mantel. He looked up and met her gaze in the mirror above his head.

"Lord Devenham, good evening." Phoebe thought she achieved just the right mixture of coolness and civility in her tone. "We had not expected to see you back this evening—I mean, at least not so early. I'm afraid Judith and Edward have gone out."

"Have they?" He sounded perplexed. "I am sorry to hear that. I have some news I wanted to share with them."

"Perhaps it will wait until tomorrow?"

"Tomorrow I will be moving back into the Clarendon. That is my news—a declaration of independence, one might say. I am getting about so well now, I really cannot impose upon their—and your—hospitality any longer."

He removed his elbow from the mantel and, leaning on his cane, came a few steps toward her.

"I had hoped we might all enjoy one last evening together. You have proven an admirable partner at whist, you know, besides being a most excellent nurse."

She knew she should have been expecting this. More, she should be happy about it. She should not be feeling such a sense of loss, such pain at the prospect of separating. She did not seem to have enough reserves of denial left to smother the reaction, however. She swallowed, trying to clear the lump from her throat. "Will you be going home to your estates now?"

"I am probably well enough to finish my journey home. My mother has been most anxious to see me for all these past weeks. If she enjoyed better health, she would most likely have jumped into her traveling chaise and come straight to London. But I will not be going yet."

He will still be in London.

"His Royal Highness the Duke of York is holding a reception on the twenty-ninth. I am required to be there. I do not wish to test my newly recovered strength by traveling from town and then coming right back in such a short space of time."

"Yes, I'm sure you are right."

His departure was going to leave a much bigger hole in her life and her heart than she had dreamed possible. How long would it take for that to heal? The hole Stephen had left had not healed yet; she had simply bricked up the opening into a wall.

"I was wondering," he said hesitantly, "if you would consider attending the Duke's reception with me. I would feel greatly honored."

Wouldn't that simply prolong the pain? She did not know how to answer. "May I have some time to think it over?" she finally asked.

"Yes. Yes, of course. The invitations are not even out yet."

An awkward silence fell between her and the earl. They stood facing each other like actors who'd forgotten their lines, each hoping the other would do or say something to which they could react.

What was he feeling? she wondered. Did he have regrets as well? If only things had been different! What if she had met him instead of Stephen when she was a young, unmarried girl dancing through her first Season with a light, joyful heart? *I would have felt ravished on the spot by those piercing blue eyes, and I would have been terrified by his reputation. So much for might-have-been fantasies,* she told herself.

But what if she had been someone different under the same circumstances that had occurred? Things might have indeed turned out differently. She sighed.

"You could be comfortable in Edward's study," she suggested. She gestured vaguely toward the door and the stairway that lay beyond it. "Several of today's papers should be in there if you care to read them."

"No, thank you. I would prefer to spend my last night here in company."

"But Judith and Edward are—"

"I know, they've gone out. You have no chaperone, and I am no longer ill. Perhaps Mrs. H? Or your abigail?" He moved slowly to the gaming table, and began toying with the chess pieces there. He chuckled, "Whoever dusted these did not have the least idea how to reset them."

He rearranged several pieces as she stood watching him. "I believe you owe me a game, you know."

"I owe you one?"

"Yes. I never exacted the punishment for your insubordination on the day we rescued Mrs. Finchley. That is your sentence—you must play one game of chess with me. Now. Tonight."

No, she thought in alarm. How could she spend the evening like that with him, knowing every minute that she wanted to be in his arms? "I don't think I can do that."

"Why not?"

"I won't be able to concentrate." That was certainly true. She lowered her eyes. "I—I am too tired. I planned to retire early."

The look of playful entreaty on his face changed swiftly to one of solicitude. "Are you certain you are all right?" He moved toward her from the table. "That was a very unpleasant scene I interrupted in the garden this afternoon."

Dear Lord, how much had he seen? She had assumed he knew no more than what he had heard at the end of it. "Yes, I am all right," she insisted.

"Will you continue to be? What will you do? How will you handle Mr. Brodfield the next time?"

"There won't be a next time."

"Do not be too certain of that. I am concerned for you."

That he did care showed plainly in his face. He was standing much too close to her, and her pulse was racing much too fast.

I must tell him now, she thought. *I cannot go on this way.* She forced out the words. "Your concern for my affairs is out of place, my lord."

"Is it?"

Facing him was too painful, so she turned and walked away toward the window, shuttered now against the night. "I do not mean to offend you, for I know you are well-intentioned. But your pursuit of me is a waste of your time."

He moved to stand close behind her. "Do you feel so pursued, then?"

It was not the reply she had expected, and it flustered her together with his nearness. She needed to move away, to escape both him and her own pounding heart. But she realized suddenly that there was nowhere to turn with him so close behind her. There was a chair to one side of the window, and the pier table on the other. She stared at the closed window shutters, seeing nothing, her head held stiffly.

"Well, yes. No, I mean—your attentions to me go too far, sir. I do not return your interest."

He had not moved from behind her. In fact, he stood so still she was not even sure he was breathing. She began to fear she had angered him, but then he spoke, quietly, in an even voice.

"Perhaps I would believe you if you could look into my eyes and say that."

Oh no, she thought. *How can I? I must—I will make myself do it. I am strong. I can do it, this one time. He will believe me then, and be gone.*

She turned around and looked into his intense blue eyes. For a moment, her resolve faltered, but then she spoke. "I am looking into your eyes," she said in carefully measured syllables. She tried to summon some feeling of anger to help her. He had pushed her to this, after all. But his face showed her the range of his feelings—longing, love, passion, doubt. *I must say it now,* she told herself.

"I am not interested in you. I want you to leave me alone." There, she had done it. She felt the betraying tears start into her eyes, and quickly turned her face away before he should notice.

"Your words say no, but your heart says yes. If you have truly fooled yourself, let me prove it to you."

She tried to push past him then in panic, but he took her into his arms and put his lips gently upon hers. She struggled for only a moment. As the kiss continued, it acted like a drug upon her reason. The stiffness went out of her and she began to savor his taste. His lips were gentle yet demanding, seeking. The response they sought fanned to life within her, rippling up through her body.

As she gave a small gasp, his kiss deepened. The searing desire she had thought was dead or at least banished forever suddenly was pouring through her again. Its power had always frightened her. It possessed her for several moments, until the remembrance of Stephen's kisses and her response to him intruded upon her pleasure. Then she was filled with pain that more than equaled her passion.

"No!" She broke away so suddenly that Devenham could

not stop her. As she pushed past him, she saw the hurt and bewilderment in his face.

"Phoebe, why? Why can you not trust me and let me care for you?" He held his hands out to her almost in supplication.

She had failed, utterly failed, to pass his test. Now he knew her feelings, but he still would not understand.

She turned her face back to him, knowing full well it was streaked with tears and full of anguish. Could a heart already broken break again? "Don't—please, don't. How can I explain? I tell you, it is my own heart that cannot be trusted."

With that, she ran from the room.

Chapter Thirteen

"Devenham, 'tis your play."

"Hello, Jack?"

A gentle nudge brought Devenham's attention back to the cards in his hand and the laughter of his companions as they sat in the card room at Brooks's two nights later.

"If you're going to be woolgathering, I demand a new partner!" teased the friend who sat opposite him.

"I never thought I'd see the day when Devenham lost his concentration at cards! I tell you, gentlemen, this is serious—very serious."

Devenham smiled and shook his head. His thoughts had been full of Phoebe, it was true. He studied the cards on the table now, trying to sort out who had led what suit and which card his partner had played in turn.

"Hush!" cried another in the group. "For once we have a sporting chance of beating him. Let him woolgather all he wants, and later we'll offer a toast to the lady, whoever she is!"

"Nay, gents, this is more serious than you think," Devenham's partner protested. "He's on his way to being ruined, can't you see? Not to mention me along with him. When a man as sharp as Jack loses his edge, he's in trouble. 'Tis Lady Brodfield that has brought him to this, mark my words. Look into my eyes, Jack, and tell me which suit is trump."

The others at the table roared at this and reached for their drinks to wash down their laughter. Devenham didn't mind. He was quite inclined to agree with their analysis of his situation, but he was damned if he knew what to do about it. Inconceivable as it might be, or even inconvenient, he was in love with Phoebe.

Even more amazing was his belief that she might be capable of loving him in return, if she would only allow herself the chance. Such a possibility damned near turned his view of life and the whole world upside down. But he was beginning to despair of ever breaking through the barriers she had erected around her heart.

"Why, look! There's old Lord Nowersby. Now there's a man whose addiction to the fairer sex has far ruined him, indeed."

This was met with a rude chuckle around the table.

"I didn't know he ever ventured out!" said one of the friends in mock amazement.

"I've heard it said that his coattails are hot to the touch and his breeches require special tailoring."

"He looks quite normal to me," came the reply. "Although I could have sworn I've heard that description applied to you, Rawson."

This comment was deemed hilarious, although Devenham did not join in the round of laughter.

"I've heard that it's his bedsheets that never cool off! They say he has procurers who bring the women right to his door!"

"Or right to his bedside? The devil, you'd never think he'd have such prodigious stamina, would you? No wonder he's so scrawny—he must never get a chance to eat."

Devenham was used to the crude banter of his friends. He found he had lost his taste for it, somehow, although he tried to maintain his tolerant smile. The next comment riveted his attention, however.

"Isn't Nowersby a confederate of Richard Brodfield's?"

A sudden, sobering silence descended on the table of friends.

"If you want my advice, Devenham," said the player to his right, "you'll let go of whatever there may be between you and Lady Brodfield. She's a beauty, there's no question. But if I may speak frankly, as a friend, she's damaged goods. Not damaged in the sense we might usually mean," he hastened to add, "but damaged nonetheless."

Devenham narrowed his eyes. "Would you care to explain in what sense you do mean, Corbet?"

"Nothing disrespectful, Devenham, please believe me. It's just—surely you know about the scandal that surrounded her husband's suicide. No one knows what truly passes between a man and his wife. Just the scandal alone is reason enough to look elsewhere, man."

"Her remaining connection to the Brodfields is reason beyond that, Devenham, trust us."

The earl's friends shook their heads solemnly.

"She has another strike against her now that Lord Tyneley is gone," said the one called Rawson. "He was the stabilizing influence among the Brodfields. Any man would think twice now before making even an oblique connection to that family."

"Explain that to me."

"Reputation, man. Reputation! There's only a certain kind who don't care if his name gets linked with the likes of them. Brodfield has been a scandal unto himself for some time, and it would not surprise me now with the old earl gone to see his mother, Lady Tyneley, kicking over the traces. The only surprise was that his half brother was apparently cast from the same mold."

These comments only frustrated Devenham. "You forget I have not been in London for more than two years, my friends. Not all the gossip you know reached us in the Peninsula or France. And in Vienna, there was so much new gossip being generated every day, any London news was likely to pale beside it, I assure you. If you truly mean to advise me in my affairs, you'd best speak plainly."

Corbet, who had first spoken against Phoebe, lowered his voice. "I'll speak plainly, Devenham, but if any repeat what I say, I'll deny every word. Think about Brodfield. Have you ever seen him in here, or in White's or Watiers', or Arthur's, or any of the more acceptable clubs? No, you have not. He's been blackballed in every one he ever tried to get into. He haunts the hells on Jermyn Street and Pall Mall. The man is a born cheat and a liar. We believe in a life of pleasure and I'd not be the one to cast the first stone, but none call us depraved or perverted that I know of, nor would they have grounds. Rakehell or libertine I might answer to, even proudly, but not such other charges. But I have heard such things whispered about Brodfield. He is said to hold strange orgies at his property outside of London, and some say he belongs to the Hell-fire Club. No one seems to know how he managed to be away from his regiment so often as he seemed to be."

"He missed his own father's funeral," said Devenham's partner. "The one time he could have gotten an authorized leave!"

"He didn't need to get leave by then—he had already sold out, from what I hear."

"I heard he was too busy with private business at Margate to attend."

"Private business? Of course! The kind conducted in bed, that is!"

There was laughter after this remark, but there was tension beneath it that had been missing when the discussion first started. Devenham did not even smile. Instead, he tossed down his cards.

"Gentlemen, I will have to beg your indulgence on this one occasion. I promise to make it up to you another time—if you like, you can make me pay double the stakes that everyone else pays. But you are right about my preoccupation this evening." He reached down for his ebony cane on the floor by his chair and stood up. "I am quite unequipped to play, and it is unfair to my partner and to all of you. I am certain you can find another fourth to replace me."

"I hope we have not given offense? None was intended," said Corbet.

"None was taken. If it had been, trust me, you would know. As for the advice you have offered, I will consider what you have said. But I would leave you with a thought to consider yourselves. I was damaged goods on the field after Waterloo. I am damned thankful I wasn't abandoned there simply because of it."

Devenham bowed and headed for the door.

Once outside, the earl decided to walk for a bit. The strength of his injured leg was increasing every day, and using the muscles seemed to help. He wanted to think, and the cool evening air seemed conducive to putting together bits and pieces of a difficult puzzle.

The more he heard about Richard Brodfield, the more convinced he became that Richard must have played some role in whatever had happened between Phoebe and Stephen, and even in Stephen's death. He did not have the faintest idea what that role might have been, and he had not a shred of evidence. But he was not going to give up his efforts to find out. Quite contrary to their intentions, his friends had helped him to renew his determination to dig into Phoebe's past until he found some answers. If he could accomplish nothing more, he at least wanted to help her to come to grips with that tragedy.

He wished he could find a way to prevent Phoebe from having anything more to do with Brodfield. His friends had reported rumors that the man had held "orgies" at his property outside of London. If Brodfield did own property outside of London, why was he so insistent on having the estate his father had left to Phoebe?

They had also mentioned his absence from his regiment, the same problem Sir Henry Torrens had mentioned. Devenham knew now that he wanted to learn not only how often Richard had been absent, but when. Finding out could prove to be a bit challenging. He would need to visit the Horse Guards again, and another consultation with Sir Charles Mortimer might prove helpful.

The evening was particularly fine, the night air cool but soft like the breath of a woman. Devenham walked along the pavements through alternating patterns of shadow and pools of lamplight, disrupted by increasing numbers of passing carriage lamps as the hour grew late. He wandered the streets for a little while longer before turning his steps toward the Clarendon.

He had kissed Phoebe twice now, and her response to him was undeniable. He had felt it clearly the first time, but the second time it had been even sweeter and far more intense, albeit brief. If only she would trust him, confide in him! If only she would share her pain. He wanted her so much it hurt, but he wanted all of her—heart, soul, mind, and body. If the pain he sensed in her was so much a part of her, then he wanted that, too.

When he finally returned to his rooms at the hotel, he was astonished to discover that Phoebe had sent a note to him quite late in the day. He literally snatched the message out of Mullins's hands in his eagerness to read it, and found a request for him to call on her at Wigmore Street at his earliest convenience.

"Blast and confound it," he said, looking at the clock. "It is far too late to send a reply. I wish now I had come back sooner. I shall simply take her at her word. If my earliest convenience tomorrow is too early, I shall simply wait upon her."

He sat down in the nearest chair, feeling quite suddenly the combined effects of both the quantity of wine he had drunk with his friends and the exertion of his evening walk. He looked helplessly at Mullins, who came over and began to help him out of his coat without further prompting and without comment.

Phoebe had herself received a most astonishing note that afternoon. According to Maddocks it had not come by the regular post, but had been brought to the door by a ragged boy who could not so much as say who sent it, but who stubbornly refused to depart until he'd been given a coin for his trouble.

From habit, Phoebe took the letter and headed toward the garden, thinking she would sit in the shade under the hawthorn tree to read the message. She stopped at the door. For the past two days she had not been able to bring herself to go into the garden. It was quite as if Richard had poisoned it. Instead, she turned back and retreated up the stairs to her room on the second floor.

The note was small, written by some parsimonious person on only a portion of a sheet of foolscap. That its author was a woman was quite clear from the handwriting, a schoolgirlish script which lacked style but appeared both laborious and careful.

Intrigued and mystified, Phoebe unfolded the paper and read:

"Dear Madame, What I have to tell you cannot be explained in a brief note. I have reason to believe that your husband is still alive. If you would know more, please to meet me at St.

James's Church tomorrow at the hour of three. You do not know me, but I knew your husband well. I believe we may help each other."

It was signed "Mademoiselle Jeanette Gimard."

Phoebe dropped the letter onto her dressing table quickly, as if it singed her fingers. She blinked in shock and surprise. Then, as she began to feel the old tingling numbness spread through her shaking limbs to overtake her body, she closed her eyes and willed herself not to give in to it.

Think, she told herself, *do not feel. Focus on what you know in your mind.*

She knew very well that Stephen was not alive. She had identified his bloodstained body herself. The horrifying image haunted her worst nightmares. Was the note intended as a cruel jest? No, she did not think so. There was a simple sincerity about the words that convinced her the author believed what she had written. She picked up the letter and read it over again.

Who was Jeanette Gimard? The woman was obviously French. How had she known Stephen? Phoebe retracted the last question as soon as she thought it, for it was simply too naive not to assume the obvious. She had to have been one of Stephen's lovers. What could possibly have led her to think Stephen was still alive? And after all this time?

Phoebe stood up and began to walk in absent circles on the flowered carpet as she stared at the letter and thought. There was only one way to learn the answers to these questions, and that was to meet the woman. But she did not want anyone to know. How could she manage to do that?

She ran through various possibilities, coming up against obstacles built into each one. She could not ask Goldie or Mary Anne to go with her, for then surely Edward and Judith would find out. Also, someone might identify her by recognizing them. She thought she could disguise herself, ironically, by not wearing mourning dress. She must have something plain in a color, that combined with a deep bonnet and perhaps a veil, would render her anonymous on the street. That did not solve the problem of getting from Wigmore Street to St. James's

Church, however. And how would she get away from the house alone?

In the end, Phoebe had written the note to Devenham. He had said he stood ready to help her, and had practically begged for her trust. Perhaps he would be willing to loan Mullins to her for a few hours, without knowing why.

The next morning she rose early according to her usual habit and after dressing made her way to the garden with a quick detour through the kitchen en route. She could not continue to stay away, for the poor cats would be hungry. She took a deep breath at the threshold of the door from the basement and forced her feet to step outside, as if she had crossed some invisible barrier.

The morning was cool and dewy, and the scents of the garden hung fresh in the air. The sun seemed to kiss the plants and sparkled in the droplets that still clung to their leaves. With a soft mew of greeting, first the calico and then the other two cats appeared, coming to her to rub their heads against her outstretched hand.

"There, did you miss me? I am sorry that I did not come. You must be hungry, or have you been catching birds and mice? I'd rather you be hungry, yes. I have some lovely scraps of mutton Mrs. H saved for me to give you. So much nicer than birds or mice. See?"

She opened the cloth bundle in her basket and made three little piles of scraps on the gravel path, one for each cat. They ate heartily, every so often stopping to look up at her as she sat watching them from the nearby bench.

She sat there for some time, talking to the cats in a soft voice and watching the changes come over the garden as the sun grew stronger. She tried to draw the peacefulness into herself, banishing the memory of Richard's hateful presence and strengthening herself for the strange visit with the Frenchwoman that lay ahead.

She found it was Devenham's presence in the garden she could not seem to banish, remembering his gentle courtesy and the pleasure he seemed to find in her company. What woman would not be charmed by such a man? She remembered, too, how he had looked when he had found Richard with her in this garden three days ago. Would he have looked as dangerous if it had been Judith or any other woman caught that way? She hoped so, but a part of her argued that the earl had developed something more than a passing fancy for her.

Maddocks's voice cut into her thoughts and made her jump. "Excuse me, madam. Major Lord Devenham?"

Of course, there he was, just as if her thoughts had summoned him. She chose to attribute her racing heart to the start Maddocks had given her. She managed to smile.

"Lord Devenham! You are indeed an early caller this morning." She stood up, gathering her basket and turning toward the house where the earl waited in the doorway. The cats vanished into the nearest greenery at her movement.

Devenham stepped out and came toward her, nodding his thanks to the butler as they passed each other. "Your note said at my earliest convenience. I hope I am not disturbing you?"

You have disturbed me from the first moment I ever saw you, Phoebe thought. He looked more handsome than ever this morning, perhaps because she had not seen him for two days.

"I have frightened away your furry companions once again," he apologized. His lopsided smile made her heart turn over.

"I have not yet had breakfast," she answered evasively, flicking her eyes away from him and looking anywhere else— at the garden, the gravel, the empty windows of the house. She should invite him to come in, to join her, she knew, but the garden offered privacy they would not have inside the house. She turned away and began to walk down the path toward the foot of the garden. "However, I did say at your earliest convenience, and I do thank you for coming." She spoke over her shoulder. "You must have pressing affairs that demanded you get an early start on your day."

"Not particularly." The gravel crunched under his feet and a moment later he was beside her. "I suppose I am such a fashionable fribble I needs must stay a-bed until noon, to guard my reputation? Someone might suspect I had not been out all night carousing, otherwise."

She had the grace to blush. "You make it sound an insult to be considered fashionable. That is not how I meant it."

"I know." His voice was low and soft. He stopped on the path and, reaching for her elbow, turned her to face him. "Perhaps I was only eager to be in your company."

Phoebe felt the current running between them the instant he touched her. She prayed he was not going to kiss her. The continuing battle within herself could not withstand such an assault. She dared not look into his face, yet she needed to know what was coming. She forced her hesitant eyes to meet his.

What she saw there was desire strong enough to make her breathless, but she also saw tender concern, and questions.

"How can I help you?" he whispered.

She closed her eyes, struggling for control over her raging emotions. How much easier it would be to just let go! To throw her arms around him and love him and take the comfort he offered. But it would be cruelly unfair. She would be using him, and in the end he would have the deepest regrets. They would both find only pain.

"There is a small thing you might do for me," she said carefully, "but I must beg you not to ask for an explanation. Could you spare Mullins for a brief while this afternoon? Perhaps it is not such a small thing."

"I could spare him," the earl answered, "but am I not to know to what purpose?"

"I need him to accompany me on a short errand."

"That is easily arranged."

"You must give me your word that you will not ask him where we went or what we did after we have returned."

He looked at her searchingly, and for a moment she was afraid he would refuse. Then he sighed, and raised her hand to his lips for a fleeting kiss. "I can refuse you nothing. You have my word on it."

Chapter Fourteen

Mullins arrived at Wigmore Street in a hackney at half-past two to pick up Phoebe as she had requested. Now as the carriage carried them to the rendezvous at St. James's Church, she leaned back against the squabs, nervous about the meeting but confident at least that few people would even see them, let alone identify them.

She had dressed in a high-collared pelisse of blue and pink striped silk and a jockey-style bonnet with a deep poke in a shade of blue that almost matched the dress. She had attached a veil to the bonnet to hide her features even more. The pelisse was more fashionable than she had wanted, but she had found nothing in her wardrobe that was plain without being too noticeably out of date. How difficult it was to render oneself invisible!

She had been forced to go to elaborate lengths to escape on her errand without raising suspicion at home. She had given Mary Anne an unexpected holiday, and had asked Goldie to accompany Lizzie and the children to the park, which she knew he would agree to do with pleasure if he was not otherwise engaged by Judith or Edward. Afterward, she had pretended to conceive a sudden desire to go to Hatchard's and told Judith that Devenham had offered her Mullins's services if ever required.

She felt very uncomfortable about lying to her sister. Judith, however, would never have understood her need to meet with the mysterious Mlle. Gimard—if anything she would have been shocked by Phoebe's intentions. Respectable women did not consort with members of the *demimonde*. For that matter, respectable women did not venture too near the area of St. James Street, that special enclave belonging so specifically to the male species. Situated between Piccadilly and Jermyn Street, the church of St. James stood sentinel at the edge of the neighborhood. And of course, respectable women *never* went anywhere alone.

Phoebe instructed the coachman to drop her and Mullins a few steps beyond Hatchard's, to avoid being noticed by any of the popular bookstore's patrons. They walked quickly along the pavement under darkening skies and turned in at the gate of the churchyard.

There was no one waiting in the yard, for which Phoebe was thankful. Apparently Mlle. Gimard had a fine sense of propriety; she had not suggested coming to Phoebe's home, nor was she flaunting her presence openly at the church. Phoebe instructed Mullins to wait outside, and entered the church.

At first, she saw no one inside the building either. Even on this dark afternoon its graceful, Wren-designed interior was filled with light from the plain glass windows except for a few shadows in corners beneath the galleries or behind pillars. She lifted the veil from her bonnet and looked at the watch she had pinned to her bodice; it was not quite three o'clock. Perhaps she had arrived first. Or perhaps the other woman had changed her mind. She would wait a little while to see. But as she took a step toward one of the pews, she heard a woman speak.

"Lady Brodfield?" The sound was hollow in the empty church. A woman emerged from the shadows at the far end of the sanctuary and came toward her.

As she approached, Phoebe could see that she was dressed very respectably in a daygown of figured muslin with a military styled spencer of dark blue over it and a dark blue silk bonnet. Phoebe was not quite sure what she had expected, but the woman's good taste surprised her. "You must be Mademoiselle Gimard."

The other woman nodded, clearly taking stock of Phoebe and making some judgment before saying anything more. "I was not certain if you would come." Her English was heavily accented.

"I was not certain if I should come," Phoebe replied. She noted that the Frenchwoman was quite attractive. She had fair skin and a well-proportioned figure. A few curls of honey-colored hair escaped the confines of her bonnet. Phoebe guessed she was only a year or two younger than herself. "Perhaps we should sit down?"

Mlle. Gimard nodded again, and they entered one of the pews. Phoebe wondered how to tell the woman that she was mistaken about Stephen.

"I must say I was quite astonished by your note," she began, speaking in fluent French that had been drilled into her throughout childhood by a long series of tutors. "What gives you the idea that my husband might still be alive?"

"I have seen him."

Phoebe felt a chill crawl up her spine despite her certain knowledge that the statement could not be true. She stared at the woman.

"It was only from a carriage window, I admit, but I would know him anywhere. It is essential that I find him. And then I thought that you would want to find him, too, madame."

For a moment Phoebe considered whether the young woman might be mad. Had her mind conjured up a vision she simply wanted to believe in? Might she be dangerous? But no. There was no madness in the woman's face, only something haunting and desperate in her eyes that touched Phoebe's heart. She thought that she should despise this woman, who had been her rival for Stephen's love along with who knew how many others, but she could not. She wondered if Mlle. Gimard had loved Stephen as much as she had.

"Mademoiselle, I am sorry," she said gently. "What you thought you saw is not possible. My husband is dead." Quite unintentionally, her eyes misted. "I saw his body and identified it myself. That was a year and a half ago."

The Frenchwoman looked stricken. "You loved him!" It was a statement of discovery, given in a peculiar tone of distress.

"Why, yes."

"Then that is another charge I have against his account." The woman looked straight at Phoebe. "He has deceived us both, madame, God help us. I love him also, but he told me that you had no feelings for him. I am sorry."

Phoebe did not know what to say. She had never thought

Stephen would lie, even to a mistress. But certainly he had deceived her. She had never even guessed at all the things she had learned after his death. To discover now that he had denied her love hardly hurt her, after so much other pain.

"It seems he did deceive us, mademoiselle, when he was alive. I do not think it possible for him to deceive us any more, from the grave."

"Ah, madame. I saw him. When I saw him from the carriage, I cried out his name, and I saw his face go pale. He is alive."

Phoebe was beginning to feel a hint of frustration. "How can you think he would be out walking in the streets if he were in hiding, supposedly dead, mademoiselle? It makes no sense."

To her distress, the other woman burst into tears. "I do not know! I have waited for him so long. It has taken me all of these months to return to England to discover why he never came. First I learned that he was dead, and then I saw him on the street. I must find him." She turned her tearful face to Phoebe. "He is the father of my child."

A fierce but momentary stab of jealousy lanced through Phoebe. Then it was gone, and she put her hand on the Frenchwoman's arm in a small gesture of comfort. "He would never have abandoned you if he had known. Your child—is it a boy or a girl?"

Mlle. Gimard looked puzzled. "It is a boy—my son, Gaston. But he did know. I was increasing when he sent me back to France. He gave me a little money and said he would soon join me. I am sorry, madame. He said there was nothing between you and him."

"Your lover was not my husband," Phoebe declared. "Perhaps the man you thought was him *is* still alive, mademoiselle." She hesitated, wondering if she should go on. Opening the wounds would bring back the pain. But something was very wrong here, and she saw no other way to sort it out.

"My husband wanted children more than anything in the world. As did I," she added in a whisper. "It proved to be something I could not give him. He had reason to seek outside our marriage for the one thing he wanted most, although I never knew he did so until after he died. He used to tell me it did not matter, but I knew better. He would never, never have abandoned you, Mlle. Gimard, if he had known you were carrying his child. He would never, never have—have taken his own life."

She looked at the Frenchwoman, wondering if the agony she was feeling showed on her face. "It is almost enough to make me wish he had been your lover, mademoiselle. He would have lived."

Mlle. Gimard shook her head. "Have you any likeness of your husband, madame?"

Of course. Why did I not think of showing it sooner? Phoebe fished in her reticule for the miniature of Stephen she had brought with her for just such a purpose. "Surely this will clear up the confusion," she said. She handed over the portrait and then attempted to dry her eyes with the silk handkerchief she had taken out at the same time.

"It looks so like him!" Mlle. Gimard exclaimed, yet she hesitated. "It is like, and yet it is not. Perhaps the artist? I am not sure. There is something . . ."

At that moment, Phoebe knew the answer. It had been Richard. Richard had used this poor woman in Stephen's name, and cruelly abandoned her. It was Richard the mademoiselle had seen from her carriage and called to in vain. It was Richard who was still very much alive.

"Mademoiselle," said Phoebe in a deadly serious voice. "My husband's brother—half-brother—looks very much like him. His name is Richard Brodfield."

"But madame—forgive me, but my lover, my *Etienne,* was the Viscount Brodfield."

"Then he lied to you." Phoebe's words came out more sharply than she intended, but her mind was racing ahead. If Richard had posed as Stephen in one affair, might he not have done so in others? *But why?*

"It is true," the other woman said reflectively, "he lied to me at the end. Perhaps he also lied at the beginning."

"By courtesy my husband was Baron Brodfield of Ruslan," Phoebe said almost apologetically. "The Earl did not hold any other titles."

"This brother, this Richard Brodfield, he lives here in London?"

"Yes."

"I must see him. Perhaps he never saw the letter I wrote to tell him the child was a son."

"The family has a large house in Charles Street. He and his mother are the only ones left there now. But do you think it wise to confront him?"

"I must. I have come all the way back to England for this purpose."

"You cared for him?" Phoebe found it almost impossible to believe, but the other woman nodded. Somewhere, deep in Richard's black soul that had always seemed the perfect antithesis of Stephen's, there must be some shred of good. Phoebe had always hoped so. Certainly, Lord Tyneley had always believed so. Perhaps Mlle. Gimard had found and touched it, however briefly.

Phoebe regarded the Frenchwoman through narrowed eyes. "You still care. Even after what he did, and what we have discovered?"

Mlle. Gimard began to cry again. She bobbed her head saying, "God help me."

This time Phoebe put her arms around the young woman. "God will help you, and so will I."

Phoebe left the church by the same door she had entered and looked for Mullins as she stepped outside. It had begun to rain and she felt a pang of guilt for making him wait in it. A male form peeled itself from the brick sidewall of the building and came toward her, but it was not Mullins. It was Devenham.

"You have been crying," he stated as he reached her. He grasped her elbow and like a perfect dance partner turned her around and back in through the church door with a single smooth motion.

For several seconds Phoebe had lost her voice in astonishment and indignation. Finding it at last, she sputtered angrily, "What are *you* doing here? Where's Mullins? I trusted you! You gave me your word."

"Sh-h." He put a finger on her lips. "I could ask you the

same question, what are you doing here? I have sent Mullins
to Hatchard's to buy you a book, since that is apparently the
excuse you used to get yourself here. Did you not consider that
someone might wonder when you came home empty-handed?"

In truth, she had not, but that did not make her feel any less
annoyed with him.

"As for keeping my word, I agreed that I would not ask
Mullins anything about this exercise after he returned, and indeed, I will not. I always keep my word. Besides, I will have
no need to ask anything by the time I am back in my rooms at
the Clarendon. We are not leaving this church until you have
explained everything to me."

She jerked her head back from his lingering finger and
glared at him. *How dare he?* "Why should I explain anything
to you? What did you do, follow us here? What did you think
might be going on? What gives you the right to spy on me, or
interfere?" She fired the questions at him like artillery missiles.

"This," he said simply, slipping his arms around her and
lowering his mouth to hers.

His kiss was brief this time, but it communicated a great
deal. This time it was neither hesitant nor gentle, but confident, demanding. It told Phoebe that Devenham saw through
her attempts at resistance. It told her that he cared enough not
to take no for an answer, and that he would not give up easily.
Above all, it told her he knew she would respond to it exactly
as he wished, as indeed she must have, for he broke it off with
a tender but satisfied smile.

She put the back of her hand against her lips and turned her
head away from him, trying to replace the hunger of her response with the anger she had felt before. "You cannot keep
me here," she said with a sharp intake of breath.

"Yes, I can. And I will, until I have my explanation." The
warning note in his voice forced her to look back at him.

He cocked one eyebrow at her infuriatingly. "Think about it.
Who knows that you are here? Even the person you were
meeting thinks you have left, and you made sure no one else
knows that you came. And God forbid if we were to be discov-

ered here like this, alone. If your brother-in-law Edward found out, he'd have us back here in a trice, awaiting the parson."

With a sinking feeling, she realized he was right. Even if she tried to run, where would she go? Out into the streets would be worse than staying here.

"Begin at the beginning," he prompted. "Why did you come here? Why all the secrecy?" When she still hesitated, his voice became rough-edged. He put his hands on her shoulders. "Do you not know why I arranged with Mullins to follow? I was concerned for your safety. I care about you."

At the intensity in his voice Phoebe felt as though something quite physically cracked inside her. She didn't know if it was her heart or a piece of the wall she had built all around it. Suddenly she began to talk, the words slipping out without waiting for her permission.

"I came here to meet with a woman," she said. "It is not what you think."

"I didn't think anything but that you might be in trouble," he replied softly.

"I couldn't let Judith and Edward know. This woman was— I mean, she thought she was—one of Stephen's mistresses. She had sent me a note, asking to meet me here. She thought—she thought Stephen was still alive."

Phoebe went through the whole story with him. She did not know when the tears began to roll down her cheeks, or when the earl took her into his arms to comfort her as she finished the rest of the tale. She only became conscious that these things had happened as she came to the end and rested quietly against him.

"You do not find this shocking?" she asked.

"My dear, you are speaking to the notorious Earl of Deven-ham. I am no stranger to scandals, you'll recall. And I must confess, some parts of your story had already come to my ears. I have been looking into it, for it did not seem to me to make sense."

"What do you mean, you 'have been looking into it'?"

"I have been making certain inquiries. But this new information about Richard's masquerade opens up many more questions."

"Why would Richard use Stephen's name?" she asked now as she had already asked herself several times.

Devenham tightened his arms around her but did not answer right away. "Not only why, but how often?" he finally said, echoing her own thoughts. "Not only how often, but when? If one mistress was his, could not the others have been also? What of Stephen's supposed other marriage? And what of Stephen's gambling debts? Were those truly his, or were some of those Richard's?"

Phoebe remained in the earl's embrace, drawing comfort from the feel of his warm, solid body. Was it selfish to grasp a few crumbs of pleasure from a relationship she could not allow? He had not recoiled from her in horror when her narrative had revealed that she was barren, but certainly now he would see that she could never be his wife. Perhaps he would even understand how foolishly she had given her heart, how blind and stupid her own passions had made her, how her overpowering love and unproductive body had driven her husband to take his own life. No matter how much of the scandal had been Richard's doing, nothing altered the fact that Stephen had put a pistol to his own head and fired it.

She lifted her head just enough to shake it. "In the end, asking questions does not bring Stephen back. What does it matter except to understand Richard?"

"Do you not feel angry that it may have been Richard's deeds that blackened Stephen's name? And after his death, when he could not vindicate himself! The very idea offends me deeply. Think of the reflections the scandal cast on your own reputation, and the pain it has caused you!"

"There would still have been scandal," she answered, "and there is no remedy for the pain."

"Yes, there is. Tell me if you feel pain when I do this." Devenham proceeded to kiss and caress her with a determined thoroughness that both aroused and astounded her. She scarcely noticed when he untied her bonnet and removed it. When her knees gave way he half carried her into the nearest pew and sat there with her in his lap. She saw her own smoky desire reflected in his eyes.

"Tell me," he said, nuzzling her neck.

She could not make her mouth form words. She shook her head.

"Give me your pain," he whispered. "Let me be your remedy."

Finally she pushed away. "No," she said. "You cannot." She stood up and moved a few steps away to be out of his reach. She retrieved her bonnet from the floor where he had dropped it and poked at her hair with unsteady fingers, looking at him reproachfully. "Such behavior in a church! Really, Lord Devenham, I believe you are every bit as scandalous as people say."

She repositioned her bonnet and tied it securely, mindful that Mullins should soon be joining them.

For a few moments neither of them spoke. Finally, Devenham said, "You should at least feel angry. You should be angry with Richard and the world, and you should fight back. Fight back! People always want to believe the worst. Instead of hiding, show them that you don't give a fig for their opinions. If it is what you want, be so virtuous and good that it shames them. Hold up your head and live your life! As for Richard, we must expose him."

"How?" she asked. The single word seemed the only possible response to everything he had just said.

"For one thing, go with me to the Duke of York's reception. Show people you are not afraid of their clucking tongues. They will gossip, unquestionably, if you make your appearance there with me. Are you brave enough to take such a step?

"I am less certain what to do about Brodfield. We have no proof of anything, just Mlle. Gimard's story." He looked at Phoebe thoughtfully and rose from his seat. "What became of Stephen's papers after his death? There must have been notices from his creditors, and the lines from his other marriage, to have set off the scandal, or was all of it heresay?"

"There were papers. Some were examined at the inquest. I suppose they are still at Charles Street. I took nothing when I left there."

"If we could see those papers—get names from them—then we could interview some of the people who were involved in this. Perhaps they would discover, as Mlle. Gimard did, that the brother who presented himself as Stephen was not, after all."

Phoebe could see that the earl was excited by the idea. The spark of desire in his eyes had been replaced by a spark of— what? Revenge? Anticipation? Why did Richard's duplicity matter to him? He stood like a man prepared to do battle, his fists clenched and his jaw set. If he thought he could slay her personal dragons like a knight of old, she knew he was sadly mistaken.

"I suppose I could ask Lady Tyneley for them," she offered without much enthusiasm. "If she won't give them to me, perhaps she would at least let me look at them."

"I don't like the idea of your going back to that house. What if Brodfield is there, and Lady Tyneley is not? What if he approaches you as he did in your own garden? Who would be there to help you?" She saw his face darken at the very thought. "You will let me accompany you."

"I am not certain Lady Tyneley would cooperate if she suspected anything was amiss. I will only go when I know she is at home," she replied quickly. Then she added, "Perhaps I will bring Mlle. Gimard. She wishes to meet with Richard, and I promised to help her. I had not thought of taking her to the house, but really, she seems very respectable. I suspect that originally she came from a good family. I do not see what Richard could do if there were two of us."

She hoped he would be satisfied with that. She did not feel challenged to fight the way he did; perhaps there was something lacking in her spirit, or else she just saw the world through different eyes. She suspected that battling her demons might be a way for him to battle his own. She had seen clearly the pain he carried from his childhood, and she was beginning to understand that the scandalous behavior behind his reputation was his way of answering the pain caused by other people's false assumptions. This chance to do battle was one thing she could do for him, one small thing she could give freely.

"All right," he said. Relief washed over her. Then he smiled, and she felt even better. "You have not yet said if you will accompany me to His Royal Highness's reception."

"I will. You honor me by asking. Who would not feel proud

to attend a reception at Carlton House and stand by the side of a Waterloo hero?"

She smiled back at him and they simply stood there, more than a dozen feet apart, until a moment later Mullins arrived, spattered with rain and carrying a paper-wrapped parcel from Hatchard's.

Chapter Fifteen

"You look positively beautiful, Aunt Phoebe. Everyone will admire you."

Phoebe smiled and tried to draw comfort from Dorrie's rather partisan approval. She was nervous about attending the reception at Carlton House and, unlike her innocent niece, she was aware that the second statement did not necessarily follow from the first. "Thank you, Dorrie. You are sweet to say so."

She sat still while Mary Anne fastened a necklace of jet beads around her neck, the finishing touch to her toilette. At Judith's insistence, she had indulged in a new evening gown to wear to the Duke of York's reception. With so much of the city's population already gone to their country estates, she had found no difficulty in procuring the services of a modiste on short notice. The woman had gone to great lengths to please her, no doubt in view of the further exodus of clients about to take place as the month of August came to an end.

The Allingtons were preparing to leave London like most of their remaining neighbors and acquaintances. In a few days, Phoebe would find herself in Kent with the family at their country estate, which was finally sporting a completely repaired roof. Such a prospect would normally have lightened her step and filled her heart with joyful anticipation, as she vastly preferred the quiet months spent in the country. This time, however, she felt suspiciously dismayed to be leaving.

She had tried to tell herself that the feeling was due entirely to Devenham's unfinished efforts to investigate and expose Richard Brodfield's villainy. Her initial lack of enthusiasm for the project had been overthrown by Richard himself. She had done as she had promised Devenham, paying a call on Lady Tyneley and taking Mlle. Gimard with her. The young Frenchwoman had succeeded in having an interview with Richard while they were there, and Phoebe had in fact managed to get her mother-in-law to let her see the papers Stephen had left behind in his desk. When the two young women left, Phoebe had a list of names she had surreptitiously copied down to give the earl, and Mlle. Gimard had Richard's answer to her son's future.

Unfortunately, the visit had proved successful for only one of them. What Richard's response had been was very clear from the Frenchwoman's pale face and drawn expression. Phoebe had prodded Mlle. Gimard until the woman finally confided in her. Richard had refused to acknowledge Gaston, saying that it was to the lad's advantage that he not do so. Phoebe was deeply offended by this, for she was certain the poor Frenchwoman was at her wit's end.

She had decided then that Richard deserved whatever scandal or legal repercussions resulted from Devenham's efforts. She was sorry that she would not be in London to see the process completed, but if she were honest with herself, she had to admit that that was not her greatest regret. The curtailment of her connection with the earl weighed on her heart far more heavily.

Tonight, at least, she would be with him. She supposed it was a fitting farewell of sorts. Judith and Edward had kindly invited him to join them for a formal dinner prior to the reception, and then there would be the reception itself. Phoebe wanted to look especially fine to honor him in front of his comrades-in-arms and the Duke of York. There was speculation that the Prince Regent himself would be attending in addition to having provided Carlton House for the event.

Once her abigail had declared her perfect, Phoebe stood up and performed a quick pirouette in front of her niece. Her dress was an elegant confection in black and white, for she had decided half-mourning would be acceptable for such a gala occasion. The low-cut corsage of white crepe was trimmed all around with small black crepe roses and leaves, which also accented the tiny sleeves. The fall of the skirt was fashioned from black crepe, with an attached ornamental white apron embroidered in black and a wide panel of white set on around the hem. This band was overlaid with an interlaced trimming of jet beadwork and headed by a row of black roses where it joined the plain skirt. Phoebe thought the dress was fashionable and extravagant to the extreme, but it pleased her immensely.

"Ooh," sighed Dorrie. "Do you suppose if I become an actress I will have such elegant gowns?"

Phoebe offered the young girl a hug in response. "What I suppose is that you will be called away to dinner at any moment, young lady, and that you need not worry your pretty head about such grave matters as the future just now."

A light knock at the door seemed to confirm this pronouncement, until the maid opened it to admit David, Thomas, and William, come to inspect their aunt. As usual they were full of questions once they had given her appearance their unanimous approval.

"Will Prinny be there?"

"Is the Duke of York as fat as they say he is?"

"Will they give Lord Devenham a medal?"

"Will the earl wear his uniform?"

"Heavens, David, don't let anyone hear you call His Royal Highness the Prince Regent by that awful nickname!" Phoebe responded in her best governess voice. "It is rude to call anyone fat, even if they are," she added, "and undoubtedly Lord Devenham will be wearing his uniform. And no, they are not giving out any medals. At least, not right now."

She suspected that her firm tone did not fool the children. They never failed to notice even the smallest betraying twinkle that might show in her eyes. This evening she probably had a sparkle as bright as the gas lights on Pall Mall.

In his rooms at the Clarendon, Devenham was finishing his own toilet, with Mullins's able assistance. Packed away in a trunk in his quarters, his dress uniform had escaped the brutal punishment of Quatre Bras and Waterloo. It had only been out of the trunk one other time since then, when he had showed it to the children at the Allingtons'. It looked fresh and crisply presentable on him now.

He stood patiently while his trusted servant brushed imaginary specks of lint from the dark blue jacket with its scarlet facings, collar and cuffs, and silver buttons and lace. Its design was far less spectacular than that of the hussar regiments or even the old style dragoon uniforms, but still handsome and infinitely more practical without all that braid. It occurred to Devenham that Phoebe had never seen him in his uniform; he wondered what she would think.

Phoebe occupied his mind a great deal lately, he thought with a smile. He was looking forward to the reception simply because she would be with him. The prospect of going through the rest of his life with her by his side had crossed his mind more than a few times, although the idea scared him like little else. He definitely needed more time to examine it. In the meantime, he thought Phoebe's receptiveness to him had improved, and that gave him hope.

He had spent the last few days pursuing information that might be useful against Richard Brodfield, for he was more convinced than ever that the man was a key to Phoebe's past. It was the past that had made Phoebe barricade her heart and deny herself a future, and he was determined to uncover it and free her. His suspicions about Richard were growing uglier every day, although he had not shared those suspicions with Phoebe. The names she had gotten for him from her late husband's papers had opened up several new avenues of inquiry.

"Right, my lord, that should do it," Mullins announced, stepping back to inspect the earl's appearance. Devenham glanced in the cheval glass and caught the look of approval in his servant's face. From the shirt points standing above his black velvet neck stock to the perfect fit of his white inexpressibles and the shine on his silver-tasseled Hessians, he was the pattern card of a proud officer of the 16th Light Dragoons. At least for a moment, he could feel like the Honourable Major John Allen Jameson once again instead of the Earl of Devenham.

"Thank you, Mullins. Enjoy your free night. You have earned it." He was ready. He scooped up his silver-trimmed shako from the small table near the door and jammed it on his head as he headed out, tucking the tasseled cap lines under his epaulet and fastening them to the button on his shoulder as he went.

He walked the short distance from the hotel to the livery stable where he had hired space for his new curricle. He had found time to go to Tattersall's and had purchased a first-rate rig and a beautiful pair of chestnuts for a rather princely sum. He would enjoy driving Phoebe to the reception in such fine style, and would gladly pay the fee to have the Duke's lads or those attached to Carlton House mind his horses during the reception.

At this moment, the livery's ostlers held the horses as he climbed up into the seat, thinking of how much his leg had improved in the past two weeks. He took up the ribbons and clucked to start the animals. The horses were not only handsome but superbly trained; he believed them worth every guinea he had paid for them. They turned the tight corner out of the livery into the mews with perfect coordination and calmly proceeded toward the entrance of the narrow alley.

Moments before they reached it, however, a wagon suddenly pulled across the opening and blocked it. Devenham was forced to draw the horses up hard. The frightened animals reared and were in danger of injuring themselves against the wheels of the opposing vehicle. Even as the earl opened his mouth to shout a protest, two figures materialized out of nowhere and clambered onto his vehicle. Before he could get a single word out, something struck his head, producing incredibly sharp pain followed by blackness.

The Allingtons and Phoebe waited an hour before going ahead with their dinner. They still expected the earl to arrive, but Judith thought Cook was close to having a fit that would leave regrettably permanent results if they did not proceed. When Devenham still had not arrived by the time they finished eating, Phoebe's initial mild concern had passed through annoyance into very real anxiety.

"Perhaps some unexpected business called him away suddenly, Phoebe dear, and he still plans to take you to the reception. Perhaps he did not have time to send a note," Judith said in an obvious attempt to comfort her. She seemed far more ready to defend the tardy earl then Edward.

"I hope he has a good explanation," Phoebe's brother-in-law muttered. "This is not much of a way to show his gratitude to us."

"Edward, I am positive he must have a reason," Phoebe said. She just wished she knew what it was.

"A reason, yes. I can think of several—none of them good. I thought he was settling down, done with stirring up scandals and trying to shock people. Could I have been so wrong?" He looked at Phoebe in distress. "I never thought he would make you a victim of his capriciousness, dear Phoebe."

"Edward! Was it not you who convinced me to take Lord Devenham under our roof in the first place?" Judith responded. "He has proved himself more kind, generous and noble than I could have dreamed. I learned a lesson about judging people for myself while he was here. Do you not lose your faith in him now, after the faith you had in him before!"

Phoebe thought the clock ticked relentlessly and rather loudly, although perhaps that was only in her head. When the hour for the start of the Duke's reception came and passed, she said quietly, "I would like to send a note 'round to the Clarendon, Edward. May I send Goldie with it?"

"Of course, my dear, of course. Write your note, and as soon as it is ready we'll send him off. In fact, I'll let him take the gig."

The note she wrote was very brief, only expressing her regrets that the earl had been unable to join them for dinner and inquiring politely if there had been a change in plans or if there was any trouble with which either she or the Allingtons might assist him. She thought it hid very well the mixed agonies of dread and doubt that were starting to torture her as the night wore on. Had something happened to him? Or had he suddenly realized he did not want to be seen with the shamed Lady Brodfield at the reception, and not known how to tell her?

The note was sent off, and she settled down to play at cards with Judith and Edward while they waited to see what results it might bring. They played five-card loo, but Phoebe could not concentrate. Their shared laughter every time she had to put more counters into the pool was hollow, as if no one could truly enjoy the game.

More than two and a half hours crept by before Goldie returned to Wigmore Street. When he finally did, Mullins was with him.

"There was nobody there when I first got there—I mean to say, both his lordship and Mullins was out, so I waited," the young footman explained hastily.

"Lord Devenham gave me the night off," Mullins said. "I'd no idea he had not showed up here. I just thank God I stopped back at the hotel—your man might have been waiting there for me till an even later hour." He stopped and looked meaningfully at Edward. "P'rhaps we should speak privately, Sir Edward?" He rolled his eyes at Phoebe and Judith.

"I want to know anything that Mullins has to say," Phoebe insisted before Edward could even reply.

"As do I," Judith agreed.

Edward nodded and the serving man continued quickly. "Lord Devenham left in plenty o' time to be here for 'is dinner engagement. Goldie and me checked at the livery, an' he did go there and pick up his carriage. Just to be sure, we went to Carlton House. O' course we knew we couldn't go in, but one o' the grooms took our message to a footman, who passed it inside. After a while one of His Royal Highness's own servants comes out and tells us the earl hasn't been there, and the Duke is none too pleased about it. I'm afraid now he is in more than one kind of trouble. But I don't have any idea where he is."

Phoebe had to swallow twice before she managed to voice her question. "Did you think he was intending to keep his engagements when he left you, Mullins?"

"Yes, Lady Brodfield, I did."

The next query was even harder. "Do you still think so now in light of what has happened?"

Mullins stared straight at her with that determined look she had come to know so well during their first days. That look conveyed more to her than his words, and while it soothed some of the pain in her heart, it left fear there instead.

"Yes, madam, I do."

Mullins's words meant that Devenham had not intentionally abandoned her. They meant he had met with some accident or foul play. Phoebe felt positively chilled as she thought of the hours that had already passed. He could be lying in an alley somewhere, the victim of street thieves. Or, there was another possibility, so terrible to consider that she could scarcely believe she had thought of it. What if Devenham had found something more about Richard? How often had he warned her that Richard was dangerous? Was Richard truly wicked enough to have taken some form of retribution against the earl?

She was appalled by the very idea, and she also did not know how to learn if there was any truth to it. There was no evidence to take to the authorities. It was terribly late at night now to barge in on Lady Tyneley demanding to see Richard. Richard was probably at a club, or home in his own bed, and what would she say? *I just wanted to inquire whether you had kidnapped Lord Devenham?*

She felt sick with worry, and also utterly helpless. Apparently the others felt the same, for they all stood about in a little worried knot, staring into each others' faces as if they might find some clue there to what they should do.

Finally Mullins said, "Well, I'm going to go back out and search every mews and alley between 'ere and the livery stable, if it takes me all night."

"Goldie shall accompany you," said Edward, "and so shall I." He looked quickly at Phoebe, who was just opening her mouth. "No, Phoebe, don't even think it. There is no way under either sun or moon that I would permit you to come with us."

There was no use arguing, Phoebe realized. Men had more freedom to move about in the streets at midnight than a mere woman had even in daylight. She would only be a hindrance to them, and of course they had no way of knowing how she felt. She thought that just now she would willingly face the most hardened criminal or suffer the most complete destruction of her reputation if either thing could put Lord Devenham safely in the Allingtons' drawing room.

She did argue with Judith after the men had left them, when her sister suggested they retire. There was no point in trying to sleep, for her mind was too occupied to permit it. She urged her sister to go to bed, and settled herself on the sofa to await the searchers' return. Heartsick, she did not know what to hope for most, beyond her prayers that Devenham was alive.

Devenham was definitely alive; the intense pain that blossomed anew in his head with each bounce of the carriage confirmed the fact most unpleasantly. He was not exactly awake, but seemed instead to be hovering in a groggy state of semi-consciousness.

He could tell by the sound and the motion that he was in a carriage, but whose it was or whither it was bound quite eluded him for the moment. He knew it was not his own—this one was closed, and it smelled of straw and blood. The impossibly uncomfortable position of his body and the hard surface he could feel beneath him led him to believe that he was on the floor.

He flexed his fingers to see what would happen and almost instantly came in contact with the hard leather of someone's boot. He also discovered that he could do little else with his fingers; his hands were bound at the wrists.

Experimenting, he shifted his feet very slightly. Apparently they were still free, although it was difficult to determine with his legs cramped beneath him. What did that mean? He tried to focus his mind. It must mean that someone wanted him to be able to walk. The owner of the boot? He had his answer a moment later.

"Do I see some small signs that you are waking up at last, Devenham? I suspect that you will be very sorry."

The low voice took time to penetrate the fog in his brain, but he recognized it. He had not forgotten the one other occasion when he had heard it. *"You may be the ones to rue the consequences,"* Richard Brodfield had said that other time in *Phoebe's garden. Was this what he had meant?*

The boot prodded him. "What, nothing to say? I didn't think a peer of the realm was ever at a loss for words." Brodfield laughed. "Then again, I never thought I'd have a peer at my feet. I'm rather enjoying this."

"Where are you taking me?"

"I suppose you would want to know that, but in the end, does it matter? You want to know too many things—too bad you did not learn to be less inquisitive. I am taking you somewhere very quiet where you shan't cause me any more trouble."

At least he did not say the docks. Men shipped aboard the slavers were seldom heard from again.

Devenham weighed his questions carefully. It was never a good idea to show weakness in front of an enemy. Abducting a peer was the act of a desperate, possibly demented, certainly unpredictable man. Brodfield undoubtedly planned to kill him—he would have to. Yet if that was his intention, why had he not done so already? The earl decided to try to draw him out.

"Why are you doing this?"

Brodfield laughed. "Do you mean to say it is not obvious? Perhaps you are not as smart as I thought. You insinuated yourself between me and Phoebe."

"You and Phoebe?" Devenham could not keep the note of incredulity out of his voice.

Brodfield's amused tone turned surly. The boot prodded Devenham again, suggestively close to his ribs. "You think that simply because she does not like me there can be nothing between us? That there *is* nothing between us? You are a fool. Have you never bedded a reluctant whore? They are the best kind."

The toe of Brodfield's boot shifted closer to Devenham's belly, but that was not the reason for the sudden nausea that swept through him. The utter depravity of what Brodfield was suggesting stunned him.

"I thought at first I'd have to thank you," Brodfield continued. "Having her name linked with yours served my purposes well enough—it did her reputation little good, especially with you both under the same roof. Too bad Allington is so insufferably respectable. At any rate, people will be all the more ready to believe it when they hear her name linked with some of the others they're going to hear. By the time they hear mine, there will be no one left anywhere who will still receive her."

"What is the point of ruining her?" Devenham was beginning to suspect that Richard Brodfield was mad.

"Don't you see? She'll be desperate, she'll have nowhere else to go. She'll be completely dependent upon me."

"You never did intend to purchase Beau Chatain from her, did you?" Devenham was feeling his way, trying to maintain a deadly calm.

"Not once I realized I could have both. Why should I? If I have Phoebe, I will have the property, too. Not legally perhaps, but in every way that counts. I need a place to keep her, and God knows my income is never sufficient. I see them both as potential for increasing it. Too bad you had to start meddling."

"I take it that you intend to kill me."

"Eventually. I need you for a little while yet. Phoebe is not likely to cooperate with me at first. I underestimated her spirit, as it happens. I have you to thank, again, for helping me see that."

"I don't follow."

"She loved Stephen so passionately, don't you see? I did not think she would ever be able to form an affection for anyone else after she came to believe that he'd betrayed her so completely. I thought her will, her heart, would be as dead as he was. I thought in her grief she might accept me. How wrong I was!"

Devenham could not see Brodfield's face from his cramped position on the floor of the carriage, but he could hear the passion beginning to swell dangerously in his voice. He was not sure what the man was going to do.

"She fled, you see? She moved out of the house and disappeared. And as long as my father still lived, I could do little about it. He would have stopped me from selling out my commission or trying to find her. Who would have guessed that he'd last so long, the bastard? I had to help him along."

Dear God, Devenham realized, *somehow the man had a hand in his own father's death.* Why was he telling him? No one would ever have been able to prove it.

"What did he think I would gain by facing French cannons in the company of scum? The army was just a more dangerous way for me to lose all my money." Brodfield was continuing almost as if there was no one there. "He was so ill already, a few doses of arsenic were quite sufficient to finish him. When he finally died, I was certain I'd find Phoebe again. She always had a soft spot for the old man. I had my friends watching for her. Then I watched, and I waited. And then I began to see that she had a *tendre* for you."

The earl could see that Brodfield's motive for abducting him was much more than simply the investigation he had begun. Unreasoned jealousy and deep-seated resentment were all part of the mix. He did not believe Phoebe's feelings toward him were at all as clear as Brodfield thought.

"Tell me, did you kill Stephen?" he asked very quietly.

"Oh, did you not get as far as that in your inquiries, Devenham? I thought you had almost figured it all out."

"Was the whole scandal fabricated? Did Stephen find out what you were doing to him?"

"I needed to ruin him in Phoebe's eyes, don't you see? He was always so righteous—the perfect son, the perfect heir, the perfect lover, the perfect husband." Brodfield's voice shook with the force of his hatred for his half brother. "But he wasn't so perfect, was he? What good is an heir who can't father an heir? Phoebe was wasted on him, utterly wasted!"

The earl recalled Phoebe's distress in St. James's Church as she had related the tale of Mlle. Gimard and her own failure as a wife. This was important. The pain in his head clouded his thinking and was sapping his strength, but he fought against it, trying to separate the pain from his consciousness. "How do you know it was Stephen who could not produce a child?"

"Ha. It was not hard to see. Like most boys we went through a chain of women, learning our way. He was the heir—he almost always got first pick. We started with a delightful dairy maid who could have made her fortune if she'd have come up to London. But none of his women ever got with child. Imagine, no bastards! I used to taunt him with the number of brats I've made.

"He always thought the next woman might be different. He

thought so when he married Phoebe. I warned him, but he wouldn't listen. Later I offered my services. Who would have known? Phoebe wanted children, Stephen wanted children, I wanted Phoebe. It would have been perfectly sensible. My father's precious bloodline would have continued, after a fashion. But no, Stephen wouldn't hear of it. He threatened to kill me if I ever laid a hand on her. Don't you find that a rare joke?"

So by rights you should already be dead, Devenham thought. He was filled with an anger so intense it drove out his pain and exhaustion. He remembered Phoebe's bruised wrists, and the scene in the garden. This thing, this worm, on the seat above him had committed murder twice in the name of lust, and had almost completely destroyed Phoebe's faith in herself as well as in the man she had loved. That itself seemed like spiritual murder. He felt quite capable of murder himself. This man filled him with such hatred and disgust that he was afraid it was a contagion. God forbid that he should become so blinded by it that he was no better than Brodfield!

The mere thought of Phoebe pushed back the dangerous anger Brodfield had provoked in him, however. The villain would have enjoyed watching him try to display his rage while he lay helplessly trussed on the carriage floor. It was as if loving Phoebe saved him from being the wretched animal he might otherwise become. It was very clear to him now just how much he did love her.

It was also very clear that he must keep a cool head if he wanted to survive. Suddenly that was something he wanted more than he ever had before in his life. He could not allow Brodfield's plans to succeed. He must concentrate not on violence, but on escape. Justice could follow in its own turn.

Chapter Sixteen

Morning did come to the Allington house on Wigmore Street, although there were times during the night when Phoebe felt certain that it never would. She had dozed fitfully on the sofa in the drawing room, awakening with a stiff, sore neck. Edward, Mullins, and Goldie had come back with nothing to report after several hours' search. The earl had disappeared without a trace.

Phoebe agreed to rest for a short while after a very early breakfast. By mid-morning, however, she was resolved to pay a call at Charles Street. She might not know what to say to Richard if he happened to be there, but at least it was something to try. She simply could not stand by and do nothing. She did not care if she awakened her mother-in-law's entire household.

"Phoebe dear," Judith scolded gently, "you have not even changed your dress from last night."

Phoebe had given no thought to her attire whatsoever. She made a hasty mental survey of quick solutions. A pelisse thrown on over her gown? A spencer? She was not sure either would button over the decorative roses trimming her bodice. She settled for a shawl which at least concealed her upper arms and shoulders.

Edward and Goldie were prepared to accompany her and she was just tying the black grosgrain ribbons of her bonnet when the knocker sounded at the front door. A moment later Maddocks appeared, bearing a note.

"For Lady Brodfield," he announced in his usual dignified tones. Only an extra pair of small creases in his forehead betrayed that he shared the anxiety of those around him. "It was left in the door."

Phoebe held her breath as she opened the note.

"Dear Lady Brodfield," it said, "my deepest apologies for not appearing last night as we had planned. I am sorry to report that I have met with an accident and am injured. Surely you know that nothing less could have kept me away. I am in Willesden and do not know how soon you may receive this message, for I must depend on those around me to see it delivered into London. If you can forgive me and wish to see me, come to St. Mary's Church near Willesden Green. I will be there or else will leave instructions for you. Yours, Devenham."

Phoebe threw down the note. "It is all nonsense, of course," she said angrily. "What could he possibly have been doing in Willesden when he was supposed to be having dinner with us?" She looked at Edward and Goldie and read the concern on their faces. "I don't believe the note is from Devenham at all, but there is one way to be sure. Could Goldie go to the Clarendon and fetch Mullins? He would recognize the handwriting."

Goldie was dispatched at once. Phoebe began to pace in a tight little circle until Edward and Judith came to stand beside her. She took their offered hands and closed her eyes. "I am afraid the earl is in grave danger," she whispered, "and it is all my fault. I have to make it right."

"Phoebe, please explain what you think is going on. You can tell us, you know."

She opened her eyes and looked into the kind faces of her sister and brother-in-law. She sighed. "It is a long story, but I will give you the short of it." Without revealing her visit with Mlle. Gimard at St. James's, she told them briefly what she and the earl had learned about Richard's impersonation of Stephen, and about the investigation Devenham had begun to pursue.

"I made a list of names from the papers that were found in Stephen's desk after he died. Lord Devenham was going to try to talk to the various people. But Lady Tyneley must have told Richard I had been looking at the papers, don't you see? He must have guessed what we were doing." Tears had begun to roll down her cheeks. Judith slipped a comforting arm around her shoulders.

"And you think this is Brodfield's way of stopping you?"

"What else could it be?"

Edward shrugged, and Phoebe knew he must feel as helpless as she did.

When Mullins arrived with Goldie, he took one look at the note and confirmed that it was not the earl's writing.

"Then it is definitely some kind of a trap. What should we do?" A fresh pain stabbed Phoebe's heart when she realized the one person whose counsel she would most trust on such a matter was exactly the one person who was missing. "Mullins, what would *he* say to do? He knows so much about strategy. Can we not try to think like him?"

Mullins squinted up at the ceiling in an attempt at concentration that would have seemed quite comical under a different set of circumstances. "What advantage do we have?" he asked at length in a voice that almost mimicked the earl's.

"We know that the arrangement is a trap?" Phoebe guessed.

"Yes," said Edward with enthusiasm. "And they do not know that we know it."

"Also, they do not know how early we have received the note."

"No. That assumes that part of the note was true. Someone is well aware that we have received it already—whoever delivered it."

Phoebe began to grow excited. "But if they—whoever 'they' may be—are truly at Willesden Green, the note deliverer has not yet had time to return there. If we were to set off at once, and go quickly, we might even overtake that person, or at least arrive so soon behind him that they would not yet be looking for us."

Edward cleared his throat. "That might be good or bad. What we want to do is spring their trap. We won't succeed if the trap is not ready for us."

"I think we need to make two approaches," Mullins said. "We send an advance guard into Willesden Green to be ready near the church. We wait a little time for the enemy to ready their trap, and then we send in their quarry. Then the advance guard shows up before anything can go wrong."

There was some discussion over the risks and inadequacies of this plan, but in the end it was agreed to. "It is the best we can do on short notice," said Phoebe. "We must act quickly, or we'll lose some of our advantage."

The advance guard was to be made up of Edward, Goldie, John Coachman, and the pot boy, young Tom, who was pronounced a feisty lad and tough. Phoebe wanted Mullins to drive her when the time came to spring the trap.

"Judith, you take Maddocks and Mary Anne with you and bring this note to the police office at Bow Street. We haven't anything else for proof, but tell them the story, and they'll send someone out, I'm certain. All we'll have to do is delay until they arrive to help us. If you can go right away, they won't be far behind us at all. Lizzie and Nurse and Mrs. H will still be here to mind the house and the children."

It was decided that Mullins and Phoebe should set out an hour after the advance guard departed, to make the two parties headed for Willesden Green seem convincingly unconnected. Edward borrowed a coat and hat from John Coachman to reduce the chance of being recognized. The hour of waiting looked impossibly long to Phoebe, so she went upstairs to visit the children.

"Aunt Phoebe, your dress! You still have it on!"

"Yes, I know," she sighed. "I am going on a little bit of an adventure. I will tell you all about it when I come back." Henrietta had crawled into her lap, and Phoebe found comfort rubbing the soft pup affectionately behind the ears.

"When will that be?"

Phoebe swallowed. "Later on today, I hope." She added a silent prayer, *Dear God, please let us find Devenham and bring him home safely. Please let our plan work.* If the plan didn't work, she did not know what anyone could do.

At the appointed time, she and Mullins headed out the Edgeware Road in Edward's gig. Paddington and Maida Hill were still little more than country villages, and beyond them open fields graced the road. It was only a few miles to the turn for Willesden.

Phoebe frowned, resenting the sunshine. It did not seem right for the world to enjoy such a beautiful day, when so much wickedness was afoot. A thick, foul-smelling river fog would have been far more appropriate than this sparkling, warm summer day. Birds soared over the ripe fields waiting for the harvest, and harebells nodded in the hedgerows.

Phoebe wished she could wake up and suddenly find herself in Kent. Then all that had happened since the end of July could be dismissed as nothing more than a nightmare. She could not deny Mullins's presence beside her in the gig, however, and she realized with a pang that she did not want to wish away the existence of Lord Devenham in her life. The true nightmare had only begun last night.

The gig took the left turn onto the Willesden road and proceeded smartly along the country lane. At a dip in the road ahead, a grove of trees shaded the rutted surface of the roadway and Mullins started to pull up on the ribbons. As the carriage entered the patch of shade, however, chaos broke loose.

A stout rope stretching across the road was suddenly pulled up tight in front of the horse, causing her to rear in panic, nearly oversetting the small vehicle. As Mullins struggled to regain control, two men leaped onto the gig. One struck Mullins a vicious blow to the head as the other seized Phoebe around the waist and pulled her bodily from the carriage.

Screaming and kicking, she resisted the man's greater strength as best she could. He was big and solid and the hand he clamped over her mouth was none too clean. She saw the other attacker push Mullins's limp form out of the gig and climb down after it, rolling it into the ditch by the side of the road.

"Keep fighting and we'll serve yer the same, miss," the man who was holding her said roughly, giving her a shake.

Even as the other man climbed back into the gig and took up the ribbons, Phoebe saw a closed landaulet emerge from the trees at the far side of the grove and come toward them. She needed to think quickly. The gig was being turned around. The trap had indeed been sprung, but not where anticipated. Willesden Green, where help lay waiting, was not even in sight from here. Already the man who had hold of her was starting to push her toward the landaulet. She could well guess who was awaiting her inside it, and it would not be Lord Devenham.

She glanced down at the hem of her dress, torn now from her struggling. Bits of jet beadwork and a few black roses hung by their threads. If she was clever, if she was quick enough, perhaps as she lifted her skirt to enter the carriage she could dislodge them, and no one would notice. She would not be able to leave a trail, but at least she could mark the place where she had been.

When Devenham regained consciousness a second time, he was in a place so dark he could not tell if it was day or night. His head throbbed and he felt exhaustion in all his limbs.

It had still been night when Brodfield's carriage had finally come to a halt in what looked to be woods in the middle of nowhere. Devenham had been manhandled out of the carriage, barely able to stand after unknown hours with his legs bent in the small space of the vehicle. As his eyes had adjusted, however, he had discerned the faint lines of an overgrown fountain, and the edges of what once had been flower beds. There were shrubs among the trees that nature had never planted. What he had taken for woods was an ancient garden, long since abandoned and now overgrown.

Neither one had seemed like a good place to die. He had looked around him, analyzing his chances if he broke away and ran. They were not good. Brodfield had two other men with him, helping with his dirty work. Devenham's hands were tied in front of him, but they would have been of limited use for warding off branches or helping him keep his balance. If he had fallen, it would have been all up with him.

Besides, had Brodfield not said he needed him for a little longer? To Devenham, that statement meant two things. One was that he might have a better opportunity to escape if he waited. The other was that Brodfield did not yet have Phoebe in his power.

The earl had barely arrived at these conclusions before one of the men had pushed him forward along a faintly detectable path. They had rounded the corner of a rocky outcrop overgrown with vines and halted before what appeared to be a heavy wooden door. Brodfield himself had pried it open on its rusty hinges, and then Devenham had been thrust forward into darkness. He had fallen, and remembered nothing more until now. How much time had passed he did not know.

So much for waiting for a better chance to escape, he taunted himself. How did he expect to get free from a tomb of solid stone? He felt tired and short of breath, and he wondered if he would die slowly there from lack of air. Brodfield would not have to worry about disposing of his body, certainly—that job was already done.

But in the meantime, he could not sit still. He felt extraordinarily restless, and even his heart seemed to share an inexplicable and uneven excitement. It was a peculiar feeling combined with his lack of energy. If he got up and moved about in the darkness, would he hasten his own demise? The only way to learn what lay around him in the dark was to explore. If only he could get his hands free. His sword and even his spurs had been taken from him.

He thought then of the ancient door on its rusty hinges; hinges were metal, and if he could locate the door and somehow pry out a corner of a hinge, he might be able to rub the rope binding his wrists against it and eventually cut through.

He felt the floor around him. It seemed for the most part smooth and flat, like flagstones. His hands encountered small chunks of rock here and there, probably fallen from the walls or ceiling. The chamber he was in was like a cave, but he could not allow himself to think about that. *Think only of your task, or think of Phoebe,* he told himself sternly. He had no time to lose. He struggled to his feet and moved carefully in the darkness, ducking a bit in case the ceiling was low. There was no way to know if he was moving toward the door or away from it, or only toward the side wall. If he could find a wall, he would simply follow it.

As he searched, the physical sensations he had been noticing intensified, and finally the truth dawned upon him. His last dose of laudanum had been many hours ago. His body was reacting to the lack of it. The throbbing in his head was probably as much from that as from the blow he had received.

He wondered, *how bad will it get?* He had seen opium-eaters in the army go through terrifying physical and mental agonies when deprived of their drug; it was how he had become aware of the problems of taking it. Over the past weeks he had slowly reduced his dose to a small amount, so he hoped to be spared their fate. He could tolerate what he was feeling now. He just hoped it would get no worse.

At length he succeeded in finding the door and locating the lower hinge. He held a rock awkwardly between his hands and whaled away at the metal until a corner finally began to project enough to help him. He settled himself into a position he thought he could maintain for some time, and began the tedious task of fraying his bonds.

As he worked, his mind reeled off questions: How long had he been here? What had Brodfield been doing since he left here? Would Phoebe be clever enough to elude Brodfield's clutches? Would Phoebe guess what had happened to him? Or would she lose faith in him, thinking he had abandoned her, insulted her, by his failure to honor their engagements?

Phoebe had just begun to cautiously open her heart, he was sure. Even if she never loved him, she might have found someone to share her future with. If that incipient trust, that small beginning, was destroyed by what Brodfield had done now, Devenham would count it as another murder against the villain's record.

Angered by the thought, Devenham pulled hard against the metal, letting the pain in his wrists override all his other discomforts. Quite suddenly the ropes gave way, bringing his chest and face hard against the door from the force of his efforts. He uttered a sharp cry of pain and surprise, then straightened and rubbed his nose.

"Blast and confound it!" he said, feeling a bit foolish as well as vastly relieved. He began to rub his wrists to restore circulation. Now he could . . . He stopped in mid-thought. Somewhere behind him he had heard a noise—a small noise, or several small noises, that chilled his blood. Paralyzed, he could only crouch by the door, listening for more, straining his ears for the squeak and the rustle he wanted desperately to believe he had not heard.

Bats! The fear attacked his body, wracked already by the opium effects. He felt tears on his face, and a wrenching self-disgust. Was he finally to be defeated by a passel of small animals and the ghost of his brother? Had he no more control than this? Brodfield would laugh to find out it was so easy. And what of Phoebe? Did she not deserve more than this? Was not her future at stake as much as his?

The thought of Phoebe acted like a powerful charm as it had earlier in the carriage with Brodfield. Devenham struggled through his fear to reach her, like a drowning man who sees the shore and suddenly finds he can touch bottom. *I will not submit to you, Jeremy,* the earl declared, defying the memory of his brother's habitual cruelty. *You are dead. I have enemies who are alive.*

He knew the bats were not his enemies. Only Brodfield was. If he could overcome his fear, could not the bats be his allies? Bats would not live in a tomb that had no exit. He had thought to try to break down the ancient door he had come in by, but it was thick and heavy, and there was the added risk that Brodfield might have left a guard. However, Brodfield's struggle to open the door told him that it normally stood closed. That meant there had to be another way out. If he was extraordinarily lucky, it might be a way that a man could use as well as a bat.

Devenham felt around him on the floor and picked up several pieces of stone. He wished there was at least a little light. Once he disturbed them, the bats would likely fly out in a rush. He closed his eyes and clenched his fists to steady his nerves, thinking of the fluttering wings and terrifying sound the bats' sudden exit would make. He would have to follow, and follow quickly, or he would lose his chance.

He moved a little way along the wall away from the door, to give himself a head start. Then, considering the possibility of a guard outside, he began to shout words that would not betray his plan. "Is anyone out there? Release me this instant! Blast you and damnation!" Blindly, he threw stones at the ceiling, hoping he would frighten the bats without bringing down any of it on his head.

He was rewarded with the sounds he had never thought he

would be anything but terrified to hear. A wave of alarmed squeaking began near him and swept through what must have been a huge colony. He felt and heard the first few bats take wing, moving away from him. Keeping one hand on the rough surface of the wall, he moved that way, too. The sound of flapping wings grew louder around him as more and more of the bats joined the general exodus.

As he followed the way became rougher and narrower, the ceiling lower. He put his hands above his head to protect himself as the bats and he moved through what must have been some sort of passage. He prayed it would not become too small to admit him. He continued to follow as long as he sensed any bat still in flight to guide him. When the last one had left him behind in silence, he offered a prayer of thanks. There was a glimmer of light at the end of the passage ahead of him.

Chapter Seventeen

Phoebe glared at Richard from her seat opposite him in the landaulet. He had made a mockery of being courteous at first, speaking and acting as if nothing at all were amiss, complimenting her dress and expressing delight at her company. He gave up the attempt after a few minutes, and the rattle of the carriage, the pounding of hooves and the jingle of the harness were the only sounds. At length, her angry silence seemed to wear on him, however.

"It was never my design to have to resort to such measures as these, Phoebe," he said harshly. "In time, you would have come to me of your own free will."

His comment so astonished her, she blurted out a reply. "To what purpose?"

"Why, to live with me, of course."

She could hardly believe he had made such an offensive statement so casually. "I would never have come to you! You must be mad to think so."

He laughed as if she had made some delightfully clever remark. "The scandal that you survived before will seem like a puff of wind compared to the tempest that is brewing around you at this moment. I don't believe your reputation is sterling enough to withstand even another small puff, my dear, especially now that you've been associating with Devenham. Such notorious company, dear Phoebe!

"Besides him there's the long list of my friends who would swear that they've also been bedding you, as long as I promise them a true chance to do so. Oh, you would have come, once you had nowhere else to turn, once everyone you depended upon had turned their back on you. Once they all believed the worst of you, you would have come, begging and grateful, on your knees."

"Never," she whispered.

He looked less amused now, as if he regretted the lost opportunity to see her so reduced. But what he said made no sense. Phoebe knew that Judith and Edward would never have abandoned her.

"You may thank your meddlesome friend for precipitating this rather drastic turn of events," he continued. "People quite rightly believe me capable of a great many unsavory deeds, but I could not, after all, allow the two of you to present a case adding murder to the list. My burning desires do not include being displayed on the gallows."

The hard knot of fear in Phoebe's stomach tightened. "I don't know what you are talking about, Richard. After I met Mlle. Gimard, it simply occurred to us that more of the scandalous doings laid at Stephen's feet might have been yours."

Richard studied her. "You really do not know, do you? Poor little Phoebe. Devenham guessed. I am not certain when, or even how, but he knew that Stephen did not kill himself."

Stephen did not kill himself. The words seemed to hang like dust suspended in the air of the carriage. Phoebe was so shocked she could barely comprehend them. She thought of the way Stephen had died, and the place, and she still did not understand. "But . . . then, how?" Her trembling hands framed the question in front of her.

"So innocent, dear Phoebe. You cannot begin to imagine, can you? There are so many worlds outside of Polite Society. You will be getting your education from a master."

He reached across suddenly to touch her chin. When she twisted her head away, he flashed her a smile so evil she thought it must have come straight from hell. "You had gone to the theater with friends that night, do you remember?"

Of course she remembered. She would never be able to forget that night.

"It was a simple matter to lure Stephen to Covent Garden. He had such weaknesses, really, he was an easy mark." Richard paused to look at her, and then he laughed. "They were not what you are thinking! I did an excellent job of ruining him in your eyes, did I not? Even now, you know not what to believe."

The pleasure and excitement in his face were like a child's. Cold dread wrapped itself around the knot that had moved into Phoebe's heart.

"Stephen's love for you and his distrust of me were his greatest weaknesses," Richard announced. "One made him madly jealous and overprotective and the other made him believe the most unlikely things, as long as they involved me. When I sent him word that I had taken you from the theater and brought you to the cat house in Covent Garden, I knew he would respond like an enraged bull. He never thought to check the story first. How I laughed when I heard later of the way he came barging into the nunnery demanding his wife! I was waiting outside when they threw him out. It was easy enough to make it look like a suicide. I had taken the pistol from his desk."

Phoebe closed her eyes and put her hands over her ears to shut out Richard's stream of hateful words. *Stephen had loved her. He had not killed himself.* She felt cold and numb and far away from the sound as Richard continued talking, but she still heard his next words.

"Once Devenham is dead, do you think there's a hostess who would dare to still receive you? You'll be amazed at how quickly the doors will slam shut upon you. Not that there'll be any hint of suspicion. Devenham's death from an overdose of opium will be as blameless as poor Stephen's suicide. You knew he was still taking laudanum, didn't you? I imagine he is in considerable discomfort right now, since he has been without it for so many hours. I doubt very much if he'll notice the strength of the solution when I finally give him some relief. Permanent relief."

Phoebe was vaguely aware that she was rocking, ever so slightly, and not from the motion of the carriage. Richard had killed one man she had loved, and now he would kill another. She realized that she did love Devenham, no matter how much she had fought against it. Now she must lose him too? Despair so total it felt physical was pulling her downward, sucking her into a black void, when suddenly she heard the earl's voice, as clearly as if he sat beside her.

Fight back. They were the words he had spoken to her that day in St. James's Church. *You should be angry. Fight back.*

Her eyes flew open in surprise.

Richard was still talking. "Of course, in some quarters the scent of danger about you will only increase your allure," he said. "There are compensations for the kind of future I am offering you, you know." He inched forward a little on the seat. "I could make you the most sought-after courtesan in London, with your beauty. We could both become very rich."

Phoebe lowered her hands. Beneath all her pain, beneath her despair, she had found a seed of anger that, shorn of all the layers that had hidden it, was now beginning to swell.

Richard did not seem to notice any difference in her. His look suddenly became sly, as if he guessed his first inducements held no appeal. "Or, there is something else I can give you, sweet Phoebe—something Stephen never could provide. You always wanted children, did you not, Phoebe? I'll give you babes, as many as you want."

"No!" Phoebe could not conceal her horror when she heard him say this. Had it always been Stephen's failing—is that what he was telling her? Their childlessness had not been her fault, and Richard had known! For two years of marriage and another year and half of grief she had believed she was barren. She had believed that her failure had driven Stephen to secretly gamble and drink and bed other women while pretending that he loved her and did not mind her barren state.

How she had wronged him in the months since his death! She had been blaming herself for the wrong crime. But her own sin was nothing compared to Richard's. Richard had orchestrated it all so deliberately. She felt her anger swell some more.

Richard smiled cruelly. "Ah, but I forget. You did not know, did you? Stephen always thought something would change."

He moved forward on his seat another inch, and Phoebe hoped a sudden lurch of the carriage would bounce him off it to a more painful one on the floor.

"I offered to service you for him, you know. It seemed like the brotherly thing to do. But do you know what he said? He said he'd kill me if I ever touched you."

Richard laughed, sending shivers along Phoebe's spine. "A hasty boast, that. I turned the tables on him nicely, I think. Do you suppose he sees us, Phoebe? How do you think it makes him feel?"

"He sees and feels nothing, Richard," she said in a curiously flat voice. "Stephen is dead."

It was the wrong thing to say. She knew it the moment the words left her mouth. She saw at last what no one had ever realized—that Stephen's half brother was mad. She could see it now in his eyes as he spoke to her of the way things would be now that he and she were together, as if he truly believed such things could be. He did not seem to take any account of the fact that he had committed grave crimes to achieve his ends, or the fact that Phoebe even now would never go along with his plans.

Perhaps he had always teetered on the brink of madness, she thought, driven by jealousy of his brother and overindulged by his mother. Phoebe could remember witnessing violent fits of temper in the house on Charles Street, and arguments between the two half brothers that had made her tremble. But she had never been as afraid of Richard as she was now, scarcely knowing what direction his mind would take next.

She was not prepared when Richard suddenly launched himself upon her.

"He is watching us, and I know how it makes him feel, Phoebe! I want you to feel it, too." The weight of his body pressed her back against the squabs, and his legs were straddling her. He was fumbling with her dress.

For a moment shock and nausea threatened to overcome her. She fought to keep her head clear. In the moving landaulet, his balance was precarious, and if she could only push him at the right moment, he might topple off her. She knew that she would have to jump from the carriage.

In an instant the right moment came as the vehicle lurched over a sizable bump. She shoved Richard with all her strength and slid out from under him toward the door. She had got the

door unlatched and open before Richard hauled her back by
the arm with a vicious oath.

"No!" she cried, kicking and fighting him. The open door
swung crazily with the motion of the chaise. "Stop the carriage!" she tried shouting, but she doubted if it would do any
good.

"Not ready, are you, vixen? We'll see about fixing that."

He had not yet managed to pinion her, and she was still aiming punches and vicious kicks in his direction. For an instant it
looked as if they might both tumble out of the carriage door.
Then the vehicle began to slow. Hope bloomed in Phoebe's
heart, only to die seconds later. Richard glanced out the door
and announced, "So, we have arrived."

In the split second that she was distracted, Richard managed
to get his arms around her. "Do you know where we are, my
dear?" he said with a wicked light in his eyes. "You may not
have come willingly as I wished, but I am quite certain that
you will stay. We are at Beau Chatain. It is kind of you to
share it with me, sweet love, although I'm certain many will
find the arrangement beyond shocking. Who would have
guessed that your tastes were so depraved?"

He laughed and pushed her toward the door. His two henchmen waited below.

"Here," he said callously, shoving Phoebe out. Her cry of
alarm was cut off by the impact as she landed against the
larger man, who instantly imprisoned her in his own arms.
"Shut her in the root cellar for now," Richard instructed. "Her
first lesson is to learn that I am master here. She must learn to
obey."

To Phoebe he added, "You may scream if you wish to.
There is no one to hear you who will care. The only servants I
keep here are ones who are well used to my little amusements.
They have heard it all before."

The cold, casual way he dropped this information chilled
Phoebe more than her fear of what he would do to her. He had
done this to others? But who? Why?

The root cellar was cool and darker than any place Phoebe
had ever been. It had been dug into the side of a grassy slope a

little way from the house, its walls reinforced with stone, and it smelled of the damp earth. The tiny cracks in its old wood plank door admitted only enough light to show Phoebe they were there. Except for that, she might as well have been blind.

The darkness was frightening, but far less so than Richard. Even this impenetrable blackness was nothing compared to the darkness of Richard's soul. Phoebe knew she would rather die than live the life of degradation he was offering her. She was outraged by all that he had done and planned to do. He had robbed her of love, and had robbed Stephen of his very life. What he was planning for Lord Devenham filled her with horror. Tears of grief sprang to her eyes as she thought of all that might have been.

She did not shed them, however. What had been done in the past could not be undone. Nothing could bring Stephen back or give the love they had shared a second chance. But *she* had been given a second chance at love, and had nearly squandered it. She dashed the tears aside and gave full vent to the anger that had been building inside her. The sound that came from her throat was more like a battle cry than a scream. The rage in her heart gave her new strength and determination. Devenham was still alive. She was still alive. There was still a chance for them, if they could fight Richard and win.

Her imprisonment suddenly seemed a God-sent respite from struggling with her demented brother-in-law. She needed to think. Her only chance of escape would be the moment Richard or someone came to let her out of the cellar. She would have the advantage there in the darkness. She would have to make whoever it was come in to get her, and then— what?

She had no weapon. She thought of the stones that lined the walls and wondered if any were loose, or could be loosened. Only the intensity of her anger would give her the strength and the will to knock a man out with one, but she believed she could do it. She searched in the darkness for the walls, moving cautiously with her hands outstretched. Her biggest fear as her eyes strained in the darkness was that she would touch something other than air or wall. She had given no thought to spiders, or rats, until that moment.

She found what she needed by stumbling over it. One of the bricklike stones lay on the floor close by the wall from which it had fallen. She judged that she was quite far from the door, for the tiny cracks of light she had seen between the planks were barely perceptible now. She settled down there to wait, the solid stone in her hand offering comfort in the great dark void. She thought about what she would do once she escaped from the cellar.

It seemed that only a few minutes passed before she heard the rattle of the door bolt and a bright shaft of light pierced the darkness. She was startled that someone had come so soon and scrambled to her feet to be ready, her fingers wrapped around the rectangular stone.

The door opened slowly, cautiously, as if someone did not wish to make a noise.

"Lady Brodfield?"

Phoebe's heart leapt with joy at the whisper. She dropped the stone and rushed to embrace the silhouette in the partly opened doorway. It was the earl.

Devenham had found his way out of the artificial garden temple, for that was what he decided it had been, by way of an equally artificial garden grotto that had been built on the other side of the natural outcrop of rock. To his intense annoyance the grotto had featured several cleverly intersecting passages open to the sky, but only one that had led out to the remains of the partially filled pond and ruined garden. Gradually he had followed what was left of the ancient paths until he was within sight of the house and stables.

A cavalry-trained scout, the earl had reconnoitered from a protected position at the edge of the abandoned garden. Beau Chatain was a stuccoed Palladian-style manor house set in the midst of a rolling, grassy lawn studded with specimen trees. A long carriage drive swept into a circle in front of the house. The stable block was at an angle from the house, off to one side with a paved yard between them. A garden designed in a newer, less formal style had been installed behind the house in what must have been a simpler alternative to razing the entire area of the old garden.

Hiding behind some overgrown shrubs, Devenham had seen Brodfield's carriage arrive and the way Phoebe had been man-handled out of it. It had required a supreme act of self-control not to rush out in anger against his enemy's superior numbers. Instead, he had been forced to wait, watching helplessly as they carried her off. The house had blocked his view of their ultimate destination, and he would have assumed she was a captive in the house itself had she not uttered the cry of an-guish and anger that led him to the root cellar.

Devenham came down the steps inside the entrance and let the door fall to behind him, engulfing them both in darkness. He took Phoebe into his strong arms and held her tightly. He could feel her shaking. "Sh-h, my precious Phoebe," he mur-mured. "I am here with you now. Are you all right?"

"Now," she said in a voice muffled against his coat. "I am all right now. How did you find me? Where did you come from? He was going to kill you."

"Sh-h, I know. I must explain later. We cannot stay here. We must get out before someone comes back. I could not get you out until no one was about." Taking her by the hand, he started to lead her up the steps, but she pulled back.

"Wait. What will we do once we are out? There is no place to hide."

"There is a whole part of the park that is abandoned and overgrown. There are many hiding places there. We could wait until night, then slip away."

"I have another idea," Phoebe said, and quickly outlined the daring plan she had conceived while sitting in the dark.

"All right," Devenham agreed. "There will be risk no matter what we do. Sometimes the boldest approach is the best, the least expected." He thought the boldest plan of all would have been to confront Brodfield in the house, but there were too many unknowns.

Running across the open expanse of grass, the pair of fugi-tives managed to reach the stables unseen. Devenham hid around the corner as Phoebe ran to the entrance. She had no need to fake the stricken expression on her face as she ap-peared there, breathless and disheveled, before the startled grooms.

"Hurry," she cried to them, "your master needs you! He's had a bad fall, down by the back edge of the far garden. I think he's badly injured."

Feed buckets, harnesses, pitchforks, and brushes were all dropped in an instant as the stablehands rushed out in the direction of the gardens. The youngest, no more than a boy, was the last to go, and as he went past her Phoebe pulled at his sleeve. "Please, help me," she begged. "I'll make sure the authorities know that you did so. I need your fastest horse."

The lad looked at her dubiously, as if he did not understand what she was about. "You'll never 'andle 'im, miss."

"Then saddle him for me," said Devenham, suddenly appearing in the doorway. "There is no time to lose." He spoke with unquestionable authority in his voice and grabbed a saddle from the blocks nearest him even as he spoke. "I want your next fastest for the lady, and the rest turned loose. Now!"

"Hurry, please," urged Phoebe, glancing back to the stable door.

The lad glanced back too, the light suddenly dawning. " 'E's not even where you sent them, is 'e, miss? Cor, what a row there's goin' to be."

"Yes, there's going to be a row no matter what," Phoebe said hurriedly. "Perhaps you should take a horse, too! Now, quickly, which ones do we take?"

She did not wait for him, but began to move along the line of stalls. Decisively, the lad grabbed a halter from the hooks beside him and tossed it to Devenham, pointing to a stall.

"That there's the master's own horse, sir. Take him." He took down another halter and hurried down the row past Phoebe to open another stall. "This 'ere's Nessie—she'll do for you, my lady."

Phoebe moved quickly to take the halter from his hands. "I can do this," she said, surprising him. "Do you get the saddle, quickly!" All the while she was listening for the sound of running footsteps returning to forestall them. She assumed Richard was in the house, but how long would it be before he noticed the commotion outside? She thought her heart must be beating so hard it would frighten her horse.

Devenham's mount was saddled and ready, and he was

busily opening the other stalls and chasing out the horses. He saw Phoebe into her sidesaddle and then turned to the young boy. "Mount behind me, lad, there's no time to saddle another one. You'll have your pick of fine jobs when this business is through."

They dashed out of the stables and headed for the carriage drive just as the angry stablehands returned from the garden. Their shouts had roused Richard, and as Phoebe looked back, she saw him step out of the house into the chaos that now filled the yard. She had no doubt that the escaped horses would delay them no more than a few minutes.

The carriage drive seemed endless. Phoebe realized that when they reached the road they would have to ask which way to go. She knew Beau Chatain lay outside the village of Hampstead, but she had no idea in which direction.

Just before they reached the end of the drive, however, they saw a carriage with two outriders turning in. Phoebe recognized the landau immediately. "Edward!" she cried.

Sure enough, the Allingtons' own John Coachman was driving the carriage, with Edward and a rather groggy Mullins inside. Goldie and young Tom were riding horses hired hastily in Willesden when it became clear the original plan had gone awry.

" 'Twas only my guess that Brodfield might have come here," Edward explained modestly. "When we saw the bits from your dress and found poor Mullins, I didn't know where else to try! The innkeeper at Willesden Green sent a postboy back along the London road to meet and give word to the police. I pray they're not far behind us." He looked at Phoebe and Devenham, his face filled with emotion. "You can't know how very glad I am to see you!"

"You cannot be more glad than we are to be here," Devenham replied, relieving the company with a moment's laughter. "However, we must go back, now that there are more of us. I'll be damned if I'll let that devil escape justice."

There was general agreement from everyone but Phoebe, who refused to be left behind at the end of the carriage drive while the others went back for Richard. Edward insisted on moving outside by exchanging places with young Tom. It was a motley crew that arrived in the yard of Beau Chatain in time to face the small mounted party Richard had just finished gathering.

Phoebe was astonished to see Edward, Goldie, Mullins, and John Coachman all produce pistols, apparently loaded and primed. The men pointed them at Richard with steady hands, and the servants who were with him nervously eased their mounts a little away from him.

Richard appeared more astonished than Phoebe for a moment, but he recovered himself quickly.

"Heavens, gentlemen, what is this all about?" he asked, feigning innocence. "We were just preparing for an afternoon's hunt."

"I'm certain you were not expecting so much company," the earl said acidly, "nor were you expecting to become the quarry. However, I'm afraid Lady Brodfield and I have chosen to decline that honor."

His horse moved restlessly, as if it felt the barely restrained impulses of the man in the saddle. Phoebe thought she had never seen Devenham's eyes look so piercing as they did now while he stared at Richard Brodfield.

"Be thankful, Brodfield, that I do not also have a gun. In my present shaky state, I feel certain that my finger would slip on the trigger. It would be such a shame for you to be dead before the authorities who are on their way ever got here."

Chapter Eighteen

Only after the Bow Street officers arrived and took Richard and his henchmen into custody did the little group of Wigmore Street heroes relax. The men dismounted and climbed down from Edward's carriage, congratulating each other with handshakes and very undignified slaps on the back.

"So they'd been wanting some evidence to hold against him, eh?"

"Said they'd had complaints 'bout him but nothing they could act upon."

"Seems he generally used doxies to carry on his activities, but a few times he brought in shop girls or maids instead. They weren't nearly so willing, and there'd been some complaints."

"Their word against his, and hushed up with a generous bit of the ready, I expect."

"Yes, I expect so. Going to be quite a scandal this time."

"Indeed. Murder, that's something. Lord Tyneley's son! The old man don't know that he's better off dead, but he is. Likely Brodfield'll hang."

Most of Richard's servants had gone with the officers to give information, with only a few left behind to look after the house and the remaining livestock. Edward's horse and gig that Phoebe and Mullins had used were discovered behind the stables. For the most part, Beau Chatain was deserted.

Edward watched the earl go to Phoebe to help her dismount. They walked away from the others, their heads bent, talking. He thought of Judith, waiting at home, worrying about them all, and thanked his stars that he had found himself such a sensible wife, who had not failed to carry out her important part in alerting the police. Unless he had learned nothing about love after a dozen years of marriage to her, he'd not be wrong to

say Phoebe and Devenham made a handsome couple. He
hoped they had the sense to see it themselves.

Judith would rejoice when he got back with the news of all
that had happened—as Wellington had said of Waterloo, it had
indeed been a very near-run thing. Edward realized suddenly
that he was more than a little tired. He was getting too old to
stay out at night till all hours and then go chasing after mad-
men and kidnappers.

Devenham walked Phoebe away from the other men to protect her ears from their rather unsuitable conversations. He
paused on a small rise of ground near the house, pointing out a
pair of large trees.

"I wondered if there were truly any chestnuts at Beau
Chatain, or if they had all disappeared long ago," he said. "I
believe those are chestnut trees, are they not?"

Phoebe nodded, but he had not successfully distracted her.
"You are kind to try to make conversation after all that has
happened," she said, turning to him. "Are you truly all right?"

In truth, he was not. He had made a brave showing during
all their efforts, but the opium withdrawal was taking its toll
on him. His head throbbed as did every muscle in his body, or
so it seemed. He felt as if he had performed heroic feats of
strength and endurance while suffering from the worst afteref-
fects of too much drink. He found it ironic that the royal physi-
cians prescribed laudanum for the Prince Regent to counter
those very same effects. There were uglier symptoms he might
yet suffer; he did not want to be with anyone but Mullins when
those began to set in.

When he did not answer, Phoebe took his hand and began to
walk with him again. "Richard said you would be suffering
without your laudanum. Is it very bad? I do not know how you
have managed to be so courageous and dashing if you are feeling very ill."

Devenham looked at her in surprise. "He knew about that?"

She turned her head away but not before he noticed she had
tears in her eyes. "He—he was going to use laudanum to kill
you. He said you would be in such misery you would never
notice the strength of the dose." She turned back to him, her

beautiful face streaked with tears. "He said it would give you relief, permanent relief."

Devenham was overwhelmed to think her tears were for him. Surely, such a thing meant that she cared for him, at least, enough to feed his hopes. But now—now was not the time to pursue them. That Brodfield had said such things to her was just another measure of his cruelty.

"Phoebe, I am sorry he upset you so. I can assure you that I would not have taken the laudanum if he had offered it. In a day or so I shall be fine, and my body will be free of the need for it. Our adventure is over. You must try to put it out of your mind as soon as possible."

He did not tell her that Brodfield's unusual knowledge of opium made him wonder if the man had been addicted to it himself, nor did he mention that Brodfield would have found some other way to kill him. He searched vainly for a handkerchief to offer her, and finally, removing his soiled gloves, with her permission used his hands to very gently wipe away her tears. How much he would have liked to take her in his arms again!

"You must admit," he said, trying to coax a smile from her, "the past eighteen hours have been a good deal less boring than the Duke of York's reception would have been."

She gave him a very shaky smile. "We are a sorry pair, are we not? Look at your uniform."

He had already taken in the condition of her gown, which he could see had been quite lovely before it became torn and soiled. Through all that had happened, she had somehow managed to preserve her shawl. His own immaculate breeches were streaked with dirt, and his jacket looked as if it had seen battle duty after all. There was a tear in the sleeve, and at least two silver buttons had disappeared from one side. His sword, his sabretasche, and his shako had been missing along with his curricle and horses since the attack on him in London the previous night.

"Poor sir! Will you tell me what you went through?"

He agreed to tell her some of it, provided she would do the same for her part. "But not now," he added with a hint of his usual mischievous smile. "Think of how many others are waiting to hear these details, and of how many times we will be forced to repeat them. Let us at least cut down on that number as much as we can."

There was no avoiding the scandal to follow. The news of Richard Brodfield's arrest spread through London faster than the Great Fire, and was carried out into the country with every carriage that left the West End in the grand exodus for the start of the shooting season.

Of course, those immediately involved in the episode found their travel plans delayed.

"I have *never* missed the start of the shooting season before," Edward was heard to lament, but he was quick to assure Phoebe that he would survive perfectly well under the circumstances.

Devenham, after recounting his part of the story in the Allingtons' drawing room upon their return, retired to the Clarendon with Mullins and was not seen or heard from for two days. When he reappeared at Wigmore Street on the second day of September, only the faintest of shadows under his eyes gave a clue that he had been ill. His curricle and prized chestnuts had been found in Lady Tyneley's stables behind the house on Charles Street, along with his saber and the missing articles from his uniform. He had sent his belated excuses to the Duke of York, and had learned that his absence was forgiven due to the rather unusual circumstances. However, the Duke now required him to appear in three days time for an audience with the Prince Regent himself.

Devenham and Phoebe tried to spare their families and friends from the most sordid aspects of their experiences. The Allington children now worshiped their aunt and the earl so thoroughly they could hardly be separated from the pair. So it was that Phoebe and Devenham found themselves walking in Hyde Park on the afternoon of the earl's reappearance while four Allington children cavorted with Henrietta under the somewhat distracted watch of Lizzie and her own object of adulation, Goldie.

"I know that Mullins is a very capable nurse," Phoebe was saying, "but I could not help worrying about your welfare, all the same, my lord. I hope you did not suffer too greatly." She took refuge in addressing him formally; she felt awkward with him now after all they had been through.

"Dear Lady Brodfield, it was nothing. A few unpleasant symptoms, and then I confess that when I finally slept, I did so for some twenty-four hours! I imagine I ought to be leaping about with a surfeit of energy quite like Henrietta."

Devenham's teasing, lop-sided smile was back in its usual place, to Phoebe's great joy. Deprived of his company for the past two days, she had suffered miserably, although she thought she had hidden the fact quite well. It was as if the deep anger Brodfield had brought out in her had cracked all the remaining barriers she had built to contain her passions. She was grateful for the reprieve in departing to Kent for whatever few extra days or hours it gave her to be with the earl.

"I hope this time she won't scare up any great flocks of birds," she said quite seriously.

Devenham laughed. "I could not agree more, but I must tell you, I don't believe that particular sound will ever again hold as much terror for me after what I went through at Brodfield's hands."

Only Phoebe had been able to appreciate the full significance of Devenham's escape from his prison in the abandoned gardens of Beau Chatain. She shuddered as she thought again of what he had faced.

Devenham stopped walking and turned to face her. Somehow, they seemed to be standing very close together. The smile had suddenly vanished from his face, and his eyes were more intense than she had ever seen them, seeming to search her own face for something—she was not sure what.

"I could not tell you this in front of everyone, but it was you that rescued me, Phoebe. It was the thought of you that gave me the courage to do what I had to."

He had used her Christian name, as he had when he rescued her from Richard. He had also taken her hands into his, and she could feel that he was shaking, ever so slightly. She began to wonder, and to hope.

"You have been through a terrible ordeal, and I do not mean just what has occurred in these past few days or weeks. I believe it began on the day your husband died, or perhaps even before that. It is only natural that the shock should take some time to wear off, that it should take you some time to recover, to heal. But I must ask you if—if you think, if I might hope, if ever at some future time—oh, confound it! Do you think there is a chance you might one day come to care for me? Would you ever consider me if I were to press my suit?"

Phoebe was amazed to see her gallant earl so uncertain of himself. Could he truly be unaware that her heart was already his? Could it be that he truly wished to marry? Surely her answer must shine in her eyes brighter than the sun itself.

"When I was alone with Richard in the carriage, my lord, it was you who helped me. Do you remember what you said to me that day in St. James's Church? You said that I should be angry, that I should fight back. I heard your words again as clearly as if you were right beside me, and I fought with strength I hardly knew I had. I think we have given each other an extremely special gift—perhaps the gift of having a future. It does not seem inappropriate to consider sharing that future together."

"Phoebe." He stared down at her and raised her hands each in turn to his lips without ever letting go of her gaze.

"I was wrong about your eyes," she said. "I thought they were blue like the sky in October, but they are really a deeper blue than that. They are more like the sky after the sunset colors fade, when the first star comes out."

"You do have the soul of a poet, madam. I thought I was the one who is supposed to compose odes to your beautiful eyes. I would write odes to your eyes, your hair, your skin, your spirit, your courage, your beautiful soul, your generous heart . . ."

Phoebe laughed and put a hand on his lips to stop him, for his intention to go on for some time seemed quite clear.

"My lord! You will create a new scandal if anyone should hear you going on so."

Devenham growled and took her into his arms. "I'll give them a new scandal," he said, and proceeded to kiss her thoroughly, standing there in the middle of the public park.

Phoebe was shocked, but she thought she might never have enjoyed anything half so much.

"I love you, Phoebe. I love you more than life itself. You had better learn to call me Jack, for that is the name my closest friends use, and you will always be closer to me than any of them."

"I love you—Jack, Major Jameson, Lord Devenham. I tried so hard not to, but you would persist. I don't know why." Phoebe reached her arms up around his neck, inviting another scandalous kiss. Her emotions were threatening to overwhelm her.

"Because that's the way I am," he said at length, pausing for breath, "and that's the way love is. And I'll tell you a secret you'll discover once we are wed. My eyes can get even bluer than this. Will you marry me?"

She nodded. "Just to see that."

"Not to mother my children?"

Phoebe caught her breath. Did he know? She had told no one of that part of the events. Her question must have been visible in her eyes, because he said, "Brodfield told me. He was a very cruel man, and to have withheld that knowledge from you was unpardonable. But I want you to know, and never doubt, that I would have you for my wife even if you could never have a child. Your Stephen knew that too—that you are too precious, too wonderful, for that even to matter. I knew he could not have taken his own life."

He cradled her against him protectively. "When you marry me, your name will be Jameson, your title will be Countess of Devenham, and we will see how quickly the *haut ton* forgets all the scandals that we have been through. They will forget that the name of Brodfield was ever connected with you. And we will show them that this Earl of Devenham has broken the mold that cast all the others before him."

"Will you wish to keep Beau Chatain?"

"Do you want to, my love?"

"No. Lord Tyneley meant well when he left it to me, but there are too many unpleasant associations. When the scandal dies down, I think we should sell it."

"You already know much about my estates, from your service as my secretary. You know I have no need of more. But remind me never to build a temple in our gardens. No temple, no grotto, no maze . . . Perhaps we shall forgo the gardens altogether. Leave the places natural—but no caves."

He laughed when he saw the stricken look on her face.

"Dearest Phoebe," he said, kissing her once more before the Allington children and Lizzie and Goldie could descend upon them. "We can have flowers. Acres of flowers. And birds and frogs, and stray cats—even pet ones. And lots of children to help us love them all. As long as we have each other."

Author's Note

The first English edition of fairy tales collected by the Brothers Grimm was published in London in 1824 and was illustrated by Cruikshank. This means that many such beloved and well-known tales as Snow White and Rumpelstiltskin were not familiar in Regency nurseries. It is entirely possible, however, that some of the stories Jacob and Wilhelm Grimm had collected by 1815 could have been retold in England by soldiers or statesmen who encountered Jacob Grimm in Paris or particularly in Vienna.

Jacob Grimm worked for his government during the closing years of the Napoleonic Wars and in 1814–1815 he served at the Congress of Vienna in addition to making two trips to Paris to recover important German paintings and books stolen by the French army. It is known that in Vienna he was the nucleus of a small literary gathering who entertained each other with the telling and retelling of folktales and fairy tales. Many of these stories were not originally intended for children, and were only made suitable after the Grimms modified, edited, and in some cases embellished them for publication. Jacob's store of tales in Vienna would have included those already published in the Grimms' first volume of *Nursery and Household Tales* and others like "The Frog Prince" about to make their appearance in the second volume.

Jacob and his younger brother Wilhelm were German scholars who, as a side interest to their primary fields, collected and wrote down folklore and fairy tales from the oral traditions of German peasants. Eventually their collection numbered some two hundred tales. Their first volume of tales was published in 1812. They published a second volume in

1815, and followed this with a third volume in 1822 that included both new and repeated stories. The expanded collection we know today as *Grimms' Fairytales* did not appear until 1857.

Ⓓ SIGNET REGENCY ROMANCE

STRONG WILLS AND FIERY PASSION

☐ **THE PERSISTENT EARL by Gail Eastwood.** Beautiful young widow Lady Phoebe Brodfield could not imagine that a man who lay helpless in a sickbed could pose a threat to a woman betrayed in marriage and who vowed never to love again. Yet as the Earl of Devenham grew stronger, so did the danger of his rampant desire—and as Phoebe's once broken heart mended, her defenses melted away.
(181913—$3.99)

☐ **MISS DORTON'S HERO by Elisabeth Fairchild.** When the lovely and young Miss Margaret Dorton awoke the passions of the dark and handsome Evelyn Dade, for whom love and war were one and the same, she had no idea that she had to not only fight her own desires but defeat his as well—in a battle to save what was left of her good name even after she had lost her heart. (182804—$3.99)

☐ **LORD KINGSFORD'S QUEST by Donna Davidson.** Taryn Burnham had been little more than a child when she fell in love with her distant cousin Woolfe. Then Woolfe vanished from her life, fleeing punishment for an angry act of violence. When he returned, there certainly was no room in her perfectly planned life for a reckless, ruthless adventurer. But there was no denying of Taryn's desire as she found that there was room in her heart for him as well as in her arms.
(180070—$3.99)

☐ **A CERTAIN REPUTATION by Emma Lange.** Censorious society whispered that the dazzlingly beautiful widow Anne de Montforte was a wanton woman. The handsome, heartless Duke of Buckingham was determined to prove that those rumors were true. Anne had to defend her honor against this man who thought she had none and most difficult of all, she had to defeat her own growing desire for a duke who used all of his talents to undo her. (183983—$3.99)

*Prices slightly higher in Canada

Buy them at your local bookstore or use this convenient coupon for ordering.

PENGUIN USA
P.O. Box 999 — Dept. #17109
Bergenfield, New Jersey 07621

Please send me the books I have checked above.
I am enclosing $_____ (please add $2.00 to cover postage and handling). Send check or money order (no cash or C.O.D.'s) or charge by Mastercard or VISA (with a $15.00 minimum). Prices and numbers are subject to change without notice.

Card #_____ Exp. Date _____
Signature_____
Name_____
Address_____
City _____ State _____ Zip Code _____

For faster service when ordering by credit card call **1-800-253-6476**

Allow a minimum of 4-6 weeks for delivery. This offer is subject to change without notice.

Ⓞ SIGNET REGENCY ROMANCE

STEP INTO A PASSIONATE PAST ...

☐ **THE COUNTERFEIT COACHMAN by Elisabeth Fairchild.** Miss Fanella Quinby finds herself being driven pell mell down the road to ruin—with no way to say whoa—when she begins considering the possibility of yielding to an imposter whose honor is as dubious as his word. (181557—$3.99)

☐ **FORTUNE'S FOLLY by Margaret Summerville.** Miss Pandora Marsh finds it hard to believe her protests of innocence as passion contends with propriety and desire becomes more and more difficult to deny. (180488—$3.99)

☐ **LADY ALEX'S GAMBLE by Evelyn Richardson.** Alexandra de Montmorency was masquerading as a man as she staked all to save everything her family had ... and when handsome, steely-eyed Christopher, Lord Wrotham, came too close to the truth for comfort, she had to decide if it was worth winning her game of pretense at the price of her rising passion. (183401—$3.99)

☐ **A PERILOUS JOURNEY by Gail Eastwood.** When Miss Gillian Kentwell flees her guardian's hot pursuit in order to escape the monstrous marriage that was arranged for her, she finds herself accepting the aid of a handsome, high-living stranger whose lips could lie as well as they kissed. (181891—$3.99)

*Prices slightly higher in Canada

Buy them at your local bookstore or use this convenient coupon for ordering.

PENGUIN USA
P.O. Box 999 — Dept. #17109
Bergenfield, New Jersey 07621

Please send me the books I have checked above.
I am enclosing $_____ (please add $2.00 to cover postage and handling). Send check or money order (no cash or C.O.D.'s) or charge by Mastercard or VISA (with a $15.00 minimum). Prices and numbers are subject to change without notice.

Card #_____ Exp. Date _____
Signature_____
Name_____
Address_____
City _____ State _____ Zip Code _____

For faster service when ordering by credit card call 1-800-253-6476
Allow a minimum of 4-6 weeks for delivery. This offer is subject to change without notice.